LAST BREATH

BRIT KS

Last Breath is an imprint of Romance Ain't Dead

PO Box #5382 Atlanta, GA 30307

ISBN: 979-8-9882277-7-9 & 979-8-9882277-8-6 & 979-8-9932413-0-2

Cover and interior art by Warickaart

Interior formatting by Quirky Circe

Map by Andrés Aguirre Jurado (aguirreart)

Character art by Madchaxxx

Developmental editing by Goldenmay Editing LLC

Line and proofreading by Earley Editing LLC & KD Proofreading

"It's not about being the leader ...it's about being the one who makes the sacrifice."
— Eddie Munson, *Stranger Things*

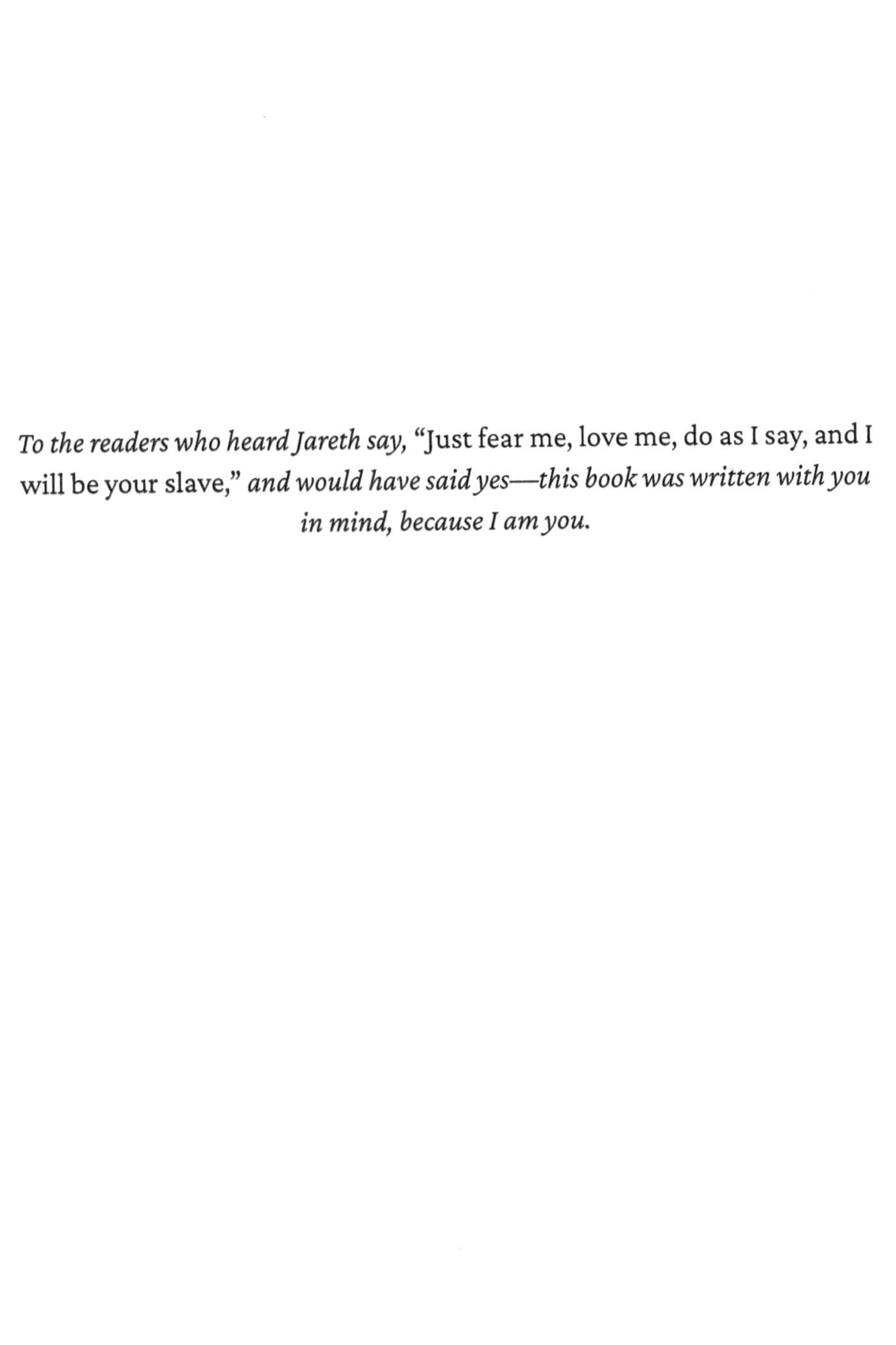

To the readers who heard Jareth say, "Just fear me, love me, do as I say, and I will be your slave," *and would have said yes—this book was written with you in mind, because I am you.*

CONTENTS

CONTENT WARNINGS

Dear Reader,

Stories—even those filled with magic, romance, and otherworldly adventure—can sometimes touch on real, painful emotions. This book explores themes of loss, love, and what it means to face the darkness within ourselves and the world around us to find what brings us true joy. I always want my readers to feel safe and prepared before diving in, so please take a moment to look over the content warnings below. Your mental and emotional well being matter more than anything, and it's okay to step away, take breaks, or come back when you're ready.

Content Warnings
- A death realm steeped in grief
- Bullying
- Child kidnapping
- Death
- Drug addiction (past reference)
- Explicit language
- Ghosts, demons (daemons), vampires, witches
- Grief
- Gun usage/other weapons
- Heart attack and hospitalization (off page)
- Open door romance scenes

Please proceed with care and
kindness toward yourself.

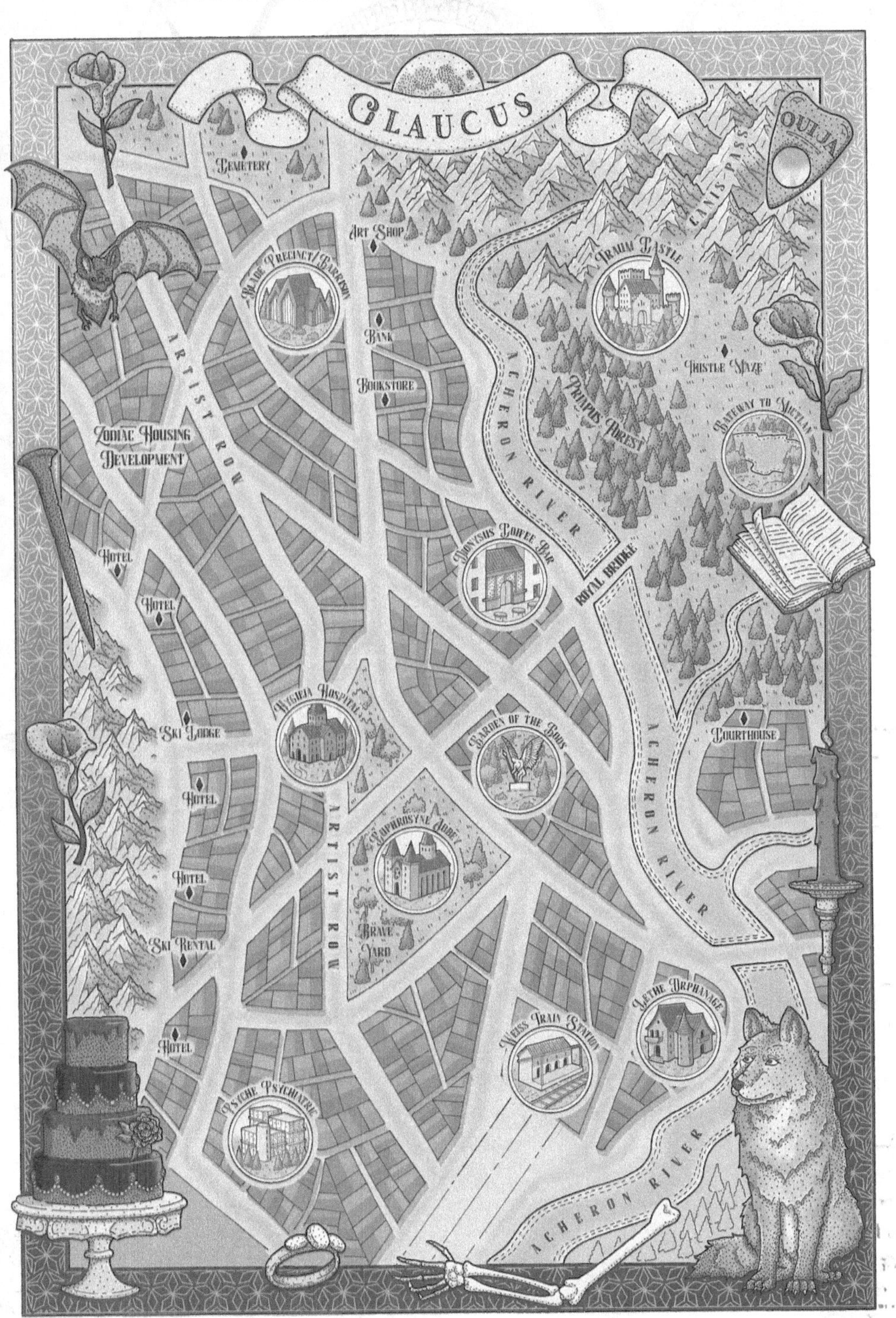
GLAUCUS
OUIJA
CANIS PASS
CEMETERY
ART SHOP
SHADE PRECINCT / BARRACKS
BANK
BOOKSTORE
TRAUM CASTLE
PRIAPUS FOREST
THISTLE MAZE
GATEWAY TO MICHLAM
ZODIAC HOUSING DEVELOPMENT
ARTIST ROW
HOTEL
HOTEL
DIONYSUS COFFEE BAR
ACHERON RIVER
ROYAL BRIDGE
SKI LODGE
HYGIEIA HOSPITAL
GARDEN OF THE GODS
COURTHOUSE
HOTEL
ARTIST ROW
SOPHROSYNE ABBEY
ACHERON RIVER
HOTEL
BRAVE YARD
SKI RENTAL
LETHE ORPHANAGE
HOTEL
WEISS TRAIN STATION
PSYCHE PSYCHIATRIC
ACHERON RIVER
ACHERON RIVER

THE ELEMENTAL WITCHES

A GUIDE

In this world, the arcane and the tangible intertwine, where magic is as real as the air we breathe. This guide introduces the five elemental witches, each embodying a unique aspect of the natural world and wielding abilities that define their connection to these elements.

LUNAR WITCH

Abilities: Masters of the unseen, communicate with spirits, traverse astral planes, enter dreams, control shadows, and sense spiritual life and death.

SOLAR WITCH

Abilities: Their power mirrors the sun's intensity, summoning fierce flames, controlling their own body heat, and infusing firearms with solar energy.

SEA WITCH

Abilities: They command the waters, manipulate tides, foresee through scrying, empathize deeply, and transform water into ice.

GREEN WITCH

Abilities: Connected deeply with nature, they possess healing powers, an understanding of herbology, and a unique bond with the Earth's flora.

COSMIC WITCH

Abilities: Masters of the air, manipulate winds, harness electricity, and skillfully bend light to their will.

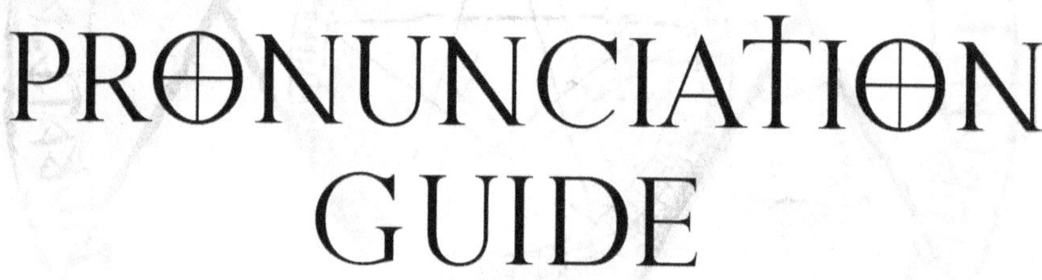

PRONUNCIATION GUIDE

Alden Lupas *AWL-den · LOO-pahs*

Anselm Raymor *an-sel-m · RAY-more*

Aradia Graves *ah-RAH-dee-ah · GRAYVES*

Aurora *aw-ROHR-ah*

Borealis *bor-ee-AL-is*

Chiron Lyra *KAI-ron · LY-rah*

Chiara Dunn *kee-AH-rah · DONE*

Desiree Dunn *dez-ih-RAY · DONE*

Dionysus *dye-uh-NY-suhs*

Domna *DOHM-nah*

Dullahan *DOO-luh-han*

Euphrosyne *yoo-FRAH-suh-nee*

Gianna "Gi" di Siena *jee-ah-nuh · "GI" · dee · see-EH-nah*

Glaucus *GLAW-kus*

Gwyn Raelyn *GWIN · RAY-lin*

Hygieia *hye-JEE-uh*

Isolde Faez *ih-ZOLD · fah-EHZ*

Ivah Graves *EE-vah · GRAYVES*

Janus Dyer *JAN-us · DY-er*

Jorina Graves Raelyn *joh-REE-nah · GRAYVES · RAY-lin*

Kosac *KOH-sak*

Leigh Raelyn *LEE · RAY-lin*

Lethe *LEE-thee*

Megaera "Meg" Erinye *muh-geh-ruh · "MEG" · eh-RIN-ee-eh*

Mictlan *MICT-lan*

Orion "Ry" Niemon *oh-RY-on · "RY" · NEE-mon*

Pallas Lyra *pal-uhs · LY-rah*

Priapus *PRY-uh-puhs*

Psyche *SY-kee*

Ravi Deyanira *RAH-vee · dey-ah-NEE-rah*

Sama Deyanira *SAH-mah · dey-ah-NEE-rah*

Selene Mhoon *seh-LEEN · MOON*

Soter Telfour *SOH-ter · tel-FOOR*

Tanith Lupas *TAH-nith · LOO-pahs*

Traum *TROWM*

Vane Bathory *VAYN · BAH-thoh-ree*

Vyvyan Bathory *VIV-ee-ahn · BAH-thoh-ree*

Weiss *VYCE*

Wilder Dunn *WYL-der · DONE*

Zeus Lupas *ZOOS · LOO-pahs*

PLAYLIST

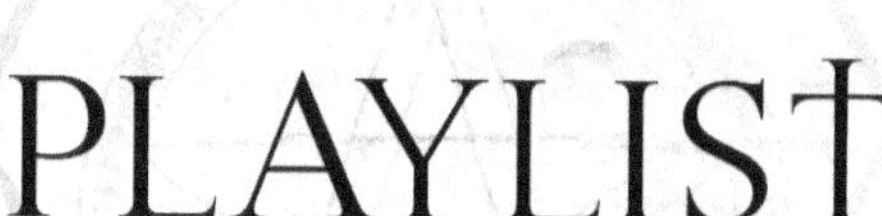

The Unquiet Grave	*Abel Korzeniowski*
Tell Me (Feat. Saoirse Ronan)	*Johnny Jewel*
your love is my drug - ambient	*Red X; pandora.*
Romantica	*Juno Francis*
Gothic Summer	*Damn the Witch Siren*
I Was Made for Loving You	*Myzica*
Eyes Without A Face	*Sinnerella*
Love Will Tear Us Apart	*Joy Division*
Another Heaven	*Curses*
Scream Drive Faster	*LAUREL*
Lay All Your Love on Me	*Pale Honey*
Devour	*Haunt Me*
Wonderful Nothing	*Glass Animals*
Afraid	*The Neighbourhood*
Follow You	*Bring Me The Horizon*
Keep the Streets Empty for Me	*Fever Ray*
The Passenger	*Hunter As a Horse*
Running Up That Hill	*Placebo*
Holding Out for a Hero	*Nothing But Thieves*
Forever Overdose	*Amira Elfeky*
Nightmares	*La Scaltra*
Seven Devils	*Florence + The Machine*
Melting Waltz	*Abel Korzeniowski*
Don't Blame Me	*Taylor Swift*

Ghosts in the River	AG
Fuckin' Heaven	GABRIELLA RAELYN
Gatekeeper	Torii Wolf
Die 1000x	Trevor Something
Where Do We Go From Here	Ruelle
The Same Deep Water as You	The Cure
Dream Woman	Suki Waterhouse
i guess u never really cared about me	Artemas
NEVER EVER	Omido
Young and Beautiful	Saint Avangeline
Church Bells	Henry Morris
Give	Sleep Token
Ceremony	Chromatics; Glass Candy
Heavenly	Cigarettes After Sex
As The World Falls Down (Instrumental)	Simone Del Freo

@MADCHAXX

PROLOGUE

LEIGH

Samhain

"NOT MUCH LONGER," I tell Ravi as my breath forms clouds in front of my face. The moon hangs full above us, and at midnight, I'll attempt something that would terrify everyone I love.

We sit together on the muddy shore of a small lake nine hundred miles north of Borealis, the country's city center, in the mountains of Glaucus. A bonfire-scented breeze stirs my long blonde hair, but the lake remains eerily still, as if it is holding its breath. The crisp autumn night promises snow, and mud seeps through my jeans as wet pine needles stick to the bottoms of my hiking boots.

"Are you cold?" Ravi asks, motioning to his fleece jacket. "You're trembling."

"Just eager to finish this and get home."

Home to the capital, where the kingdom functions well enough that I can slip away for personal reasons. Home to Wilder, who thinks I'm here mourning my ancestor Aradia, rather than trying to resurrect her. Home to wedding plans that have been ongoing for over two years because we're both too busy with our respective jobs to focus on the details—thank the gods for Gianna, who's been our saving grace in handling everything we keep forgetting in the chaos of crowns and Council meetings. Finally, *finally*, we will get to say our vows in March at the Iron Parthenon in Borealis, and I can hardly believe it's real.

But first, I must fix the mistake I made last winter. The one that's been eating me alive.

At midnight, when the barrier between the living and the dead is thinnest, I will invoke the gods to bind Aradia's soul to mine. It's my fault she's trapped in the despair of Mictlan. As a Lunar Witch, I am responsible for helping my ancestors resolve unfinished business and cross over to Heaven. I helped my father cross last year; despite the emotional challenge of letting him go, the process itself wasn't difficult. But when it came time to guide Aradia, she refused to leave. She said, *I don't know what waits for me when I leave this place. All I know is that I want to be here with you. It has brought me joy to watch you grow into the queen you are today. By your side is where I belong.* I should have insisted; found a way to convince her. Instead, I let her linger—and souls that don't cross over eventually fall into Mictlan.

After telling me about the War Letters and helping me bring peace to our country, Aradia's continued counsel and encouragement gave me so much confidence in my identity as a queen and Lunar Witch. How could I abandon someone who sacrificed everything for our kingdom? She deserves better than an eternity of despair in a realm rumored to be bleaker than Hell itself. When Ravi found stories about Mictlan in my father's history books, I knew we had a way to save her.

Ravi shifts awkwardly beside me, getting more anxious by the second. "Are you sure we should do this? This ritual—it is dangerous."

"The time for doubt has passed." I have spent months studying Prince Hypnos. Historical accounts say that the prince, another one of my ancestors, came to this very lake hundreds of years ago and convinced the gods to bind his dead bride's soul to his own, bringing her back to life. If he could do it then, I can do it now—for Aradia.

"Something's off about this night," Ravi says. "The energy isn't flowing —it's *waiting*. Like the lake is setting a trap. Maybe we should rethink this?"

I reach for my bag, which holds the supplies we need for the spell. "Don't be a wimp."

"I'm not. It's a fact that this lake is haunted."

He's right, but we already knew that before we came here. This lake has always unsettled me, even as a kid—like something in my bones senses the violence that took place here a hundred years ago, when Lunar Witches were drowned under laws I later repealed.

"Ravi, I could use some positivity right now," I say as I pull out the white candle and a painted bust of Aradia. The voices of other trapped souls grow louder in my mind. Ancestors beg me for help, desperate to heal from the traumas that keep them from going into the light. I take a deep breath and push them aside, promising to help them later. My focus has to be on Aradia and the spell I'm about to cast.

"I'm doing my best, but—" Ravi jumps and then looks around with wide eyes.

"Did you hear that?"

I check my phone—one minute until midnight. "We are out in nature. It was probably an animal. Now, can you please help me? Or if you aren't going to, then you can leave. I'm already nervous enough as it is without you being so high-strung."

"Leave? Without you?" Ravi blinks. I give him a look that brooks no argument. "I'm staying."

Good. I'd rather not be in the woods alone if this spell doesn't work and I fail Aradia a second time.

Sliding my lighter out of my hoodie pocket, I flick the ignition wheel, and light the purifying candle.

With a reluctant sigh, Ravi stands and brushes mud off his khakis. Taking the candle, he reaches for the portrait and holds both steady so I can focus on the invocation spell I have written on a folded piece of paper in my pocket. The ritual instructions make contacting the gods seem straightforward enough. Whether they'll actually respond, though, is uncertain.

Unfolding the paper, I force a smile. "Ready?"

"Let's get this over with."

"I call upon you, Great Mother of us all, bringer of fruitfulness, through seed and root, through leaf and flower, through life and love." The words flow as a vengeful wind whips around us. "Descend upon the body of your servant and chosen queen. Free Aradia from Mictlan, bind her soul to mine, grant her flesh and bone, and may we remain tied together until my dying day."

The ground shakes. I scream, reaching for Ravi as he reaches for me.

Ravi drops the candle but clutches the portrait. The flame dies in the mud, plunging us into darkness as clouds swallow the moon. I breathe heavily, watching, waiting for what is to come.

"Did it work?" he asks seconds later.

I close my eyes and listen. Only wind and mournful cries reach my ears. No response from the gods. They gave Hypnos back his bride because he was royalty, and I'm part of his bloodline, but Aradia isn't here. Perhaps the gods didn't hear me?

Panic rises in my chest, my heart pounding faster than a caged bird's frantic wings. The spell was meant to create a controlled telepathic link between me and the gods. They would tether my soul to Aradia's in Mictlan, forming a connection I could use to pull her back.

"Let me try again—"

A bright purple light spreads from the lake's center, like ink bleeding through water.

Magnetized by the otherworldly beauty, I step into the frigid lake. "I think it worked—"

"Get out," Ravi shrieks. "That's not Aradia. You've torn open a portal!"

"To the gods?" Hope stirs within me.

"Mictlan." He blanches. "You called to the gods, but the dead answered instead."

My blood turns to ice. A gateway to the realm of despair? I rush toward shore. My spell was meant to invoke the gods, not the ghosts. Usually, I have advisors, researchers, and Aradia herself to help me with urgent magical matters. But I'm at a total loss here. I studied how to call on the gods, not how to open—or close—portals to other dimensions.

"How do we close it?" I ask.

"I don't know."

This can't be happening. After years of building stability, I might have put everyone and everything in jeopardy in just one night. The peace

Wilder and I worked so hard to achieve—all of it is at risk because of my guilt.

"We should call for help," Ravi says, offering his phone. "At least tell Wilder."

"No." The word slips out sharper than I intend. I can't explain to anyone—especially Wilder—that I've been lying about this entire trip. The deception festers like acid in my stomach. He would lecture me about acting without thinking, and gods, he'd be right. I lied to his face, claiming this was a simple getaway from royal duties, while I was planning something this reckless, this *dangerous*, so close to our wedding. We are so near to our happy ending, and we have earned it after everything we've been through. I refuse to take that from him.

Ravi frowns. "Fine. Don't trust your *fiancé*." His words sting, because they're unfair—this isn't about trust. It's about *protection*. Protection from me and what I've done. "What about Jaxson?" he asks. "Or the Council? Someone should be here in case anything comes through."

I shake my head. I can't tell the Council that their supposedly stable queen just ripped open a portal to the realm of the dead. Their faith in me would disintegrate like a sandcastle in a storm.

The purple light in the lake pulses gently. Nothing has come through it yet. Maybe nothing will. If we can handle this ourselves, then why create unnecessary worry? The Council, Jax, and the Glaucus Blades would mobilize half the kingdom before we even understood what we're facing. Wilder would insist on investigating the portal himself.

No, we have to fix this ourselves.

"We keep this between us," I say, settling onto the muddy shore and pulling out my phone. "I bet there's something online about closing portals, even if it's indirectly related. I'm sure there's a forum about magical spells gone wrong. Sit down and help me research."

Minutes pass as we scroll through articles, most of which refuse to load because of our shitty reception in the mountains. Finally, two sites load clearly.

"Here," I say, relief flooding my voice. "'Interdimensional portals reflect the nature of the realm they connect to. The danger level depends solely on what world has been bridged.'" I look up triumphantly. "And this one says the same thing. 'Portal stability and threat assessment are determined by the destination realm's properties.'"

Ravi groans. "But, Leigh, I'm reading about other inhabitants of Mictlan here. It's not just lost souls. There are mentions of Dullahan, harpies—"

"Creatures of despair?" I wave him off, even as nausea rolls through me. But the point is not to panic, not until there is something tangible to panic about. "Mictlan isn't Hell, Ravi. It's limbo. That's why it is nicknamed the Nothing. The souls there are hopeless ghosts not dangerous daemons seeking destruction. Even if some escape, what's the worst they could do? Make people sad?"

My attempt at calming the situation does nothing to smooth the crease between my distant cousin's brows. "I don't know. This mentions—"

"Look," I cut him off, standing on shaky legs and brushing mud from my jeans, "we'll encase this entire lake in shadow magic. Keep it hidden from any passersby until morning, then figure out how to close it safely. No one gets hurt, no one panics."

That goes for me, too.

Ravi grudgingly locks his phone screen. "You really think that's enough?"

"We have to try."

I raise my hands, a tingling spreading through my fingers as darkness responds to my call, flowing like liquid across the lake's surface until the portal's glow is fully covered. To anyone passing by, it will look like an ordinary mountain lake reflecting the night sky.

"There." I back away, hoping I sound satisfied. "Problem contained. We'll deal with it properly after some better research. My battery is low, anyway."

As we walk up the dirt path toward the castle, I glance back, biting my bottom lip. The shadow veil stays perfectly in place; it will alert me if anything passes through it and conceal any sign of the purple light underneath. But I know the truth—a portal to another realm has been opened, and it's only a matter of time before this secret is exposed.

"MAYBE WE'RE LOOKING in the wrong place entirely." I push aside another useless book with a yawn. Pale dawn light filters through the large bay windows of Traum Castle's library, my family's mountain chalet. We've been researching for hours with nothing to show for it. "What if the answers aren't here but in there?" I gesture toward the window and the forest of pine trees hiding the lake below.

Ravi looks up from his laptop, bloodshot eyes wide with alarm. "Absolutely not."

"Listen, we've been at this for hours. Every article about portal closure is either theoretical or deals with Hell gates." I rub my temples to dull the headache that's been building since we started this search. "No one writes specifically about closing a portal to Mictlan. No recent successful missions to reference."

"That doesn't mean we go inside a death realm."

He's right. I don't want to go there either, but we may not have a choice. We need to shut the portal before anyone finds out. If something comes through and someone gets hurt because of what I did, I'll never forgive myself.

"Maybe," I slowly offer, "there's something in my father's journals back at Rowan Palace. They led us to the Hypnos story that brought us here in the first place."

Ravi's phone rings, cutting off any response he might have had.

"Turn it off. We don't have time for—"

"It's Wilder."

Fire burns through my veins, banishing exhaustion. "Answer it."

Ravi clears his throat. "Hello?" He nods, then extends the phone. "He wants to talk to you."

My chest tightens. There's no way Wilder knows what I've done, the trouble I've caused.

"Hey, baby," I manage, trying to sound normal. "My phone's been on Do Not Disturb—"

"Don't panic." The words still my racing thoughts. "Queen Jorina suffered a heart attack during the Dark Dinner. Mom thinks it was a coronary spasm. She's been trying to reach you."

A knot in my throat chokes off my response. My grandmother. Oh gods, is she okay?

"Leigh, are you there? Goddammit." There's a brief pause before he shouts, "Soter, bring me your phone."

"I'm here," I whisper.

"Did you hear what I said?"

"How is she?" The words barely escape my lips.

"My mom is with her, but until I get more details ..." Papers rustle in the background. "Leigh, we need you here. I know you needed your space, and I hate to cut your trip short, but please come home."

I wrap my arms around myself, trying to hold the pieces together. Of course I'm coming home. But panic hijacks my brain.

We haven't closed the portal. Do I risk leaving it open?

The image of my grandmother, frail and alone in a hospital bed, surfaces memories of waking up like that at Hebe Hospital when my father and Fynn died, with no family there to hold my hand through the pain.

"We'll catch the next train," I promise.

"What about the portal?" Ravi whispers urgently.

I meet his eyes, seeing my own exhaustion reflected in them. We've been awake all night without finding anything useful. The answers aren't here, but my father's extensive collection back home might have the key. But just in case, he should stay.

"Tell your mom to keep sending updates until I get there," I tell Wilder.

"I'll send Isolde to meet you at the station. She'll take you straight to the hospital."

"Thank you."

"Don't worry. Mom's taking excellent care of her. Everything will be okay." His steady confidence anchors me, but my eyes also burn with tears. We're supposed to be happier than ever right now—we're getting *married*. But if he finds out I lied about this trip, he'll think it's because I don't trust him. That couldn't be further from the truth. I trust him completely, with my entire being as well as my heart. I lied to protect *us* and this perfect bubble we're in. But if he finds out, he'll drop everything to help me fix this mess, derail his training with Soter, and turn our wedding plans into a crisis. I'd rather get lost in Mictlan than watch him spiral. I can handle this without him. I will. No matter what it takes.

"I'll text updates," he says.

After hanging up, I turn to Ravi. "You need to stay and monitor the situation."

His brown skin pales. "What?"

"My shadow magic will alert me if anything comes through. I will notify you if there's any danger." I wobble as I stand. My adrenaline is wearing off. "A few days, tops. Just until I can find something in my father's journals."

"I can't stay here. People will start asking questions if I don't return to Borealis."

"I know, I know." I reach for his hand. "Please, Ravi. I can't leave this unguarded, but I can't abandon my grandmother, either. She's unwell, and I can't be in two places at once."

His shoulders slump. "I don't like this."

I nod. Neither do I. "If anything—and I mean *anything*—seems off about that portal, you call me immediately. We will notify the Blades if necessary. But that's a last resort. We need to prevent chaos from erupting."

"Leigh—"

"A few days," I repeat firmly. "Then this will all be over."

I gather my things, guilt gnawing at me. I'm lying to Wilder about why I'm in Glaucus, abandoning a potentially dangerous magical anomaly, and leaving my cousin to guard a portal to the realm of the dead without help.

Everything will be fine, I tell myself. *Nothing's happened yet. Just a few days, and I'll know if I am overreacting.*

Though the shadow magic remains calm, something deep in my chest warns that I'm making a terrible mistake.

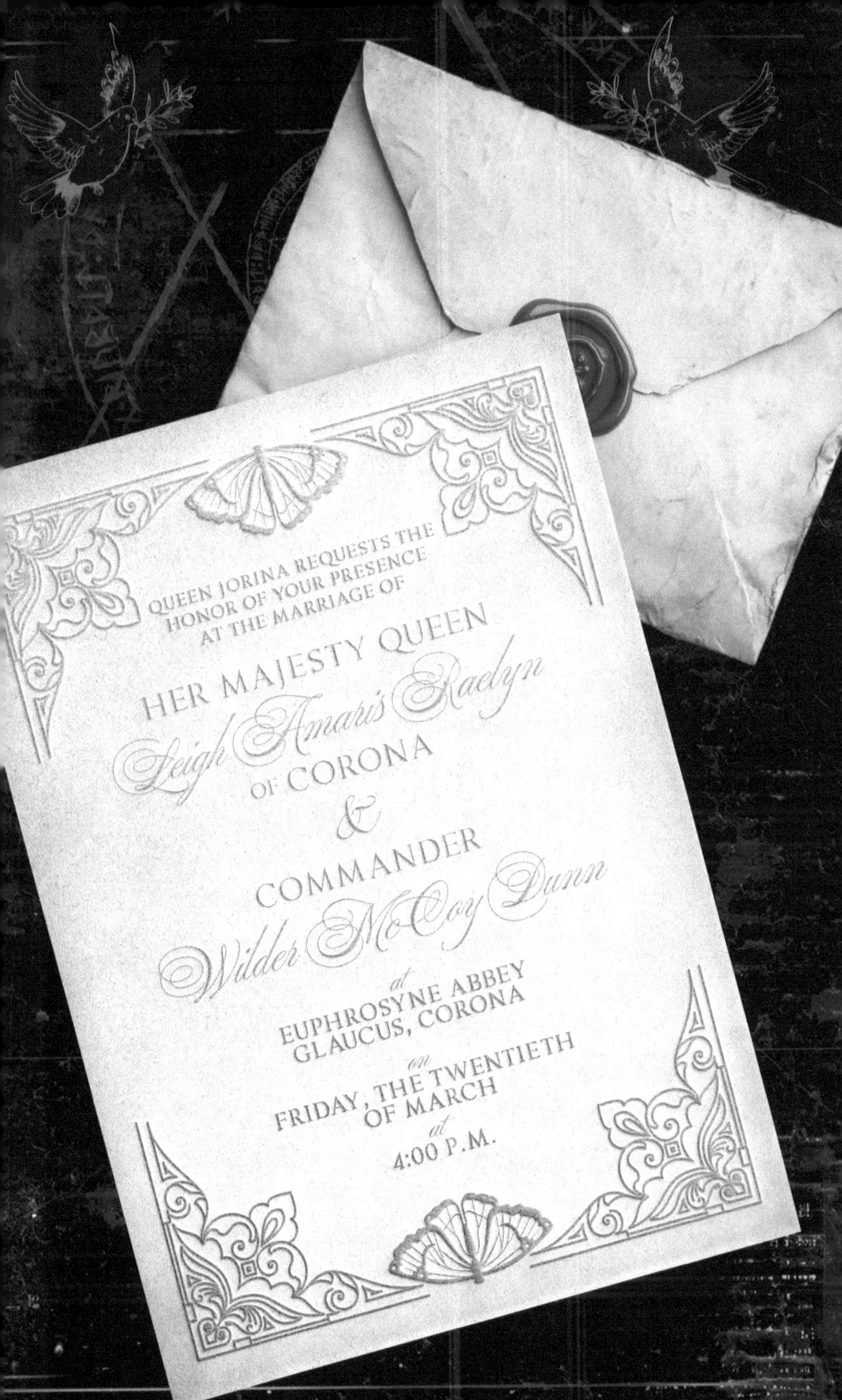

QUEEN JORINA REQUESTS THE
HONOR OF YOUR PRESENCE
AT THE MARRIAGE OF

HER MAJESTY QUEEN
Leigh Amaris Raelyn
OF CORONA
&
COMMANDER
Wilder McCoy Dunn

at
EUPHROSYNE ABBEY
GLAUCUS, CORONA
on
FRIDAY, THE TWENTIETH
OF MARCH
at
4:00 P.M.

XVI
THE TOWER

CHAPTER ONE

LEIGH

Four and Half Months Later

I'M IN HELL.

I've been socializing for hours. Wilder and I were asked to greet groups of guests, dividing and conquering the thousands of people who came to celebrate us and our love. I've shaken so many hands that my grip has gone numb. Not to mention, my nose itches from all the perfumes I've inhaled. The bright pink of the ballroom where we're hosting our welcome party is the icing on the cake, and it tests my gag reflex. I hate pink.

Pink flowers. Pink antique couches. Pink ribbons hanging from the overhead chandeliers.

"Don't you love it?" Gianna asks, her topaz eyes sparkling. As my maid of honor, she's responsible for this colorful mess, and I regret giving her free rein over this weekend's color scheme. If I hadn't been so busy with my grandmother's post-hospital care and researching how to close the portal, I would have picked a softer palette—something neutral with pops of color, like green to match Wilder's eyes.

But Gi has transformed this space into a scene straight out of one of her beloved fairy tales, complete with dozens of white rabbits darting between everyone's feet and hopping all over the chairs the guests have left empty. I feel like I'm trapped in a zoo.

I force myself to smile at her. It's my own fault for not giving my final input on the planning. Ravi and I have been frantically researching how to close the portal to Mictlan since we opened it nearly five months ago. We kept hitting dead ends until a few weeks ago, when I found—in some of my father's research—that the spell to close the gateway is in Aradia's journals, which are locked away here in Traum Castle. Ironically, we are back to where we started.

There was too much going on at home to justify another trip to Glaucus so close to the wedding. The Council and Wilder would have been suspicious; I would have had to admit how reckless I'd been in trying to bring the dead back to life. So instead, I changed our wedding location to Glaucus at the last minute.

I told Wilder that I wasn't thrilled about the wedding photos we'd get if we stayed at the venue in Borealis. With a mountain backdrop, our wedding photos would be showstoppingly gorgeous, so the ceremony must happen in Glaucus. It's not a lie—the mountains are picturesque—but being here also allows me to get back to the lake without raising concern.

Over the past few months, a few daemons have slipped through the portal, breaching the shadow boundary I set around the lake. Luckily, they were all lesser daemons, and the Glaucus Blades killed them all before they caused any damage. Since they haven't been dangerous, I haven't told anyone where they came from. Still, the threat remains, and it's growing. If I manage to close the portal tonight, everyone will remain blissfully unaware of the situation. The Blades will submit their reports about strange daemon activity, never realizing their queen caused it all. I need to close the portal before something worse gets through, and I have to do it tonight.

I want tomorrow to be about Wilder and our future together. No distractions. I've dreamed of this day since I proposed to him on that rooftop. I want nothing more than to commit to each other in a room full of our family and friends, kiss like no one's watching, and then walk out of the abbey doors without a care in the world.

I want to be a bride whose biggest worry is whether her dress is wrinkled after the long train journey from the capital, not whether creatures from a death realm might crash the reception.

Tonight feels like I'm racing against time to prevent a disaster of my own making, but tomorrow will be the happiest day of my life.

According to my father's research, Mictlan's biggest threat is the Dullahan—armored rangers who serve Kosac, the Death God who rules there. Dullahan haven't been seen yet, but I feel the risk of the ticking clock. For months, I've felt like I'm playing a game of daemon roulette. It ends now.

"Leigh?" Gi prompts.

"It's so pretty," I manage through gritted teeth.

Gianna beams, and I exhale. Poor Gi poured her heart into planning this entire weekend. I know she's determined for this wedding to outshine the two she never had. Gianna has been engaged twice—once to my brother before he passed away, and once to a jerk we went to school with—but she's never walked down the aisle herself. Her happiness matters more than my initial discomfort.

"I'm so relieved you love it. It was nearly impossible to pull off within your tight time frame, but luckily, I had help," Gianna exclaims. She grabs a flute of sparkling wine from a server dressed in a white tailcoat, then hands it to me. I've already had more than enough to drink. Drinks were constantly offered to me and Wilder before our guests tore us apart, stealing our attention from each other.

I scan the crowd of spring colors, and exhale longingly. It's been a while since I last saw him. Originally, I envisioned a small, intimate wedding focused on Wilder and me, but Gianna brushed me off. *You only get married once*, she'd insisted, *and when you do, you do it big*. Not wanting to argue, I agreed.

A happy Gi is a happy Leigh.

"Help?" I ask, noticing Wilder across the room talking with Ry and Isolde. My heart swells. Goodness, he looks so handsome in his suit. "Help from whom?"

Gi rubs her button nose, looking guilty as shit. I narrow my eyes. "I know you don't like her," Gi says carefully, her tan complexion turning waxen, "but you have to understand, you were so busy with your grandmother's recovery, and I needed an extra set of hands ..."

"*Who?*"

Gi doesn't look at me when she says, "Felicity."

My stomach hardens. "Felicity *Graves*?"

"Yes."

I sneer. My cousin Felicity and I aren't close. She only visits me and the family when she wants something, so the fact that she helped Gianna plan my wedding tells me I'm about to be asked for the biggest favor yet. I tighten my grip on my drink. As the daughter of my grandmother's late brother from a second marriage, Felicity is technically next in line for my throne until I have children. Over the past few years, she's become bolder, asking for a higher allowance and more royal responsibilities, and I don't like it.

I make a mental note to deal with Felicity after the wedding.

I pretend to yawn. It's time to meet Ravi, help him find the spell, and close the portal. Wilder's busy with friends; maybe he won't notice I've slipped away if I do it now. "I should go get some sleep. Thank you so much, Gi. Everything tonight was beautiful and special."

Gi frowns. "It's not even ten o'clock."

"Doesn't the bride need her beauty rest?" I ask.

Gi's jaw sets. "Are you really going to bed, or trying to fuck around with your fiancé?"

I choke on my spit. Gi pats my back, waving off a few concerned guests.

"I already told Wilder I'd see him in the morning," I wheeze.

"I'm sure he accepted that with the subtlety of a jackhammer."

When I told him I wanted to sleep alone tonight, Wilder complained that I always break the rules so I shouldn't have trouble breaking this one. He's right, of course. I want more than anything to sneak into his room and fuck his brains out one last time before we make it official. The thought of him wanting to tear off my clothes as much as I want to tear off his is maddening. But I stayed firm despite how much it kills me, because the excuse that traditionally, royal engaged couples spend the night apart before the wedding is the lie that will allow me to handle the portal without him knowing. He'll be happier inside the castle with the rest of our family and friends, blissful and excited as all grooms should be the night before their wedding.

"Wilder is fine with it," I lie.

"If you say so," Gi says, and I roll my eyes. "But, before you leave, you need to come with me to talk to Felicity. I told her we'd find her before the party ends."

"I'm okay, thanks." I sound bratty, but I don't have time to get caught up in Felicity's drama.

Eleven years older than me, Felicity spent our childhood criticizing everything about me. She incessantly commented on my uncouth princess behavior, my wild hair, and my mismatched clothes. The worst came after my father and Fynn died. While I was still reeling from the loss, Felicity gave an interview discussing the "tragic nature" of their passing. She told the entire kingdom how nervous she was about Corona's future with me next in line for the throne.

I'm sure she hasn't changed.

Tonight at the rehearsal dinner, I avoided making eye contact with her across the table and kept my distance when we moved to the ballroom for the party. I'd hoped to avoid her altogether, but that was wishful thinking.

Gi narrows her eyes. "All you need to do is thank her. Is that too much to ask? If she hadn't helped me with the names of caterers and hotels for your guests, I never would have been able to pull this wedding off in time."

"Felicity lives here, Gi. It's not as if she went out of her way to give you those names."

Gi leans in close. Her spicy perfume holds me hostage as she says, "Leigh, if you don't accompany me right now to thank your cousin, I will put laxatives in your morning coffee." My oldest friend flashes me a cold smile. "Taking photos will be awkward as hell when you can't get off the toilet."

Sensing she's serious, I scowl. "Remind me why we are friends?"

"Ah, I see Felicity." Gi waves. I follow her line of sight.

I suppress my groan as I slip my arm through Gianna's. The sooner I thank Felicity, the sooner I can leave. "Let's get this over with," I grumble.

My forced smile falters. Felicity isn't alone. Admirers surround her—all men—each of whom she probably promised she would choose to have at her side when she becomes queen.

"Ow," I whine when Gi elbows me in the ribs.

"Stop scowling, will you? I've heard from reliable sources that she gives great gifts."

"Ugh. I can afford all the nice things I want. I'm the *queen*."

Gi pouts, and my resolve crumbles like streusel. "Humor me. Felicity said she's super excited to see you. I think she's matured since you two last saw one another. Maybe she will surprise you?"

I'll believe she's changed the day dogs can talk. "Maybe."

I inhale a deep breath, feeling the seams of my white dress tighten. I can do this.

Felicity stops talking with her friends. My cousin, a Green Witch who looks more like my grandmother than I do with her long dark hair, sapphire blue eyes, and a reserved heart-shaped face, grins maniacally. I need to get out of here.

"By the stars, Leigh, don't you look fancy," Felicity greets, kissing me twice on each cheek. Her lip gloss is sticky, like syrup. She wears a pastel pink baroque-style dress, which is her signature color. I'm guessing she was involved in decorating the venue. White silk gloves cover Felicity's hands and elbows, and her yellow diamonds are modest, yet we both know they are extremely expensive.

"Well, it is my wedding," I reply with a hand on my silky hip.

Gianna frowns. "*Be nice,*" she mouths.

"I'm so happy you found your person," Felicity gushes. Her male companions nod as if on cue. "For a while there, my mother and I didn't think you'd ever settle down. At least, not with anyone other than that Bennett fellow." She pretends to look for Bennett among my guests, though I know she's aware he isn't here, considering she helped Gianna with the wedding preparations, which likely included the invite list. "Shame he couldn't make it, but no one wants to watch the love of their life marry another man."

I choke back ugly laughter. Felicity hasn't changed a bit. "I am hardly the love of Bennett's life." Last I heard, he'd met someone.

A huge smirk forms on Felicity's face as she speaks. "I only meant that the way you two behaved when you were kids made it obvious he was obsessed with you. My mother and I still talk about how you two had sex in a closet at Fynn's engagement party." She laughs humorlessly, and her men laugh along with her.

My breath stalls, while Gianna flinches. I can't believe Felicity brought up Gi and Fynn's engagement party in front of her. Father and Fynn *died* that night.

"I mean, talk about a scandal," Felicity continues. "But you were always one for breaking the rules. It's funny how you enforce them now."

My fingers twitch with the urge to put this bitch in her place, but I'm not about to create a scene at my party. Gi has already moved away and is locking eyes with her girlfriend across the room. "You know what, Felicity? Thank you so much for coming. Your help with planning this event has been invaluable. Excuse us."

I steer Gi out of that rattlesnake's nest.

She exhales. "That girl is toxic as fuck."

A laugh bursts out before I can stop it. "A leopard can't change its spots."

"I don't get it; she was so nice on the phone."

I offer Gi a water from the nearby buffet table. She gulps it down.

"Probably so she could get an invite to the wedding and torment guests about how she helped plan it," I reply. "Let's just pray she doesn't start singing."

Gi snorts. "Please, don't ever die. I couldn't stomach her as queen."

My stomach tightens. "Don't worry, that won't happen anytime soon."

The glow of Gi's skin returns to normal. "I can't believe you are getting married tomorrow."

I beam at my oldest friend. "Neither can I."

"Wilder is a lucky guy," Gi says, tears welling in her eyes.

"I thought you didn't approve?" I tease. Since their trip to Aurora together two years ago, Wilder and Gi have grown very close. How could they not be, especially after he rescued her at gunpoint? I glance over my shoulder and catch Wilder watching me as if he has X-ray vision. I blow him a kiss. "I'd better go."

Gi hugs me tight. "I love you."

"Love you."

I aim toward the exit with Wilder's heated gaze still on me.

CHAPTER TWO
WILDER

RY'S LIPS ARE MOVING, but I couldn't care less about what he's saying about the food. My focus is on Leigh leaving the party and how I haven't had a chance to talk to Jaxson or anyone else about the daemons invading this city because of all the guests I had to greet tonight.

I quickly look away from Leigh, scanning everywhere for Soter. He's here with several other Borealis Blades, providing extra security for the wedding, but he's also here to help Glaucus Blade Commander Wendy Detzer find where these daemons are coming from. The case has been open for nearly five months—it's time to close it without causing panic among the public.

Part of me wants to pull Soter aside, get an update on his progress, and offer help. It's his first case as Borealis Blade Commander. But Leigh deserves my full attention this weekend. Whatever's happening with the daemons will have to wait until after the honeymoon, but let's pray the case gets solved well before then.

"Where's Leigh going?" Isolde asks, catching my attention.

I twist to see Leigh saying a few parting words to her mother, edging closer to the exit.

Frowning, I move to intercept her. She wants to sleep alone tonight, but who said anything about sleeping? My grin widens. I have so many things I plan to do to her before we pledge ourselves to one another at the abbey. She's been distracting me all night in that dress—the material so revealing I doubt she's wearing anything underneath. I've made a private bet with myself to find out.

These formal parties have never really been my scene. The sparkling wine is too sour, all fizz and pretension. When I tried to order a beer earlier, Isolde acted as if I'd committed high treason. Did I overlook some unwritten royal protocol?

All I want is to be alone with Leigh. Nothing else should matter. Not the daemons, not Soter taking my job, not this ridiculous party—just her.

I take another step toward the exit. Leigh pauses mid-conversation, her gray eyes meeting mine and narrowing with recognition. She knows exactly what I'm thinking.

My smile sends a playful message: *If you try to run, I'll catch you.*

Leigh shakes her head, offering a sly smile.

She needs to relax and let her hair down, so to speak. She's been on edge for months. Maybe she feels pressured to make everything perfect this weekend, especially after Queen Jorina's heart attack on Samhain. We've postponed our wedding multiple times, and now that the day is finally here, Leigh seems distracted. She's been avoiding the subject since we got off the train this morning. Earlier, she gave me some excuse about archaic traditions and not sleeping together, then planted a mind-bending kiss on me. Still, before I could do anything about it, like checking out the honeymoon suite early, she giggled and ran off to get ready for the rehearsal dinner, leaving me alone and turned on as hell.

Leigh has been going through a lot lately, and I understand the struggle since I'm facing my own identity crisis. After years of active duty as a Blade, I retired two days ago—walking away from the career I'd been training for since my Emergence. I'd even made commander earlier than I ever thought possible, but I gave it all up without hesitation for her. For *us.*

Now I'm having a hard time figuring out who I am without the badge. Being a Solar Witch means being a Blade isn't just a job, it's literally in my blood and part of my magical nature. When I enrolled, the Blade Academy made it clear that I needed to protect and serve. Even years after the Labor Laws were abolished, old habits die hard.

If Leigh knew how much I miss it, she'd think I love work more than her. I don't; that could never be true.

Even now, I can barely believe she wants to marry me. *Me.* A nobody from the working class, who half the people in this room called Wilbur when we first met, as if I look anything like a Wilbur. Born part of the Nebula class with dirt under my nails and calluses on my hands, I never imagined a world where I'd end up with the Queen of Corona.

Yet here I am, about to become her husband. Sometimes I wonder if she's settling, choosing me because she's too busy to find someone better. But then she looks at me with genuine adoration ... She looked at me the same way during the speeches tonight, like I'm her anchor in the storm—that's when I know what we have is real.

She needs to remember how to be happy again. What happened with Aradia was not her fault. And I'm going to help her get there.

I click my tongue when Leigh leaves the party. She wants to be chased.

Ry grabs my sleeve before I can follow her.

I glare at him. "What?"

He frowns, golden curls making him look years younger than twenty-seven. "You didn't hear a word I said, did you?"

Yeah, I was too busy thinking about the Blades and getting Leigh naked to care. "Sorry. Habit."

"I'll overlook how rude that is since this weekend is about you and just repeat it: Jax has been on the phone for the past ten minutes, and he looks worried. Is he okay? He's seemed kind of off all night."

I follow Ry's gaze. Jax stands away from the crowd, dark brows furrowed.

Is Wendy giving him a hard time? Jax isn't on Domna duty tonight, but if there's been an update on the case, she won't hesitate to call him.

"Jax has seemed uneasy," Isolde comments, her eyes fixed across the room.

"Yeah, I guess," I agree, although he and I haven't had much time to talk, not with people chatting me up every five minutes and keeping us apart.

Isolde bites her glossed bottom lip, focused on whatever has her attention. Before I can follow her gaze, she walks off. "Be right back."

Ry's eyes remain fixed on Jax. "Wendy's been pressuring him about the daemons. She's desperate to find the gateway they're using to get here before the Glaucus Precinct evaluation next month. It doesn't look good that outside forces from Borealis have been brought in to handle this."

The Council's pressuring Wendy to solve this daemon case before the wedding, but something's off. These daemons are different—harder to track, more elusive—like something magical is hiding the gateway they are using to get here. The Council doesn't want to hear that, though. To them, facts are just excuses. They've thrown money at Wendy's Blades, thinking that'll fix everything, but you can't just buy your way out of a supernatural problem. Meanwhile, Jax is drowning in work, and having Soter—who he can't stand—on his turf isn't helping anyone.

Ry straightens. "Incoming."

Jax joins our group. Finding Leigh will have to come later; I need to check on my friend first. "What did Wendy say?" I ask.

"Wendy? Oh, she's tired and pissed as hell," Jax replies, half-heartedly.

"Another daemon sighting?"

Jax shakes his head. His eyes look guarded, but he blinks and is all smiles and laughs. "I thought we had strict orders not to bring you work stuff?" he teases.

I frown. "If there is a problem, I deserve to know. So does Leigh."

"Last I checked, you retired." He plucks invisible lint off his gold paisley dinner jacket. "Sorry, buddy, but what Wendy tells me is classified, and you're not married to the queen yet."

My expression hardens. "Jackass."

Jax laughs, but it quickly fades as someone steals his attention. I'm nearly to the point of grabbing him by the shoulders and demanding answers.

"There you guys are."

My sister wears a revealing red dress that matches her crimson eyes. "I didn't know Leigh was such a big fan of pink."

Jax's throat bobs. "Hi, Desi."

Desiree smiles. They may be exes, but they still talk regularly. Like me, she hasn't seen Jax face-to-face in a while. He hardly comes back to Borealis these days, almost as if he's hiding up here in the mountains. "Jax, can you believe we weren't seated together at dinner? I had to make small talk with that tiresome Felicity woman. She kept telling me my drinking blood was making her lose her appetite. I almost bit her just to shut her up!"

"You look well, Jaxson," Vane says. My sister's vampire mate, who stands taller than Jax, is dressed in a flashy green-black suit and layers of ancient gold jewelry. He makes everyone, including me, look underdressed. Jax's eyes immediately lose their brightness, and his confident stance wavers. Honestly, I've never seen him so on edge. Is something going on beyond the case?

"You too," Jax mumbles, and I wince at his disingenuous tone.

Vane pulls Desi close and kisses her temple. She grins like the luckiest girl in the world while Jax's face goes ashen.

I can't watch this; it's just too painful. Jax looks like a wounded animal. Is Desi the reason he's been acting strange? Last I checked, he had a boyfriend. Did that end?

I'll ask him about it when we are alone later.

"I'll be right back," I say as I step away from the group.

Grabbing a smooth pink ribbon from one of the flower arrangements, I wrap it around my hand, tighter and tighter. Time to catch my bride.

I LEAVE THE BALLROOM, but Leigh isn't in the hallway. She probably went to bed like she threatened, though I'd hoped to catch her first. This maze of a castle has at least a hundred rooms—I can't believe she called it a chalet.

I turn the corner toward Leigh's bedroom, and centuries-old stone walls rise on both sides of me. My mom paces the hallway with her phone pressed to her ear. Her brown hair flows down the back of her butter-yellow column dress, a welcome contrast to the harsh braid she usually wears at the hospital. She doesn't notice me.

"Yes, I received the scans," Mom says to whoever's on the other line.

My jaw clenches. Is she working?

"You were right to call me. It looks—"

I clear my throat, and Mom's shoulders tense. She made me a promise. No work during my wedding. I should never have expected her to follow through. Work is all she's ever done. Slowly, she turns around, her smile wavering. "Doctor Crux, let me call you back," she says, ending the call with the Altum Healer.

"I thought you were taking the weekend off." My tone is as flat as her stare.

"I am."

I chew on the inside of my cheek. "Then what was that?" I gesture to the phone.

Mom averts her gaze. "It was nothing."

I don't know why I'm surprised. Mom has made and broken many promises over the years, but this is *my wedding*. I figured that for this, of all things, she would finally show up for me. I hate how wrong I was.

"Come on, honey, don't be mad. It was just a phone call," Mom says dismissively. She laughs, but I don't laugh with her. My parents have always put their careers first. They sacrificed our family's happiness, which is exactly why I quit my job—because I vowed never to be like them.

"Mom, I believe the hospital can manage things without you for a few days."

She sighs. "Yeah, maybe." She goes silent, and I'm about to leave when she asks, "Where are you going? Is the party over already?"

"I'm looking for Leigh," I say, crossing my arms over my chest.

"Is everything okay?" Mom asks in that gentle tone—the one she mainly uses with patients.

Pushing my hair out of my face, I nod. "Yeah." She understands that Leigh has been struggling since losing Aradia. I've just been pretending it's not as bad as it really is. Mom's good at reading people, too.

She studies me a little longer, her clinical gaze searching for cracks. Satisfied that I don't need her to patch me up, she grins. "I saw your bride heading that way"—she points behind me—"maybe six minutes ago."

"Thanks." I turn around, but she grabs my sleeve.

"Wait, I want to talk to you. Your dad—" She opens her beaded bag.

I glance down the hallway. "Can it wait?" I want to see Leigh one more time before we exchange vows at the altar.

Mom snaps her purse shut. "Of course."

I kiss her cheek. "Desi and Vane are in the ballroom. You should go mingle."

"Sounds fun."

Feeling satisfied, I leave Mom behind and pick up my pace. Smirking, I run my fingers over the silky ribbon in my pocket.

Leigh, what are you up to?

CHAPTER THREE
DESIREE

JAXSON GLARES at Vane like he's stolen his favorite toy. *Me.*

Vane is deep in conversation with Ry, ignoring how Jax is sizing him up, as if he could somehow throw my six-five vampire husband out the nearest stained-glass window and into the Acheron River below. I shift uncomfortably. What's his problem? I thought we were all friends.

I scan the ballroom for Jaxson's boyfriend, Anselm, to help me run interference. I've seen pictures of him on Jax's social media, but he's not here. My stomach drops. He was invited. Wasn't he? I don't recall seeing him at dinner either.

If they broke up, Jax would have told me—unless they ended things because of me. That could explain Jax's hostility toward Vane.

Jax and I broke up years ago. We don't see each other often, but we talk regularly on the phone. Not once has he mentioned still having feelings for me or ending things with Anselm. I wouldn't even imagine it, but the haunted look in his whiskey-colored eyes tells me he has something painful to say, and once he does, there'll be no taking it back.

I cross and uncross my arms, trying and failing to listen to Vane talk about the live performer we booked for Little Death. I can't focus with Jaxson standing there. The energy coming off him is overwhelmingly suffocating.

I should either say something or pull Jax aside and ask him directly what's going on. I haven't seen him this anxious since right before he dumped me because he was worried Wilder would find out we were dating. He's hiding something, and I can only hope I'm wrong and it has nothing to do with me. Because there's no way I can hurt him again; he's my best friend. I'm fully committed to Vane, but I want to let Jax down gently. I couldn't live with him hating me.

I put distance between myself and Vane. No point in rubbing salt in the wound if Jaxson still has feelings. This weekend isn't about us. It's about Leigh and Wilder. I won't make a scene.

"I didn't see Anselm at dinner. Is he coming tonight?" I ask to test the waters.

"He's not," Jax says, his tone uneasy.

Why not? Is it because he got held up at work, or because he's no longer Jaxson's plus-one?

Vane glances at the space I've put between us, his eyes narrowing. I smile awkwardly.

"Ah, look, there's Vyvyan," I say to divert Vane's attention until I realize Vyvyan is glaring at Jax, who is back to scowling at Vane. Good heavens. If she stirs up drama, I'll have to leave my brother's party. I'd rather chew off my own foot.

"Vyvyan, I can see your boobs," I practically shout, and as intended, everyone's attention shifts to her chest. "That dress is so sheer. You might as well be naked."

Vyvyan grins, soaking up the attention. Vyvyan and I have a history. She once tried to kill me when she was the vampire queen, worried I'd threaten her partnership with Vane. We've gotten past that, and now both of us carry the Bathory royal name. But she's still fiercely protective of him. She tolerates me, and I do the same for her.

"It's as if you've never seen a woman's body before, Desiree. I thought you were some kind of healer?" Vyvyan deadpans, not taking her eyes off Jax, who has his arms crossed and is staring at his feet.

Vane follows her gaze. My unease intensifies.

Vane can sense emotions and thoughts, sometimes even glimpses of the future. He's definitely reading all of Jaxson's thoughts right now. His eyes are unblinking and focused, as if he's dissecting each of Jax's secrets with a surgeon's skill.

Jax glares at him. Vane grins back—that knowing grin that says, *I know all your dirty secrets.*

Jax's fists clench.

The air between them crackles with years of unresolved issues, mostly involving me. Vane Turned me, Jaxson wanted me to take the cure and be with him. Again, I thought we had moved past this. Vane's grin widens, challenging him. Jax's shoulders bunch up, muscles tensing like a hungry animal ready to pounce. He's moments away from swinging his fist at Vane's pretty face.

My heart pounds against my ribs. A few guests have started to notice, their conversations faltering as they sense the shift in the formerly jovial atmosphere.

Dammit. They can't do this. Not here. Not now. This is supposed to be a party, not their battlefield. I know Jax is hurting—the breakup, if that's the reason behind his sour mood, must've destroyed him—but he needs to back the hell off.

Vane's not the one who broke his heart.

Anselm is, and Jax is seeking comfort with me because I am familiar and safe.

Vyvyan bares her fangs. "Do you have a problem, Jaxson?"

"Not with you," Jax says tightly to the tiny vampire.

"Then you should stop staring at Vane like he's cheated you at cards if you don't want to have a problem with me." Her nails look poised to strike his face.

"Vyvyan," I warn with forced lightness. This is all a misunderstanding. "I'm sure he wasn't."

Ry flashes me a sympathetic look, then quickly moves toward Pallas across the room, leaving me with this hostile mess. I consider begging him to stay. I'm not trying to get between Vane and Jaxson. Choosing sides between my husband and best friend would create a bigger rift between them, but if Jaxson is upset because of me, then I need to try to diffuse the situation. I want us all to get along.

"I beg to differ," Vyvyan snaps at me. "My eyes are sharper than a tack. He was staring like he was plotting to gut Vane, then toss you over his shoulder and make a run for it."

"He was not."

"I'm just enjoying the party," Jax replies calmly, but the turbulent look in his eyes betrays his calm façade. "But, Desi, could we—"

"I don't blame you, Jaxson. Desiree does look delicious tonight." Vane reaches for me with a predatory smile. He tugs me closer, lips grazing my ear as he whispers, "She *tastes* delicious, too."

Every muscle in Jaxson's body goes rigid. I'm too stunned to speak.

"We'll talk later, Desi," he snaps before storming off.

Fuck. I need to fix this. I don't want Jax mad at me. Vane didn't need to say what he did.

"Congratulations," I hiss at Vane. "You won Jerk-Off of the Night." I'm not embarrassed by Vane's comment; I'm open about our relationship. I hate having to remind Jax that I'm married to someone who can read his mind and use it against him. Jax is upset about something, and I want to find out what it is. If it's about me, I'll remind him why we don't work, and he will realize he was having a lapse in judgment.

I follow Jax. Vane sighs behind me.

"Don't walk away from your king," Vyvyan snarls.

"My *king* can handle it." Fucking vampires. Their territorialism rivals mated wolves.

"Ask him for the truth, and we can all move forward," Vane calls after me.

I walk away, flipping him off as I go. I hate it when he messes with people's minds and plays games with what he finds out. Vane may be immortal, but it wouldn't hurt him to show some human compassion.

I catch up with Jax on the nearest balcony, where he's brooding over Glaucus's modern-baroque cityscape. Mountains rest beyond, and the Acheron River rushes below, its sound barely covering his anxious heartbeat.

When Jax turns to face me, my breath catches. Anguish etches jagged lines into his face.

"I just need a minute, Desiree."

"What the hell is going on with you?" My hands are on my hips. "And don't you dare lie."

We aren't toxic exes. We respect each other.

"Desiree—"

I flash my fangs. "Answer me."

Jax huffs but still says nothing.

"Vane and I are together. I thought you were okay with that. It's been years."

Jax opens and closes his mouth. "Vane is a dick, but he's not why—" He groans. "Look, what I'm about to say may seem out of the blue, but I—"

"Jax, please tell me you and Anselm didn't break up because of me. You were so happy …"

"Desiree, you should know that Anselm and I … I've wanted to tell you for so long, but—"

"That doesn't look like Vane Bathory unless you've replaced him with a younger, more volatile version," a male voice interrupts.

I turn, fangs bared, and spot Alden, the Wolf King of Lua, grinning like a fool with his beautiful wife Tanith by his side. She's piled her long, ebony braids into a bun on top of her head. Alden looks sharp in a crisp navy-blue suit—too bad he's anything but.

I squeal and launch myself at them. "I missed you two!"

"We missed you, too, Desi," Tanith chimes in with her sweet voice.

"Where's little Conall?" I ask, pulling back.

"With the nanny," Alden replies, nuzzling his wife's neck. "I get to enjoy Tanith all to myself tonight."

Tanith blushes, the scent vibrant yet vulnerable, but she doesn't push him away. The wolf couple is painfully in love—not that I blame them. Alden nearly lost her forever when his older brother, Zeus, had her Turned into a vampire to jumpstart an invasion Alden wanted no part of. My blood restored her werewolf nature.

"Alden, later," she whispers. "We have an audience."

"So? I'm a king, you're my wife. Plus, you love *performing*."

I shudder. "Alden, do us all a favor and keep it in your pants."

I'm hyperaware of Jax standing inches away—I've always been too aware of him.

"Are you sure? Maybe Jax needs a release for all this obvious stress," Alden quips.

Jax smiles slightly, but then his phone dings. He checks it, and a muscle twitches at his temple.

"Shit. I have to go." He's already moving toward the door.

I stare after him, torn between following and dealing with Vane's smug expression back in the ballroom before Jax and I face each other again.

CHAPTER FOUR

SOTER

WHERE THE FUCK did Jaxson go?

Commander Wendy Detzer messaged just minutes ago about another daemon breach—demanding every Blade's attention. My heart pounds with excitement rather than fear. This is why I'm here at Wilder's wedding. Wendy's team hasn't been able to find the gateway these daemons are using to cross into our world. A new breach means a new trail, and my chance to solve my first case as Borealis Blade Commander, earning the respect of my peers in the process.

If I can find Jaxson in this crowd.

Standing in the open doorway, my eyes shift from person to person. Most of the guests are drunk, with flushed faces and unsteady movements. I recognize many of them. They're the same people who attend my father's parties back home in Borealis. I usually get invited to those parties, as long as I stay quiet and let my dim-witted half brother, Keris, an elected councilman, do all the talking. That's what happens when you're the title-less bastard son of one of Borealis's oldest witch families.

Now that I've been promoted, that's about to change. My father will be proud of me after I solve this case. When I finally gain his approval, I can openly be with the woman I love.

I spot Keris across the room with his arm around a pretty, dark-skinned witch—his latest conquest. Father stands beside him, shoulders tensing in his suit as I walk closer. Despite the silver pentacle commander's pin glinting on my lapel, he still won't speak to me in public. According to him, I'm nothing until I do something to *earn* my title.

Focus. I need to find Leigh and Wilder. Wherever they are, Jax should be nearby as the best man.

The bride and groom are gone. Typical. Those two can't keep their hands off each other. Their happiness stings, but I have to admit that Wilder worked hard for everything he has.

Now it's my turn.

I push farther into the party. Black figures form an ominous cloud among pastels and pinks. Warring scents of cologne and perfume smother me, mingling with the sweetness of cake frosting.

Jaxson isn't replying to my texts, which is why I'm back here after giving this room an all clear twenty minutes ago.

Jax needs to stop socializing and get back to work. Wendy is meeting us here to show us the new footage from the CCTV. I hope he brought a change of clothes to go daemon hunting. That gold jacket is a bull's-eye.

"Excuse me, officer? I need to report a crime."

Isolde steps into my path, wearing a fitted halter dress. Her golden skin shimmers like the jewelry layered around her delicate, tattooed neck. My feet stop moving.

"Wow, you look …" *Stunning* isn't a strong enough word. Neither is *beautiful.* She's breathtaking. I reach for her, but she takes a step back, glancing over her shoulder.

Right. No touching unless we are alone. How could I forget?

I frown, and she exhales. "I'm sorry."

"It's fine."

It's far from fine. I'm fucking in love with her—have been since our first day at the Blade Academy. Each time she distances herself publicly, it hurts more than taking a bullet.

Years have gone by since Wilder caught us together. We went behind his back, and yes, it was wrong. But it wasn't. I initially pursued Isolde to manipulate Wilder; getting inside his head was a skill I had, and I was good at it. He was stopping me from graduating at the top of our class, and I wanted to throw him off his game. Except that didn't happen. I messed up; I fell hard. She'd never admit it to anyone but me, but she fell for me, too.

Everything between us always felt right. It still does.

I had planned to make our relationship public after I got promoted to commander because I thought no one could comment on what we did. However, Isolde has been acting unusually distant. It doesn't help that she's a bridesmaid in Wilder's wedding while I'm here working instead of being her date.

I bite my cheek until I taste blood. Damn. I really need a cigarette.

"Have you seen Jaxson?"

Isolde blinks, black liner accentuating her apologetic copper-colored eyes. She's always sorry. I'm so sick of hearing *sorry*. I want her to own her feelings and openly claim me. I'm not a nobody—I'm the Blade Commander. But maybe a title isn't enough. I still need to prove I'm better than Wilder to show her we belong together—even more reason to hurry and solve this case.

She shrugs. "Last I saw him, he was with Desiree."

"That doesn't help me." I need specifics, not vague answers.

I should persuade Wendy to meet with me without Jax. He's clearly not committed to his job. Jax has always been a party guy with no real responsibilities—so, naturally, he's hard to find when duty calls. I wondered if two years living here and working as Domna might have changed him, but I guess I was wrong.

"Is everything okay over here?" Pallas approaches in pristine party clothes that clash with his ridiculous purple hair. He's off duty tonight, like Jax and Isolde.

Fire flows through my veins. Pallas has been a thorn in my side ever since Wilder brought him to our precinct years ago to work with us. He constantly butts in between Isolde and me, as if she needs saving. The girl carries a gun and fights with fire, for god's sake. He's being sexist.

"Fuck off, Pallas. Isolde doesn't need rescuing," I snap.

Isolde's brows draw together, but she stays silent, scowling at me.

"What?" I demand.

She shakes her head. "I was thinking about slapping you but that would be animal abuse."

"Huh?"

Pallas snickers. "She's calling you an ass."

I open my mouth, then promptly close it. Fighting usually feels like foreplay between us, but not tonight. I'm too charged up—the case is calling. When I stop the daemons from coming through whatever rift is open in this city, she'll want to come clean about us. She'll finally see me as someone worth being with. Then Pallas will have to swallow his forked tongue.

"If you see Jaxson, tell him I'm looking for him." I spin on my heel and bump into a firm chest.

"There you are," Jaxson growls, pushing me back. "Funny how you were told to find me, but here I am finding you."

Pallas smiles, clearly enjoying my dressing-down from someone lower in rank. My hands ball into fists. I look at Isolde. She stares at the floor. Yeah, I'm an embarrassment to her.

"I was looking for you when I ran into Sol," I reply through gritted teeth.

"Don't call her *Sol*," Jaxson snaps, clearly in a foul mood. "She's not your friend."

Sol keeps her mouth shut. Figures. No one defends me. They'd worship Wilder and lick the mud off his boots. He's the commander they love and respect, while they'd rather leave me stranded.

Whatever. I'll earn their respect, then decide what to do with them. Maybe I'll fire them all for mutiny.

"Let's go, *Domna*." I head for the exit without looking back at Isolde.

I'm nothing to her now. But I will be.

CHAPTER FIVE
LEIGH

ONCE I KNOW no one from the party is following me, tension lifts from my shoulders. I slow down to catch my breath, exhaling a long sigh, relieved to finally be alone.

Ravi needs my help to find the right spell in Aradia's journals to close the portal. The answer is hidden somewhere in them; we just need to focus long enough to find it before dawn. If we don't—

Calloused hands brush my hair as something silky is placed over my eyes, stealing my sight.

Adrenaline sizzles beneath my skin. Before I can call for help, a deep, familiar voice whispers, "Where are you running off to, princess?"

My breath trips over itself at the hot and rough sound. *Wilder.*

"Well?" he presses, drawing the blindfold snug. His hands are all control, his body heat steady behind me.

My fingers explore the fabric—soft, smooth, decadent. "What are you doing?" My voice is unsteady as he walks me backward, my back pressed to his chest, his pulse as untroubled as ever. He always does this. Wilder's always calm while I'm a bundle of nerves. "Where are you taking me?"

Urgency nags at the edge of my mind—portal, wedding, Gianna's endless to-do list. I can't afford to get distracted, not tonight. Yet, with just a few words, he has me trembling with anticipation. Damn him. He blurs my world at the edges, leaving only himself in sharp focus. There's so much left to do before tomorrow, yet everything feels insignificant when I am in his presence. I should tell him to stop messing around, to let me go, insist I need to go to bed, but I'm also curious about what he wants and longing to stay close to him, as always.

"You'll see," he practically purrs.

"How? I can't see shit."

Wilder chuckles.

"*Wilder.*"

"Don't you trust me?"

I give a slow nod. Of course I do. Doesn't he realize I'd trust him with my life by now? I'm keeping secrets, but it's not about trust. It's about protecting his happiness. I haven't seen him this carefree in ages. I want it to stay that way. I refuse to let my actions ruin our wedding or our relationship. We've come too far.

There was a time when I feared what he'd do if he knew my secrets. Lunar Witches belonged to a hunted, persecuted magical sector, but Wilder chose me. Fell in *love* with me, shadows and all.

He's the light to my darkness, and I would be rootless without him.

He must sense my mood shift. "I'm sorry I got caught up talking to Jax and the others. I swear our wedding takes precedence over work." The concern in his voice sounds genuine.

Does he think I left the party because I saw him talking to his friends and assumed they were discussing Blade business? I frown. That couldn't be further from the truth. Even if they were, it wouldn't upset me.

Wilder stopped being a Blade, saying he did it for me, for us, even though I wish he hadn't. I appreciate the gesture, but being a Blade was his passion. Still, he can't be convinced that's true. I've tried, but I could always try harder. I don't want him waking up regretful five years from now.

"Maybe you should let me sleep," I tease, "so you can go finish talking to Jax. Maybe there's been a break in the case."

He laughs—a dark, delectable sound. "Is this a test?"

"No."

His grip on my hip feels deliciously possessive. "If you want me to show you just how badly I want you, I'll do it."

My foot catches on the hem of my dress, and I stumble, but Wilder's hands on my arms tighten to steady me. The Blades are patrolling; Ravi is on spell duty. I can allow myself to be in love for five minutes, unless

Wilder is planning some elaborate wedding scheme, and I am blindfolded as part of a prank.

"I've had enough socializing for tonight," I murmur nervously.

He tsks. "Good, so have I. What I have planned is just for the two of us. And don't lie and tell me you're too tired. I've been waiting all night to get you alone."

I stop thinking about portals and daemons. Nothing else matters except him.

Lust has my core clenching. "Are we still in the hallway? Can people see us?"

My hands reach for the blindfold, but Wilder captures my wrists. "Leave it. I like you like this."

"Like what—"

"Vulnerable. Mine to bend and shape as I please."

He kisses my neck, mouth lingering as I gasp. "What are you going to do to me?"

"Whatever the hell I want. Is that a problem?"

I bite my lip.

"Shouldn't we go somewhere private …" I strain to listen, trying to hear beyond my thundering heart, searching for footsteps or laughter. But there's only Wilder.

He presses closer. "Here's fine."

Wilder gathers the hem of my dress, sliding the silk up my thighs. Cool air teases my naked flesh. No underwear—never possible with fabric this delicate—and now I'm startlingly, appetizingly bare. He parts my thighs, his mouth at my ear, scraping teeth against my skin. I tremble for him, knees weak.

"Tell me if we are alone," I breathe.

"Does it matter?" His fingers graze my slit, feeling the dampness there, and then a low, primal groan rumbles against my skin. I grow even wetter in response. "This is your house, your party, and you're going to be *my wife*. Let them watch."

I'm floating, moored only by Wilder's touch as everything else disappears.

"O-okay," I answer with a breathy moan. I'm unsure if I'm responding to his question or reacting to his claiming touch.

I should stop—queenly decorum, lingering responsibilities—but his thumb finds my clit, circling slow. All thought dissolves.

"I think you're excited by being watched," Wilder teases. "Look how wet you are for me."

"People will talk," I try, half-hearted—a whimper more than a demand.

"What did I say?" His smile is audible. He's baiting me; he cares too much to really risk being caught.

His thumb keeps stroking, slow and persistent, igniting a fire within me. I breathe in his scent—earth and smoke, the essence of him—grounding as my body trembles.

One finger slips inside, then another, working me open. He's unhurried, unrushed.

Wilder's an expert cartographer, mapping my body with aching precision, charting every place that undoes me until I'm trembling, breathless, ready to beg.

The sounds that escape me are low; need swells with every movement of his hand.

He senses my struggle between want and constraint. "Don't hide. Let me hear you."

"Faster. I need you," I gasp, shamelessly moving my hips to grind against him.

He circles my clit faster. I curse inwardly—decorum shredded.

"Oh, fuck," I cry, voice raw as tension coils so tight I can barely breathe. Fuck, fuck, *fuck*. Wilder doesn't stop. I grip the expensive material of his jacket. Wilder's lips crash into mine, swallowing my wanton moans.

Fumbling blindly, I search for the button securing his pants. I'm desperate to touch him. Finding what I want, I slide my hand down to free him. My palm wraps around his hot, hard, heavy dick. He groans, sending shivers through my body.

"I thought you were nervous about people seeing?" he hisses. "Are you done being shy?"

I'm liquid magma. "Mm-hmm."

Wilder's laugh is triumphant. "Good. I want everyone to see how lovely you look when you come. Is that what you want?"

I know we're alone. I know his games.

"*Please,*" I breathe, rocking my hips for friction, aching unbearably.

"I can't say no to you." He slides his fingers deep, curling until I let out a desperate sound that makes him do it again.

I gasp as he gently bites my lip, tugging it between his teeth. I'm speechless, just a wet, pulsating mess in his hands. He's leaking pre-cum into my palm, craving more. Just like I am. I want to taste him.

"Your hands … gods …" I manage to gasp out, unsure if I even say it aloud.

"What about them?" Wilder grinds out, holding me so close I can't escape.

I'm shaking, breath coming ragged. "Fill me," I whisper, so needful it's almost a sob. "I. Need. More. More than your fingers."

I shriek as Wilder lifts me by my hips. My legs lock around him, my back hitting the wall hard enough to rattle paintings, and what was that other sound—books?

He fumbles between us, then lines up, notching his thick crown at my entrance. He teases for just a moment—devilish—then thrusts in quickly but firmly, filling me to the brim. We've been having sex for years, yet each time he enters me, the shock of fullness and the perfect contradiction that he could never quite fit but somehow always does catch me by surprise.

Wilder curses, clutching my hips, pressing into me. Both of us are caught in the moment, only breath, tension, and the delicious ache of him stretching me.

"You're everything," Wilder rasps. He moves his hips slowly at first, until he finds a steady rhythm. "So fucking tight … So perfect for me."

He slams into me again and again, pinning me to the wall. My body arches with desperation as he drives faster, each thrust sending pleasure spiraling higher until I'm right on the verge of euphoria.

Wilder groans. "This is such a pretty dress."

"Ruin it," I gasp between words.

"What was that?" Wilder's voice is thick with lust.

"*Ruin me*," I demand, jerking my hips. "You're so deep—I can feel you everywhere."

For one wild, reckless heartbeat, I almost beg him to forget the brew, give in, fill me, and make me his in every way. Let me carry a piece of him inside me. The craving burns sharp and bright. We've whispered about a family in the dark, flirted with the idea, but neither of us is ready for that commitment—not yet.

He fucks me harder, and the wet slap of our bodies is wickedly indecent music that makes me clench around him, anticipating our dramatic finish.

My moans spiral higher, incoherent, nails digging into his shoulders as I build, and build—

"Leigh. You may want me to ruin you, but you've *ruined* me," he pants, voice rough, hips stuttering.

I clench around him. Yes, right *there*.

"So close—I can't—holy fuck ..."

Wilder moves faster. "You *can*." He's solid inside me. "Come for me."

Like a meteor, my climax is white hot. My inner walls clamp around him. Shuddering, I cry out as my release tears through me.

It doesn't take much more time before Wilder's hips jerk. His body tautens, and he twitches inside me, coming in hot, thick bursts. He groans, the jagged sound ripping from his throat, and he's clutching me so tight I almost can't breathe.

My heart is a galloping horse, yet the rest of me collapses, boneless in his grasp.

Wilder presses a soft kiss to my shoulder. "You know how to put on a show."

"More like we do."

Wilder sets me on my wobbly feet. My heels teeter, but I use him for leverage.

Rough yet gentle fingers glide across my face. "Let me untie you."

Wilder undoes the knot, and the blindfold falls away. My grandfather's wood-paneled study comes into view. It's untouched, as if he didn't die over thirty years ago. Even his tobacco pipe still rests on the desk. The door is shut.

"So, we've been alone this whole time?" I ask, smiling. *Knew it.*

Wilder laughs as he fixes his clothes. His hair is a lost cause. "Disappointed?"

A little.

"I should get cleaned up," I say, rubbing the intense wetness between my legs. Ravi is waiting. "You should go back to the party. I'll see you tomorrow."

Wilder tilts my chin up with two fingers. His jade eyes bore into mine. "Just a sec."

"Yeah?"

He smiles with a sleepy yet satisfied grin. "You're perfect."

"You have to say that to me because I'm going to be your wife," I joke.

A groove settles between his brows. "I *get* to say that because you'll be my wife."

I roll my eyes, but my limbs are buzzing. "I should go."

Wilder's grip tightens, but it doesn't hurt. "Are you going to tell me?"

"Tell you what?" I meet his intense stare, dead on.

"Where were you going in such a hurry, Leigh? In the opposite direction of your room, no less."

He's fucking impossible. "I— I—"

Wilder distances himself from me. "I thought we were past this?"

"Past what?" I reach for him, trying to ignore how my heart breaks a little. If I didn't need to close this portal, I'd spend all night with him like this, naked, just the two of us. But the portal is open, and everyone—including Wilder—is safer not knowing I caused it. Tomorrow will be perfect. We'll say our vows, kiss, dance, and I won't let my mistake ruin what I know will be the best day of our lives.

"The lies."

Before I can defend myself, voices echo outside the room. Someone screams our names.

Wilder lifts a brow. "Does that sound like ..."

"Janus!"

Wilder and I burst from the room to find President Janus Dyer in the hallway, wearing her purple party suit and a wild-eyed expression.

"What is it?" I ask, heart in my throat.

"The apocalypse is here."

CHAPTER SIX
GIANNA

"HELLO, are you even listening to me?"

The bartender stares at me like I've grown whiskers and a tail. But I ignore him, arranging the crystal tumblers into the perfect pyramid.

"If you arrange the glasses like this," I explain over the distant hum of celebratory conversation, "they'll be easier to grab and look aesthetically pleasing in photos and to the guests."

The bartender doesn't say a word, and I frown. Why do all the people I hire look at me with the same blank expression? I'm beginning to think everyone is inept.

"Gi, I think he gets it," Meg says beside me. Her dark eyes, magnified behind her glasses, hold concern—not for me, but for the man I'm currently terrorizing with my perfectionism.

Leigh trusted me to make her wedding weekend memorable. And dammit, that's what I'm going to do, but judging by the apologetic look Meg gives the bartender on my behalf, maybe I don't have to act like a cartoon villain while doing it.

"Carry on," I tell the bartender, who quickly resumes filling orders.

Taking Meg's hand, I lead her to the buffet table. I haven't eaten all night, and before I can relax and dance with her, I need some food. While I was trying to grab a bite earlier, I saw the president rushing out. The problem at the bar tore me away before I could ask anyone about her sudden departure.

I stop in my tracks. The canapé platters look sparse. Are we out of salmon puffs? With a groan, I scan the crowd for the caterer.

"I think she ran off in tears after your last encounter," Meg teases.

"I was offering constructive feedback." I'd politely informed the caterer that the servers need to wash their hands after petting the rabbits. No one wants tularemia.

"You mean criticism?"

My stomach tightens. "Is that what it sounded like? It's a safety precaution."

Meg shrugs, and her solid blue dress sways. "One that everyone knows. Besides, didn't you say you weren't going to obsess over wedding details tonight? That you'd let the staff handle things and have fun? You've done enough. Let your assistants take over from here."

"I'm trying." But I want everything to be perfect.

Meg lifts a brow.

I let out a sigh. Yes, I've promised to stop saying yes to everyone else's demands and start focusing on my own needs. Except this party is the exception. Leigh's my *best friend*, and she's getting *married*.

I scan the thinning crowd—there's no sign of Leigh or Wilder anywhere. I hold back a snort. I knew she wasn't going to bed alone.

"How about we dance now?" I ask, pushing my hunger aside. "You love this song." It's a string version of a pop song Meg always plays when she and her sisters close their family bar back home in Aurora. Alec is there now, unable to close the bar for the entire weekend, and Phe, the youngest, is due to give birth to her first baby any second now.

"I'd love—"

"Gi, can we talk?" Ry appears behind me, his energy tense.

I jump and glance at Meg. Usually, I keep our interactions limited to the typical *hi* and *bye* to avoid any awkwardness. If he's here to discuss our relationship, he's a year too late.

"I'm busy," I say firmly. "Meg and I are going to dance."

Ry gives Meg a small smile. She observes him through narrowed eyes. They've been best friends their entire lives, and when they share silent communication like this, I'm awkwardly reminded that I'm the odd one out. It's been this way since I moved to Aurora. I manage a smile.

"What's wrong?" she asks him.

Ry winces. "Sorry, Meg, it's classified."

I tilt my head. "But you can tell me?"

Ry steers me away from Meg and into a secluded corner. When he faces me, he quietly says, "There's been a daemon breach."

My hand covers my mouth. "Here?" Is it going to impact the rest of the weekend?

"Not far from here, but that's all the information I have. I'm going to a meeting to find out more, but we can't let the guests know. Make sure people, especially Leigh's mother and grandmother, don't notice the queen, Wilder, and the president are missing. We want to avoid hysteria. You see, this isn't the first time these daemons have appeared. They've shown up at random for months. The Glaucus Blades haven't been able to find the rift. That's why, when Leigh moved the wedding, reinforcements were brought in from Borealis. So can you help keep people occupied here long enough for the queen to get a handle on things?"

My heart races. Did Leigh move the wedding from Borealis to Glaucus because of these breaches? I thought she had sentimental reasons for wanting to reschedule everything. Why didn't she tell me the truth? Haven't I proven myself trustworthy? I did all this for her.

"Gi, did you hear me? I know we're asking a lot—you're not a paid employee. Do you want me to ask someone else?"

I heard him. Ry wants me to distract the wedding guests. No one must notice that Leigh, Wilder, and Janus Dyer are gone. I'd watched Janus storm out earlier; her complexion drained to ash. Now I know why.

Off in the distance, Meg sways to the music. Leigh's mother is dancing with a bald councilman, a genuine smile lighting her face. It's the happiest I've seen her in years. To keep Cynthia and everyone else happy, I can do this one last thing. Then, I can let myself have fun.

"I'll take care of it."

"Thanks." His voice gentles, but not for me—for Leigh and Wilder.

As he turns away, I reach for him reflexively. When our fingers brush, his skin feels electric, and I jerk back. He frowns. Right—I lost that right long ago.

Still, letting Ry go was one of the hardest things I've ever done. I had loved him so much. Part of me still does, but we didn't work. He hasn't been my boyfriend for thirteen months—not since the day he proposed. I cared for him, but I had *just* broken free from everyone's expectations. His proposal felt like he was trying to tie me down to his vision of our future, to *someone* else's idea of who I should be. It proved he didn't truly know me or understand what I needed. I said no. After two failed engagements, I wanted air.

I've always felt like a pawn. My mom and Elio pressured me to take VT, even though they knew how addictive vampire tears are, so I would have enough power granted by the drug to keep up the magical façade to hide my Nebula mark. Fynn asked me to marry him when he found out he wasn't Gwyn Raelyn's child or heir and needed a suitable wife if he was going to keep up the lie that he was the next king instead of Don Raelyn's son. I understand why he did it; we were using each other, hiding our parents' infidelity, but it still hurt. Then Hammond took advantage of me to climb the social ranks in Borealis by linking himself to the president's daughter. I've had enough of others using me. I want to focus on myself and live by my own rules.

Things with Meg are easier than they ever were with Ry, Fynn, or Hammond. We have a rule: no strings attached. The goal is to have fun. Even so, her steadiness draws me in, and she makes me feel seen in the most intoxicating way. If I let myself, I could lose myself in her, but that goes against my current no-strings-attached motto.

"Will you come back to update me on the breach?" I ask.

Ry blinks, returning to a conversation he thought had finished. He got what he wanted: me saving the party. I can do damage control, but I still want to know what will happen with the daemons.

"We'll see."

He turns away, his well-fitted suit reminding me of when I teased him about needing the right clothes to date Mayor Stellan Navi's daughter. He shrugged me off then, but it warms my heart to see he took my advice instead of cursing my name after I hurt him.

Meg's hand rests lightly on my shoulder a moment later. I lean into her quiet strength.

"What was that about?" she asks, no jealousy or suspicion in her tone, just genuine interest.

I sigh. "I have one more task to take care of tonight before we can have fun."

"You could have said no." Her voice is soft but direct.

I brush aside the discomfort and put on a smile. "It's okay. I'm happy to help. Besides, Officer Pain in My Ass asked me to entertain the crowd while everyone else takes care of the official state business. I got the better deal."

Meg quirks a reassuring smile. She's been the most attentive date—never pushy, happy to lend a hand; meanwhile, I've been ghastly. More focused on the event than her enjoyment. I'm surprised she hasn't hightailed it back to Aurora.

"I have an idea," I say as I spot Felicity and her entourage. Engaging her is the last thing I want, but desperate times call for desperate measures.

I stride to the band and grab the microphone. People hush instantly.

"Let's give the band a hand." I pause for applause. "But something's missing, isn't there? How about a special number from the bride's cousin, Felicity Graves."

The room gasps. Felicity eyes me warily but she can't resist the spotlight all the same.

"Felicity's a world-class opera singer. If we beg, maybe she'll wow us with a song." I grin while Meg stands nearby, tight-lipped but also protective. She's cautious of Felicity after earlier, but it seems she understands that sometimes you need to play a longer game. Tension leaves my body.

Cajoling ripples through the crowd. Felicity sweeps up, accepts the mic, and launches into her routine. "Why yes, I'd love to. Do you know 'Hex and Hymn of the Divine'?"

The band obliges. Felicity sings.

Damn. I almost wish she were terrible, but she hits every note perfectly. Her powerful voice echoes off the walls, weaving through the riveted crowd, who hang on every word.

Crisis handled, for now.

Meg finds my hand. "Wanna dance?"

Nothing sounds better than Meg spinning me across the floor.

Except I don't move. Part of me wonders what's being decided behind the Blade's closed doors and whether it will change everything I've worked so hard to build for Leigh this weekend. Leigh's mother and grandmother are bright-eyed and chatting as they watch Felicity perform. They can't know anything's amiss. It would ruin their happiness.

"I should wait to see if Ry returns," I say to Meg, who frowns.

I'm a terrible date.

CHAPTER SEVEN
WILDER

WE BURST into a room down the hall from Leigh's grandfather's study. Jax and Soter are already there, along with Commander Wendy Detzer, who immediately thrusts her digital tablet into my hands.

"Your Majesty, Madam President, Commander Dunn, thank you for coming so quickly. I hate to interrupt your party, but this information can't wait."

We stand side by side in the castle's sitting room, a place where Leigh's family has traditionally celebrated Yule. It's an expansive room where twin leather sofas in a rich red wine color face each other before a large stone fireplace. Soft rugs add warmth, and thick tartan drapes block the windows. Leigh and I haven't spoken a word since I confronted her. I don't understand why she does it; I always find out.

"What the hell is going on?" I look at Soter, whose lips are pursed, then at Jax. His posture is stiff, and he's turned away from Soter, like they're in some childish pissing match.

"Wendy insisted that we wait for you so we can all watch the footage together," Jax said, his tone clipped. "We would have alerted you about this new breach sooner, but I couldn't find Soter."

Soter's jaw clenches.

"What's this about an apocalypse?" I ask Wendy.

"Rest assured, sir, we have things somewhat under control," Wendy says. "But you need to see this for yourself—some things can't be explained."

Chills run through me as I press play on the digital device. The CCTV footage showcases a hooded horseman galloping through downtown

Glaucus with a small, crying child tucked under its armored arm. Unease twists my stomach as the horseman carries the child over the pedestrian bridge and into the wooded forest, disappearing.

Replaying the footage, I ask, "This is a daemon?" It's unlike any I've seen before.

"Yes, sir. We believe it is," Wendy replies. "Its genetic makeup is similar to that of the Harborym or any other greater daemon. It's just unrecognizable."

The figure on Wendy's screen differs from the other daemons they've killed in recent months. Those were smaller and more animal-like than man. This creature might be eight feet tall.

A heavy hood hides its face, but thick armor covers its chest, arms, hands, legs, and feet. The horse it rides is larger than any I've ever seen, with a coat as black as midnight, looking sticky, as if it were bathed in blood. And its eyes ... I shiver. I'll never forget them. They are red—redder than Desiree's—and they fucking *glow*.

"It's a Dullahan," Leigh whispers.

We all turn to her. "A what?" Soter asks.

"A ranger of death. They belong to Mictlan, the realm where lost souls go. Dullahan serve Kosac, the Reaper of Death." She protectively folds her arms over her chest. "I don't expect any of you to know, having just learned about them myself, but death is drawn to life, and there's nothing more vibrant and purer than a child ..."

A hush falls over us.

"Please give that to me." Janus points to the tablet. I hand it over to her.

She hits replay, her eyes fixed on the screen as Jaxson tries to get a better look at the footage over her shoulder.

"Wait, so this rift isn't a portal to Hell, but to Mictlan?" I ask, my heart rate picking up speed. "We've been approaching this all wrong, treating it like any other daemon summoning circle we've encountered when it might emit a completely different type of energy. Maybe that's why we've had trouble locating the source."

Leigh averts her gaze.

"Dullahan aren't in the *Daemonic Codex*," Soter says, an annoyed bite to his tone. He shoots a look at Wendy, who has been nodding along to everything I've been saying. "It would have been nice to know we were dealing with creatures from a realm other than Hell before now. How could you miss a detail this huge?"

"It was an honest mistake, Commander," Wendy replies firmly.

"Yeah, simmer down, *Commander*," Jax grumbles at Soter. "You're new to this, while Wendy and I have spent countless sleepless nights chasing these daemons. I can assure you that nothing pointed to us needing to look for a rift between our world and Mictlan rather than Hell. So back off."

Taking the tablet back from Janus, I press replay on the digital footage. The red-haired commander, who reminds me of Marlowe—who couldn't make it to our wedding because she's on another continent still trying to find herself—stands with her hands on her hips. Her light eyes are lost in thought as I examine the creature again for signs of weakness.

"Who is this child?" I ask. If the Dullahan serves this Kosac, why target him specifically?

"A little boy from the Lethe Orphanage," Wendy replies, her voice thick. "His name is Fynn Cygnus and he's four years old."

"Wait, what?" Jaxson exclaims, snatching the tablet from my hands. The footage of the Dullahan flickers in his concerned eyes. That orphanage must be in Jax's jurisdiction. He's going to beat himself up over this. "How did that thing break into the orphanage? There's security—those kids were supposed to be safe there!"

"Easy. We're going to do everything we can to get him back safely," I assure Jax. Turning to Wendy, I say, "Send an extra unit to the orphanage. Just in case the Dullahan comes back."

Wendy nods, already pulling out her phone. "On it."

"Where did the creature go after the orphanage? Is this the only footage we have?" Soter barks.

"We don't know; the footage cuts out here, where the sidewalk meets the trees," Wendy says. A vein in Soter's temple throbs. "The second the creature enters the forest, the cameras stop. I bet the rift is somewhere in there. I hate to say it, but I think the Dullahan took the boy back to Mictlan."

"What?" Leigh gasps.

"A baby," Jax whispers, his hands shaking. Jax has two younger brothers whom he helped raise. Although he wasn't excited about the responsibility of looking after them in high school, he loves them. He's always had a soft spot for kids. "He's just a baby. Four years old and probably terrified out of his mind—"

"We need to move," I say at the same time Soter says, "Let's go after the daemon."

He glares at me.

"Are you suggesting we go inside the rift?" Wendy asks.

We both nod. Soter's mouth pinches. I narrow my eyes. What's his fucking deal? He's acting like a child himself. I figured his promotion would give him confidence and ease his temper, but it's had the opposite effect.

The incident happened nearly thirty minutes ago; if we don't act soon, the trail will go cold. Some horseman, monster, Dullahan, whatever it is, entered the town, dashed to the orphanage, and snatched a child. If we want Fynn back, we need to go now.

There's a knock at the door. Janus opens it, inviting Ry and Isolde inside.

"Gianna has everything under control," Ry says.

"Thank you," Janus replies.

"We need to save Fynn. Standing around talking about it solves nothing," Jaxson urges.

"The plan is to save the child," Soter begins, "but we need to *find* the rift first. I say we split into teams. Isolde and Ry are with me—"

"It is also worthwhile to learn how to fight one of these Dullahans, so we know what we're up against when we send a team to retrieve the boy," I say. "Do we think sunstone bullets will still do the trick?"

Soter catches one of his two lip piercings between his teeth. "You're not Blade Commander anymore, Wilder. I am. So stop talking about *we*. There's only *us*." He gestures to everyone except for Janus, Leigh, and me.

"Fynn?" Leigh's nails dig into my arm as she stares off into nothing. "His name is *Fynn*? And he's in Mictlan?"

I turn.

All the color has drained from her face. She's trembling. *Fuck.* I'm just like my dad. How many times did he forget I was in the room when a case consumed him? Too many to count.

I steady Leigh's hand in mine. "It's going to be okay."

She just shakes her head, unable to speak.

How could I forget I'm no longer a Blade? My wedding is tomorrow. The rift and missing boy are critical, but I trained Soter for exactly this kind of crisis. If I don't trust him to handle it, what does that say about me as his mentor?

That I'm too obsessed with work to comfort my distressed fiancée when she needs me most.

"All you need to do, Wilder, is figure out if this wedding is still happening or not in light of this situation," Soter says, stealing my attention from Leigh.

"Of course it is," I snap.

Soter grunts. "Then you aren't going anywhere except to bed. We can handle it from here. Wendy shouldn't have shown this footage to you until after we solved the case anyway." He says that last bit pointedly to Wendy, who narrows her eyes at him.

I glare. Soter's right about Leigh being my focus, but he doesn't need to be such a dick about it.

"We tell no one about this," Janus announces.

"Respectfully, don't the people deserve to know?" Isolde responds from her seat on the couch.

Janus jabs her with a glare. "If word gets out, we know someone in this room leaked it."

"We should get moving," Soter says. "Team up—"

"Wilder, will you please help?" Jax asks, desperation in his tone. "We could use you."

Expectant eyes turn to me, waiting, but my attention is on Leigh. She's staring at a family portrait. Her brother is in it. Her eyes water, and my chest tightens. She needs me now more than ever, and I'm a piece of shit for not prioritizing her before.

"Handle it without me." Each word is akin to swallowing glass.

Soter nods.

Anguish twists in my gut. My hands itch for action, for purpose—for the familiar comfort of doing what I've trained to do. But this is the right decision. Someone needs to stay behind with Leigh, and that someone is me. I've made my choice.

"Go now," I tell them. "We'll wait for your updates."

Isolde glances down at her party dress. "I need to change."

Wendy nods. "Quickly."

Sol, Soter, and Ry leave.

Janus approaches Leigh cautiously. "Tomorrow is a big day. You need to be ready. Rest."

"But that boy ... Fynn." Her voice cracks, and so does my heart.

"The Blades will find him," I reassure her.

Leigh winces. It's a struggle for her to prioritize herself. "Okay."

Janus leads Leigh toward the door. "I'll send your mother up to be with you."

"I'll go with her," I tell Janus.

"You shouldn't see the bride the night before the wedding," Leigh argues.

My jaw tightens. Circumstances are different for us. She's hurting.

When Commander Wendy steps out to take a call, Jaxson approaches me. Leigh leaves without looking back, too caught up in her thoughts.

"We could use you, Wilder." I slump into a nearby chair as Jaxson goes on. "This case is too big for Soter to handle alone. Fynn needs the best going after him. Soter's too green, Wendy's too cold. I just ... Wilder, *please*."

"Whoa, calm down," I say, sitting up straighter. "I trust Soter, and you should, too. Besides, you're on this case as well. Believe in your abilities. I've heard nothing but praise from Wendy every time your name comes up. You can do this, Jax."

"I only trust you."

"I need to be here for Leigh. That boy having the same name as her brother spooked her."

Jaxson looks at me, disappointment clear in his eyes. "If Leigh is right for you, why does she want you to give up something you love? Being a Blade is in your blood."

"Leigh isn't making me give up anything. I'm doing it for her."

"Make me understand."

"My parents were great at their jobs, maybe even the best, but at what cost? Desiree and I barely saw them. When we did, they were exhausted and miserable." I don't comment on how I almost succumbed to the same temptation five minutes ago. "That's not the husband I want to be. I'm not sacrificing my happiness for my career. We've postponed this wedding multiple times already. If it doesn't happen tomorrow, I doubt it ever will."

Jax inhales a shaky breath. "I get it, but you're not Moran, and Leigh isn't your mom."

"And that missing boy isn't Marcus or Xavier," I reply, mentioning his younger brothers.

I leave to check on Leigh, but Jaxson's words echo after me. Am I making a mistake?

CHAPTER EIGHT
CYNTHIA

I TIDY Leigh's room for tomorrow's festivities, smoothing her bedsheets and organizing the scattered jewelry on her antique vanity. Janus came and found me at the party not long ago. She asked me to go to Leigh, insisting she needed her mother but refused to say why. By the time I found her, Leigh was distraught, so I convinced her to take a hot shower to help her relax. Hopefully, she's scrubbing away her worries.

Entering her closet, I pick up the dress she wore tonight and place it in the hamper. The garment bag holding her wedding dress hangs nearby. I was there for her first and last fittings with the designer, and the dress is nothing short of elegant and refined, just like her. Even during her wild phase with boys and booze, Leigh still exuded grace. She's carried herself like a queen her entire life and deserves all the happiness I almost took from her.

Looking at her dress reminds me of my own wedding—and the lies that followed. When I agreed to marry Gwyn, I was already pregnant with Don's child. Gwyn and I lied to everyone about Fynn's parentage, choosing to protect our son and our family's reputation rather than admit the truth.

Lying to Fynn will forever be one of the biggest regrets of my life, but before Leigh helped her father's ghost cross over, Gwyn helped me work through a lot of the shame. Thanks to him, my daughter and I now have a relationship.

I love Leigh, but I still miss Fynn every day.

My son. My perfect boy.

Except it's not about Fynn. This weekend is about Leigh, so I feel responsible for helping fix whatever's bothering her. I owe it to her after years of neglect.

The shower shuts off just as someone knocks on the door. I walk past the dress to answer, blinking back tears for my broken family.

"Yes?" I say, coming face-to-face with Wilder. His eyes are red, and he looks tired and resigned. Did he and Leigh fight?

"I came to check on Leigh. Is she here?"

I narrow my eyes at him. "Did you two fight?"

Wilder balks. "No."

I study him. Satisfied he's telling the truth, I say, "You two can survive one night apart." Wilder opens his mouth to protest, but I shake my head. "I mean it, go back to your room. If I find you camped out on the floor when I leave, I will not hesitate to drag you downstairs by the skin of your ear. My daughter needs rest."

Hesitation flickers across his face. But eventually, he nods. "I'm here if she needs me."

"She knows."

I close the door as Leigh steps out of the bathroom and sits on her bed in a silk robe. Her hair is unwashed, hanging in limp waves. She's distracted. I sit beside her silently, studying her eyes, which are so much like her father's. It hurt me to look at them after his death.

"Cold feet?" I ask softly.

Leigh blinks. "What? Sorry, I was lost in thought."

"Say the word, and we'll run away," I say with a smile, though I am serious. No one ever gave me a choice when it came to my marriage. I was raised to be Gwyn Raelyn's wife—serious, studious, and accomplished. Desperate to please everyone around me, I earned perfect grades, mastered multiple instruments, and did everything possible to become the queen Gwyn would need me to be.

Although I eventually grew to love Gwyn deeply, it didn't start that way. I want Leigh to learn from my mistakes; she shouldn't put other people's feelings above her own. She's a queen, not a saint.

"I'm not running away." Leigh laughs. "I love Wilder. I'm just ..." She smiles at me. It's distant. "Going to go to bed. It was a long day."

"I know." I cover her hand with mine. "You can tell me. Did something happen between you two? It must've been serious and very public for Janus to come find me."

Leigh groans and falls back onto her bed. "Wilder and I are good."

I purse my lips. "Leigh, I can tell you're not yourself."

She scowls at the ceiling. "I just have a lot on my plate. You were a bride, you get it."

"I was, but I wasn't moping about the night before my wedding."

My daughter gazes at me, her brow furrowing. "Wait, have you been crying?"

I blink. Part of me wants to cut the conversation short. To push her away, like I usually would. But I am done being sad and angry. Hiding my feelings to spare others is not what I want to teach my daughter.

"I was just thinking about your brother."

Leigh sits up. She hesitates, then pulls me into a hug. "He should be here. They should *both* be here."

I hug her back. "I'm glad you are."

"I'll always be," Leigh whispers.

I hold her tighter. "I love you, my beautiful girl."

She's the first to pull away. "I really should get some sleep."

"Wilder came to check on you while you were in the shower." She glances toward the closed door. "He went to bed. I don't want him sneaking in here. This door will stay shut after I leave. Promise?"

Leigh snorts. "Promise."

With a final reassuring smile, I leave her room, my heart pounding. Something whispers in my ear not to go, to stay with her until she falls asleep, but Leigh isn't a kid. She's a queen.

CHAPTER NINE
LEIGH

AFTER MY MOTHER LEAVES, I spring into action. Dropping my robe on the floor, I hurry into my closet. I put on my jeans, fasten my bra, then grab the first shirt I see. It's cold, and the weather in Mictlan will probably be even colder, so I reach for one of Wilder's sweatshirts. It smells like him—woods and smoke—and it calms my racing heart. Gods, I wish I were curled up with him right now, not about to attempt the unthinkable. With a sigh, I finish the outfit with a pair of white sneakers. Everyone thinks I am asleep, and I plan to keep it that way. No one must ever find out I'm going into Mictlan to rescue that little boy. At least not until he's safe back home.

I opened the rift, and my failure to close it is costing an innocent child, who shares my brother's name, his life. I must find Fynn and seal the rift before more people get hurt. But I need Ravi's help.

I crack open my door, peek into the hallway, and once I'm sure the coast is clear, I pocket the ancient brass key and dart down the corridor toward the library. I am quick but light on my feet, so the ancient floorboards don't give me away.

I refuse to dwell on how I am lying to Wilder—on the eve of our wedding, no less. But it's not just him; I'm lying to *everyone*. If I had admitted the truth in that meeting with the Blades, everyone would have panicked. Wilder would have wanted to cancel our wedding, the president would label me unfit and call for an immediate vote of no confidence in me, like she did in Aurora. It's not like I hid the rift to be cruel; I want to keep my friends and family safe. No one will suffer because of my mistake.

Ravi and I will take care of the rift, and everything will go back to the way it was.

Reaching the library door, I twist the knob and go inside. Maybe, with any luck, Ravi found the spell to close the portal while I've been dealing with the Dullahan threat.

Ravi looks up from the journal he's reading, surrounded by shelves of leather-bound books. "Leigh?"

"Find anything?" I ask in an urgent whisper.

Ravi digs the heels of his palms into his eyes. "Not yet. I sense I'm close, though."

I nod as my heart sinks. "Care to take a break? We need to talk."

"Is there time for that?"

"A Dullahan stole an orphan boy." Ravi blanches at the reveal. "I need to save him. Tonight."

"Fucking hell, Leigh, this is officially out of hand. I'm guessing you didn't tell anyone about the rift, if you're the one going inside it."

I release a silent, strangled cry. Yeah, I could have told the Blades the truth. I could also tell them that there were nights when Wilder was working late that I'd wake up from missing him with my fingers buried between my legs, gasping for breath. There are some things you keep to yourself.

"I caused this," I say, my voice leaving no room for argument. "*I am* fixing it."

Ravi hesitates, studying my face. His expression is tight with concern. My pulse pounds in my ears. I think he'll refuse, maybe even alert Wilder or someone else. He sighs, shoulders slumping over the desk in what I assume is resignation.

"Ugh. Fine. What do you want me to do?"

"Come with me to the lake. In case there are more Dullahan in the forest, I don't want to be alone."

Ravi reaches for his sweater that must have fallen off the back of his chair. The weight of what I'm about to do—entering a new realm, confronting mournful spirits, saving a child—settles on me like an anvil on my shoulders.

Fynn needs me. And I won't fail him like I failed my brother.

Ravi shrugs on his crewneck that reads GLAUCUS, CORONA.

I narrow my eyes at the souvenir. "Did you get that at the train station? It's not like you aren't coming back. Did you really need a memento?"

"I thought we were leaving," he says, dodging my question with lowered eyebrows.

"We are." I turn on my heel, exiting the library.

Together, Ravi and I sneak down the hall, tiptoe down the stairs, and out one of the side doors that leads toward the lake. No one stops us. Though, a minuscule part of me wishes someone would.

The imagined look of disappointment on my loved ones' faces pushes me forward.

Fresh spring air fills my lungs as we race toward the stables. A paved path connects the stables to the Thistle Maze, and we follow it until Priapus Forest looms ahead of us. At that point, the path turns to damp dirt beneath our hurried feet.

"Do you feel that?" I ask Ravi, stopping suddenly. The energy emitted by the rift is stronger than it was in November.

Ravi halts beside me, head tilted in the direction of the lake. "I do."

"Come on." We need to hurry if I am going to make it back in time to marry Wilder.

The constant hum of energy presses against my mind, growing louder until we leave the clearing between the trees. I push my shadows aside, and we gasp together.

The purple at the center of the lake looks more vibrant than before. Could it be from the Dullahan using it not so long ago? It doesn't matter because I am about to go inside and maybe get answers to some of my questions as I search for Fynn among the sea of souls I find there.

"Ready?" Ravi asks.

"Ready."

I remove my shoes, tie them together, and grip the laced pair tightly in my fist. Ravi does the same, his expression grim as we stand in the darkness. I wade into the water first, gasping as it nips at my skin. Ravi follows closely behind, his teeth chattering loudly in the silence.

"This still feels like a bad idea," he says, but I swim forward.

No turning back now.

After a deep breath, I submerge beneath the water. My skin prickles and burns, but I kick my legs and spread my arms, clenching my jaw against the cold.

The gateway looms ahead—a shimmering purple surrounded by black.

I swim upward until my head breaches the surface. Ravi and I gasp for air.

"I'm going in," I declare, bones aching from the cold.

"Maybe I should come with you."

I study Ravi's face. Determination burns in his eyes, while there's a slight tremor in his blue-tinged lips. Ravi may be my cousin, my ally in magic, but I need him to stay.

"N-no," I manage through chattering teeth. "Go back to the castle, find the spell to close the rift. If I am not back by morning, alert the Blades, and close it without me."

"Why morning?"

"If it takes longer than that, something went wrong."

I'll be safe if I keep out of sight from the Dullahan and other rangers like the harpies. Kosac rules there like a king, much like the devil rules Hell. But unlike Hell's active torment, Mictlan inflicts hopeless despair—like entering the depths of depression. Still, if I want to find Fynn, I must endure it. Time flows differently there, with days in Mictlan feeling like mere hours here.

"I can't let you go alone," Ravi insists, kicking his long legs to stay afloat.

I shake my head, sending water droplets flying. "If we both go and something happens, then who will close the gate?" I place a freezing hand on his shoulder, my legs fanning beneath me. "I need someone I trust to keep my people safe if I can't." Felicity's snobbish face enters my thoughts, and I push it away.

I will be fine. I'm not leaving my people in her care.

Ravi falls silent for a moment before reluctantly nodding. "I'll figure it out.”

“I know you will.” I manage a smile I don’t feel. “And, Ravi? If … if something does happen, tell Wilder I love him. Tell him to be happy.”

Before he can respond or comment on the tears forming in my eyes, I submerge beneath the water, following the light trail before kicking my feet and swimming straight into the rift and the unknown.

I’m coming, Fynn. Hold on.

CHAPTER TEN
DESIREE

ONCE FELICITY STARTED SINGING, I lost my celebratory mood.

Vane and I retreat to our room upstairs while Vyvyan takes a lonely bridesmaid up on her offer to be her evening's blood source. Tomorrow will be long, with wedding events starting at eight in the morning, but I hope to find time between now and the after-party to talk privately with Jax.

He's upset. And before he could tell me the truth, we were interrupted.

If Jax and Anselm broke up because of me, he needs to say so. I'm terrified of breaking his heart a second time, especially since he's already falling apart. He deserves better.

I need Vane to stop antagonizing him. Jax is going through a lot. We're not getting back together, but I also don't want him to feel like we can't be friends. His breakup shouldn't have been a surprise to me. Why didn't Jax tell me the truth?

"What's troubling you?" Vane asks, shrugging off his fancy jacket as he walks into the closet. I kick off my heels, leaving them scattered on the beautiful vintage rug. I curl my painted toes into the soft fabric.

My phone vibrates. I pull it out and toss the spiderweb-beaded pocketbook onto the bed.

MISTY

Send pictures! Miss you.

I smile. Years ago, after Misty shut me out for being Vane's progeny—a secret I was willing to keep forever—I never thought we'd be friends again. But not long after I moved back into the Nest following my stay in Lua to help Tanith heal, Misty reached out. We talked, cried, and promised never to lie to each other again. The relief I felt at having her back still lingers in my chest.

Vane exits the closet. He notices my discarded shoes with a scowl. He despises messes. "Desiree." His single word carries a warning. We've discussed how *cleanliness is next to godliness* more times than I can count. I've never understood how that applies to vampires. We are closer to daemons than angels, are we not?

"Sorry, Dad," I joke, bending to pick up one heel. When I stand, Vane's crimson eyes lock onto me, rooting me in place.

I swallow hard.

"Say that again. See what happens."

I smile innocently, like the little shit I am. "Say what?"

"You know what."

"You don't like it when I call you *Dad*?" I laugh. "What about *Daddy*?"

Vane's pupils dilate before he closes his eyes briefly, as if fighting himself.

I saunter toward him, rising on tiptoes to whisper low and steady. "Do you want to punish me, Daddy?" Deliberately, I drop the shoe in my hand. It thuds on the floor. "Oh boy, what a pigsty."

Vane exhales sharply. I turn away with a laugh, continuing to finish my bedtime routine. But Vane grabs me, scoops me up, and throws me onto the four-poster bed. With a shriek, I bounce against the mattress.

He cages me beneath him. Anticipation coils low in my core, sharp and sweet.

"It's not wise to provoke a vampire, Desiree."

The wetness gathering between my legs is impossible to ignore. "Is that a threat?"

Vane smirks. "Threats don't seem to work on you anymore. Maybe I should try punishments instead." He flips me over on to my stomach, then jerks my hips up. The blankets muffle my gasp as he yanks my skirt up, exposing my bare ass to the cool air.

Our sire bond allows me to *feel* his emotions as if they are my own.

Right now, he's justifiably annoyed but also mad with desire. I wiggle my butt, taunting him.

"You're right, I've been a bad girl," I tease. He stills. "Maybe I need a spank—"

Vane cracks a hand against my flesh. A gasp leaves my lungs, but the brief sting transforms into a rush of blissful sensitivity. My skin is hyperaware of his every touch.

"Again?" he taunts. "Or do you promise to behave?"

"You sound more like my dad than my mate," I reply, muscles clenching for more of that addicting heat.

This time, when he spanks me, the sound sears through me like wildfire. A high-pitched whimper escapes me before I can stop it. I float; nerves buzzing as slick heat spreads and dampens my inner thighs. I need more of him, his hands, his mouth—every inch of him claiming and filling me.

"You *do* enjoy being punished," Vane observes.

I'm not looking at him, but I feel the bed shift. Is he leaving? *No.*

"Are you fucking edging me?"

My body is strung so tightly it hurts. I could snap. My hips strain for friction, for him, for anything. The hunger is deep, pulsing, and impossible to ignore.

"No, please ... I'll be good. Just touch me. I need you."

Vane peers over his shoulder, offering a smile that makes tears of arousal fall from my eyes. He unzips his fancy carry-on bag. "On the contrary, I'm getting you something to help take that edge off."

"What is it?" I sit up, and the throb between my legs worsens.

Vane reaches into the bag and pulls out a sleek black box. He breaks the seal and takes out what looks like a wand with a blunt, circular head. No way. He's not serious, is he? Before I can ask, he presses a button, and a rough, vibrating sound scrapes my ears. My breath sputters.

"A vibrator? You brought a *vibrator* to my brother's wedding?"

His smirk widens. "I packed with your pleasure in mind, sweetheart."

"Why not just touch me yourself?" I challenge, trying to hide my sudden shyness behind a façade of bravado.

Vane chuckles. "Are you nervous, Desiree?"

I roll my shoulders back. Am I? I've experienced all kinds of kinky sex with Vane, and I've used vibrators before, but never with someone else, never with someone watching my every reaction so intently.

There needs to be honesty between us, so I admit, "Yes."

Vane's eyes warm. "You are in control here. What do you want to do?"

I bite my lip. I don't want playtime to end. "Give it to me." I reach out my hand.

Vane smiles. He hands me the silicone-covered device. It's heavier than expected, yet soft in my palm.

"How do you want me?" I ask.

"I'll take whatever you give me." He settles into a tufted cognac-colored chair beside the window. His shoulders are relaxed. He crosses his legs, resting his hands in his lap as a decanter of blood breathes beside him.

I wet my lips. "So self-sacrificing."

Setting the vibrator on the bed, I reach behind me to unzip my dress. The bodice loosens as I peel it down my chest, deliberately slowing my movements as I roll the fabric over my hips before kicking it onto the floor. Vane's upper lip twitches. I smile. Ruffling his feathers is my favorite thing to do. He's right about me being a brat.

I slide my underwear down my thighs until I am completely naked.

My clit throbs as I reach for the wand. I press the button, and the buzzing sound returns. It's too intense, so I adjust the dial, turning it down until it produces a low, agonizing pulsing. Perfect.

I rise onto my knees, turning my back toward Vane, giving him a generous view of my ass. His arousal hits me through our bond, every bit as hot and demanding as my own. I spread my thighs, straddling his imaginary hips, and slide the vibrator between my legs. The toy grazes my skin, and the first surge of vibration tugs a moan from low in my throat.

I roll my hips, glancing over my shoulder. Our eyes lock. He's as starving for this as I am. Rocking forward and back, I exhale his name on my next breath. Fuck. It feels too good. My free hand grips the duvet as I ride the little toy, back arching and breasts heaving. We never break eye contact. I'm art come alive, crafted just for him.

"Is this what you wanted?" I rasp.

His ragged breaths shake his chest. He's barely holding himself together. "I've never seen anyone or anything as adoringly perfect as you."

"I'm not perfect."

One of his hands strays to his thigh, gripping hard. "To me you are."

I moan. I love it when he says sweet things like that.

As I continue moving against the vibrator, waves of pleasure crash through me. I gyrate my hips with urgency; my orgasm is so close, a tightening deep in my core. Vane's jaw clenches. Through our bond, I can *taste* his arousal, like pomegranate seeds bursting on my tongue. It's a dizzy rush, hurtling me toward release.

Fuck. I can almost feel Vane inside me.

"Vane," I cry, raw with need. "I want you."

"Soon, my love."

My breaths are fractured bursts of air. I press down harder, chasing the friction. My world shrinks to the sound of the thrumming toy. I'm so close it *hurts*. Hips rocking harder, I reach for release.

"I want to see you fall apart for me," Vane commands. "Say my name when you come. I want to hear it."

The ache inside me has me by its teeth. I grind helplessly, gasping for more.

"Vane." His name tears from my lips. Pleasure rips through me. I'm lost in the slick, shattering sensation. Everything is too much, and still not enough. I come, loud and messy, but I know Vane loves every second of it. It's what we both wanted.

When the final shock wave disappears, I collapse onto the bed. Nudging the wand with my knee, it rolls away, still buzzing somewhere nearby. I breathe heavily into the duvet, unable to move.

Vane's hand gently brushes over my back, grounding me as I descend from the intense high.

"You liked performing for me, didn't you?" he asks, prideful.

I manage a small nod against the cover, still too dazed to speak coherently.

"Can you handle more?"

I nod again, more eagerly this time. "Gods, yes."

"No gods, Desiree, just me."

Vane's strong hands position me onto all fours, and anticipation shoots through me like electricity. My breath saws in and out, and Vane runs a finger between my legs. I'm embarrassingly wet. He hums satisfactorily.

"Hurry," I whine.

Vane sheds his clothes with vampire speed. Heat radiates from his usually cold body as he grips himself, pumping once, twice. I'm pushing my hips back. Only he can give me what I'm desperately craving. With a chuckle, Vane kneels behind me, hands spanning my hips, holding me steady. He drags himself through my wetness, soaking his dick with my arousal. I arch, offering myself more.

He presses forward, a low, shaken groan spilling from his lips as he pushes inside, deeper, with exquisite slowness. I fist the bedding again, head bowed, pulse roaring in my ears as I take him inch by inch. The stroke of him is steady and relentless.

Fucking *finally.*

He chokes back a curse as I widen my stance, angling for more. "You have no idea how hard it is, keeping control of myself when you're like this," he murmurs.

"Then don't."

"Be careful what you wish for."

Vane jerks forward with fierce ferocity, leaving no hesitation to let me get used to him, and each movement is more demanding than the last. I gasp, taking him deep.

"I'm addicted to the sounds you make."

I moan loudly for show. He laughs.

"Roll your hips for me." Vane keens when I do as he asks. "That's it. You were made for me, Desiree. *Me.*"

His words turn my bones to jelly. My elbows drop to the mattress. Each of his exhales grows more rabid than the last. He curses, grip tightening as his control frays. I love riling him up past the point of no return.

"Tell me how badly you wanted this."

"I was starving for it." I crave the rawness of his dominance. "*For you.*"

The tension inside me tightens, demanding release. I'm drowning in sensation, so good I could die again and be happy.

"F-f-uuuuck," I curse. He's pounding into me so hard I might break.

My body hits a crescendo. I fall over the edge, the world around me dissolving once more. Vane doesn't stop as I ride out my orgasm; he continues to fuck me until the air leaves my lungs. He announces his release with a low growl, pumping me until I'm overflowing.

"*Desiree,*" he breathes my name, completely spent.

I exhale contentedly. My bangs are stuck to my sweaty face.

After what feels like seconds—or minutes? What even is time? Vane slips away from me. I wince at his absence. My vampire king goes into the bathroom. I drift off to the sound of rushing water.

A SUDDEN WARMTH jolts me awake. I find Vane cleaning our liquids off me with a warm, damp cloth. His gentle touch, so different from his overpowering control during sex, makes bats flutter in my belly.

It wasn't long ago that I cursed Vane's name and everything he stood for. I believed Vane had regretted turning me into a vampire, only to discover he had distanced himself to protect me from being alienated by my vampire peers. Now I can't fathom my afterlife without him. Vane's the blood flowing through my veins; every dead heartbeat echoes with his essence.

"I love you," I whisper, blowing wisps of hair away from my face.

Vane kisses down my spine. "You're my twin flame."

A slow smile spreads across my face. I turn to look at him. His eyes roam over my naked body before settling on my face. "If that's true, I have a favor to ask," I say.

"Anything."

"Be nice to Jaxson. No more teasing or pushing him. You can read his thoughts, so you know he's dealing with a lot over Anselm."

He smirks—damn him. After what we just did, I half expected Vane to throw a fit for bringing up my ex, but with him, I'm always on my toes.

"Will that make you happy? If I coddled your ex?"

I pause. "If he's in pain, we shouldn't parade our relationship."

"Is your happiness dependent on Jaxson's?"

Is that what he thinks I'm saying? "No."

"I'm not trying to fight with you, Desiree. You care about him, and I am confident enough in your love for me not to let that anger me, but I am not about to dampen my feelings for you to spare his. Are you sure you even have the whole story?"

I roll over, propping myself on my elbows. "I'm worried about him. He isn't himself."

"Maybe he's changed."

I blink. "Vane ..."

Vane sighs. "Jaxson has been your friend for a long time. But, Desiree, you two are adults. You are allowed to move on, and so is he. If that bothers him, then you owe him no explanation. You are so afraid of losing him that you don't see that one day—"

My stomach twists. "Wait. Are you mad at me?"

Vane frowns. "I just want you to remember you are living for *you*. Not me or even him."

"I-I know that."

"Good."

I nod, no longer wanting to waste any more breath on Jaxson. "Should we kiss and make up? I want to go back to five minutes ago when we were tangled up together and everything was perfect."

Vane captures my lips in a tender kiss that evolves into much more. He nudges my thighs apart, torturously pushing inside me once more. The pace is tender, languid, as our fingers intertwine beside my head.

The gentle knock of the headboard against the wall punctuates our soft yet firm beat. I moan into his mouth. Anyone sleeping on the other side of that wall likely hates us, but that won't stop us from spending the night worshiping each other like the monsters we are.

XIII
DEATH

CHAPTER ELEVEN
LEIGH

I'M FALLING THROUGH DARKNESS, scrambling, swimming, trying to find a way out of this underwater prison. The pressure against my chest squeezes the air from my lungs. No sound comes out when I scream. My heartbeat slows to a crawl. I'm surprised I'm still alive. How many mistakes do I have to make before I learn? Maybe witches can't traverse the rift.

If I don't find air in seconds, I'll drown between worlds, my mission unfulfilled, and Fynn will be doomed to remain in Mictlan, just like Aradia.

The tremors in my limbs are already fading. Numbness creeps through my extremities.

No. This can't end here. My wedding is tomorrow. Wilder is waiting for me at the altar. Closing the portal has to happen now. I need to reach Mictlan.

Fynn *needs* me.

I glimpse what might be light, and I kick harder. It might be imagined, but still, I swim toward it with what's left of the adrenaline in my veins.

Please be real.

The light intensifies, and suddenly my chest expands. *Yes.*

Breaking the water's surface, I gasp for air. My limbs are leaden as I tread water. Dread pools in my belly. I'm still at the lake.

Am I still in Glaucus, or does Mictlan resemble my world? I vaguely remember Ravi mentioning a passage from Aradia's journals that described Mictlan as a dark mirror of our realm. But this place feels cruel, somehow. It's definitely colder. My teeth won't stop chattering. Trees surround the lake, just like at home, but these are skeletal with branches like gnarled fingers.

It's creepy as hell.

An unearthly cry pierces my ears from above. I've never heard a sound like that before, like a bird but bigger. The cries grow closer, circling like a predator hunting its prey.

I can't remain exposed.

I swim to shore and drag my body onto the muddy ground, collapsing into the dirt. I can't catch a long enough breath before the screeching caws again, sounding just overhead. I scramble to my feet and reach for my shoes, only to find they're gone. I look behind me. I must've lost them crossing the rift. Is this a joke? I don't want to run around barefoot. The ground is icy and wet.

Typically, one of my ancestors' ghosts would offer a snarky response when I do something stupid like this, but for the first time since my Emergence and without the help of suppressants, the voices in my head have gone completely silent.

"Hello?" I whisper.

Nothing.

Shakiness returns to my limbs. The ghosts are fucking gone.

My skin prickles as I clutch the mud, feeling deeply unsettled by the silence. Something's wrong. This place has disconnected me from everything I am. My magic doesn't work here. For the first time in my life, I am cut off from everything I know and love. Will I be able to rescue Fynn without any magic?

Another screech.

I hurry to my feet, running toward the dark line of trees. Water slides down my arms and legs. The sweatshirt I'm wearing weighs dozens of pounds. It does nothing against the unnaturally cold air, and it's starting to rain. A droplet lands on my lip, and it tastes metallic. Wrong.

I slip between pines. The bone-colored bark scrapes against my wet clothes as I press my back against a tree. Despair claws at my chest, amplifying my worry. This place feeds on hopelessness. I need to stay strong.

Where would the Dullahan take a small boy? To Kosac, but where is he?

Don't ghosts inhabit this place? My research shows Mictlan has nine levels of suffering, which are similar but different from Hell. This must be the first level, but with two centuries of uncrossed souls—thanks to the persecution of Lunar Witches preventing them from fulfilling their ancestral duties—where is everyone? Either I'm alone or they're all hiding from me ... or from something worse than me.

"If I stay here, I might as well give up now," I mutter through chattering teeth.

I trudge through the forest, ducking from tree to tree. The creature's wings still beat overhead. My skin prickles, not just from the cold, but from the whispers that seem to drift on the wind, speaking words or warnings I can't quite catch.

The mud gives way to a gray grassy terrain that crunches beneath my feet like brittle bones. It's as if all life has been leached from it, leaving death masquerading as growth.

I look up and see an open field where the Thistle Maze would be in my world. The clouds part, revealing a single spire breaking through the mist —Traum Castle, but different. Thorns and vines choke its crumbling walls. It looks malevolent and abandoned.

That's where Kosac is; where Fynn is. I'm sure of it.

I pause. To reach it, I have to cross this open field. Except, I've seen enough movies to know stepping into the open is suicide, but the route by the river will take too long.

I have no choice but to make a run for it.

Using the elastic around my wrist, I pull my hair back and burst into a run.

My lungs burn with each breath. I pump my arms, eyes fixed on the distant tree line, trying to ignore the whispers following me.

Almost there.

A screech pierces the air, and I speed up. Beating wings rush toward me, and something that reeks of decay and sulfur breathes down my neck.

No. This isn't how my story ends.

I ran track at Sussex Prep. To block out my terror, I pretend I'm in the final stretch of a 400-meter, not running for my life.

The screeching becomes deafening. My limbs ache with exhaustion, but I can't help it—I glance back.

A bloodcurdling scream rips from my throat.

The creature has a woman's head with short black hair and a lean, muscular torso, combined with the wings and talons of a giant bird. *Harpy.* Agents of punishment, and I'm trespassing on their land.

Something stabs the bottom of my shoeless foot, and I fall face-first into the dirt, cursing as jagged rocks rip open my palms and shred my jeans. Blood wells up, hot against the cold ground.

A thunderous boom shakes the earth, followed by a high-pitched whistle.

Shit. I struggle through the dirt, debris grinding into my wounds.

The harpy lunges with its talons extended, eyes burning with ancient malice.

I push myself up, muscles howling with fatigue. Blood drips from my hands and knees. Still, I run. Run like my life depends on it.

Almost at the trees—

Thornlike talons sink into my shoulders, and piercing pain explodes through me. The wind rips away my scream as I'm yanked skyward, blood spattering the gray grass below. I flail and twist, but we only rise faster, swallowed by the swirling storm.

The darkness consumes my voice, and Mictlan welcomes another into its depths.

CHAPTER TWELVE

RAVI

I SIT ON THE BEACH, forcing my breath to steady after watching Leigh vanish into the black water. My gaze stays glued to the center of the lake, to the spot where she disappeared. Beneath my soaked clothes, chills race down my arms.

Dive in. Go after her, one of my ancestors' ghosts urges.

The only thing keeping me rooted to this muddy shore is the promise I made—to find the spell to close the rift. I have until daybreak before I risk alerting the Blades.

She's been gone five minutes. Five fucking minutes in the realm of the dead.

I push to my feet. My limbs are leaden with dread. If anyone finds out I let the queen enter Mictlan alone, there'll be hell to pay. My sister Sama and I—still outsiders here, no matter how welcome we've been treated—would become perfect scapegoats.

Cynthia and Jorina might call us family, but grief can turn people cruel. Wilder won't hesitate to arrest me and lay the blame at my feet if something happens to his fiancée.

Find the spell. Bring her home. Run if necessary.

Inside the castle, pre-wedding celebrations rage on as I head back to the library. The guests laugh and toast, unaware that a child has been stolen by a Dullahan, oblivious to the fact that their queen is inside a death realm. The joy in the air feels obscene, almost grotesque.

"I swear, the lack of propriety associated with the monarchy these days is inconceivable," a sharp voice complains around the corner ahead.

I slow my steps; something in that tone makes my skin crawl.

"Nebula and Epsilon cohabitating as if they were equals—it's disgusting!"

Felicity. I peek around the corner and my stomach drops. Leigh's cousin stands in a dress that looks like a cake, surrounded by several men, her aura green with jealousy.

"I understand my cousin's desire for peace, but it simply isn't right. She shouldn't be allowed to make the rules. Not when she's a no-good Lunar Witch." My heart stops. "I promise you, if I were queen, we'd have order, not this circus. Can you imagine? Any children Leigh has will be part Nebula! If my father were alive, he'd be sickened."

"Are you sure you're next in line?" one lackey asks.

Felicity's glare could freeze molten magma. "Are you referring to Ravi and Sama?" The disgust in how she spits our names sends ice through my veins. "Easily disposable. They'd be the first to go if I were queen. They may not be ahead of me in succession, but they come after me, which makes them a threat."

She disappears around another corner, but I can't move. My heart slams against my ribs. If something happens to Leigh tonight, Felicity inherits the throne.

My hands tremble as I check my watch. Twenty minutes. Still too early to call the Blades. I promised Leigh I would wait.

But Wilder isn't a Blade anymore.

Fear drives me toward the west wing. Leigh will be furious that I involved Wilder. She doesn't want to cause him unnecessary worry. I'm already worried myself, but I won't let anything happen to her, either. Not with Felicity watching, already plotting to get rid of both of us.

Easily disposable. Her words haunt my thoughts as I break into a run.

Leigh needs to understand what awaits her if she doesn't make it back alive. Wilder will bring her back safely. We should have told him about the rift on Samhain. As capable as Leigh is, she's not a trained fighter. Wilder won't let her fail.

Several moments later, I find myself outside Wilder's door. Gods, he'll be livid. But Leigh could be in danger right now. I try the handle and quickly find it unlocked.

Inside, his room is perfectly organized. His suitcase is empty, with clothes hung in the wardrobe with military precision. Not like me—my suitcase sits beside my bed, always packed, ready to run. I have spent my whole life as a Lunar Witch, moving from place to place, never safe. If I fail Leigh, I'll die trying to outrun a past I never truly escaped.

I open my mouth to call out for Wilder, but his deep voice interrupts the quiet, thick with sleep. "I left the door unlocked for you."

"It's Ravi. I need your help."

The bedside lamp switches on. I squint against the sudden brightness.

Wilder sits up in bed with a frown. His tattooed chest is on display. "Ravi?" He rubs his eyes. "I thought you were Leigh."

"Leigh's in trouble." No use sugarcoating it.

Alarm flashes in his eyes. "In trouble, how?"

I hesitate. "It's hard to say."

Wilder throws back the sheets and jumps out of bed, moving quickly toward the door. I look away. Thank the gods he's not naked. I've had enough shock for tonight.

"Where is she?" he growls, his voice edged with danger.

He reaches for the handle.

"Get changed; I'll explain on the way." I block his path from leaving. "And dress warmly."

He looks ready to shove me aside, but Leigh isn't in the castle. He'll never find her without me. With a furious exhale, he turns toward a patinaed dresser, yanks open a drawer, and pulls out a long-sleeved shirt, dragging it over his head. "Explain now."

Don't tell him.

He'll blame you.

You should leave now.

I push the ghosts' voices aside, though my knees tremble. "Leigh went through the rift. She's in Mictlan."

Wilder freezes, his jacket halfway on. "She did *what*? And wait, how the hell do you know about the rift?"

I swallow the lump in my throat. Maybe I should have gone straight to the library, but Felicity …

"Leigh told me, right before going through it—after that missing boy." I keep the part about being there when Leigh opened the portal to myself, for now. I need him to help Leigh, not abandon her for lying. "Come now, and I'll show you where it is."

Wilder drags his hands through his hair, nearly yanking strands out. "The Blades were handling it. Why couldn't she accept that and stay safe? When did she go in?" he snaps.

My guilt intensifies into defensiveness. "Since you retired, maybe Leigh hasn't had the same faith in them. Not without you around." I am twisting the story to fit my needs, but we shouldn't waste time arguing about this. Leigh needs help.

He frowns, eyes stormy. "So it's my fault for wanting to put her first? She takes matters into her own hands because of that?"

"Jaxson's team has been searching for months. No luck finding the rift," I counter, voice tense. It's not their fault; they can't see past Leigh's shadows. Only a Lunar Witch can. Still, we need to go.

"Yet Leigh finds it in one night?" His words are thick with suspicion, his aura darkening to deep blue.

"We really need to get moving," I urge. "Leigh needs you."

For a split second, raw terror flickers across his face before his expression hardens. "She better be unharmed when I find her or else it's your fucking head. I don't care if you are family. You could have stopped this." He disappears into the closet and returns a few moments later wearing black boots and holding his cell phone.

"Take me to the gate."

I nod and follow him into the hallway. Wilder's long strides make me half jog just to keep up as we rush out of the castle. His jaw clenches, but he says nothing.

"I should lead; you don't know where you're going," I offer.

"Then do it."

I bite down hard to swallow my retort. He's being a jerk because he's scared for Leigh. So am I. Every minute she spends alone in that realm is another minute she might not come back. We never should have kept the rift a secret. I never should have let her go inside alone.

"Ravi," Wilder says, stepping outside, "how did Leigh know where to find the rift?"

I hesitate. If I tell him the truth now, will he leave Leigh behind? If I lie, he might give up searching altogether. My future—and Sama's—depends on him finding Leigh and bringing her back safely.

I tell him the truth. As I talk, his breath quickens, each inhale edged with fury.

"Five months?" he explodes, nostrils flaring. "You've both known about this for nearly five fucking months. Is this—" He exhales through clenched teeth. "Is this why she wanted to move the wedding here at the last minute?"

I hold my tongue, which says a lot.

"Fucking hell, Ravi," he mutters, glaring at the trees. "What else has she kept secret?"

I still don't respond. His questions aren't for me.

"This way." I direct us down a winding path through the Thistle Maze.

CHAPTER THIRTEEN
WILDER

I KNEW Leigh was hiding something from me, but this? A daemon rift between realms that *she* opened and concealed with her magic is beyond anything I could have imagined. The Blades have been trying to solve this case for months. Leigh sat through a series of Council meetings about it and managed to keep a straight face. The realization of how deep her betrayal truly goes is unimaginable.

She and Ravi visited Glaucus months ago after failing to cross Aradia's spirit over. I thought she needed time to grieve, but apparently, the trip was all part of a plan to bring Aradia back.

The Dullahan, the Nothing, Mictlan—these names meant nothing to me this morning. But Leigh's known about all of them for months. Now, a child who bears her brother's name has been taken, and she believes it is her responsibility to save him since she opened the gate. Leigh's a diplomat, though, not a soldier. If she had only trusted me with her plan, I could have helped her. I could have alerted the Blades. They could have gone after the boy immediately if she had just shown us where the rift was, and I could have kept Leigh safe. We are getting married, and she thought I was so wrapped up in our wedding that I wouldn't be able to help.

She's my future wife. I'd slay dragons for her. I'd do anything she needs.

"Here we are," Ravi announces.

We reach the muddy banks of a lake so dark it seems to swallow the night itself. I scan the shoreline, searching for any sign of magic. "Where is it?" I ask.

Ravi shrugs in his damp, blue crewneck. "You're looking at it."

I blink. "The gateway is the lake?"

"Not the entire lake—just its center, deep below the surface." With a flick of his hand, Ravi brushes the shadows away with his magic. "Much better."

I exhale slowly as a purple, pulsing light appears. "Leigh went through that?"

Ravi nods. "She swam, yes."

"Without a firm understanding about what's on the other side?" I'm not sure whether to be impressed or pissed.

Another nod.

Fuck me.

"Leigh told me to tell the Blades where she went if she wasn't back with Fynn by dawn, but I couldn't risk anything happening to her before that."

I give Ravi a harsh look. "You mean, aside from disappearing into a mysterious realm full of *daemons* and *dead* people?"

Ravi drops his gaze.

Now that I know where to look, I can make out the faint energy field surrounding the small lake's shore. It's no wonder the Blades couldn't find this place; the gateway is like a spider's silk brushing against my fingers. Even the hoof prints left by the Dullahan in the mud are barely visible to the naked eye.

I take out my phone. Ravi glares at it as if it were my gun. "Who are you texting?" he asks. "Leigh said to wait."

Leigh isn't here. I text Jax our coordinates.

"Wilder," Ravi protests. "I gave her my word."

My glare is sharp. "Leigh made me promises, too."

Ravi clamps his mouth shut.

Yeah, that's what I thought. I can't hate him for his involvement in Leigh's deception. He's loyal to her, which makes him an ally, but he made a terrible mistake by keeping the rift a secret. If Leigh doesn't come back, he will be filled with guilt for the rest of his life.

"Wait, Wilder, what are you ..." Ravi's words fade as I step into the water. I hiss as the icy current seeps through my clothes and bites into my skin. I reach for my solar magic, letting it coil through my veins, warming me from the inside out. Familiar heat spreads from my core to my limbs, forming a barrier against the biting cold.

"I'm going swimming," I shout over my shoulder.

Ravi wades in next. I dive beneath the surface. I blindly swim through the dark depths toward the lake's center. My solar magic continues to pulse within me, a small sun keeping hypothermia at bay.

My lungs scream for air, yet I push farther. I've wasted enough time already. Leigh may be in trouble, may be hurt, and the longer I remain in this world, the greater the chance I have of losing her forever. There's no living without her.

Breaking through the water's surface, I inhale sharply. I shake my head, flinging soaking-wet hair from my eyes. A second later, Ravi emerges beside me. Beads of water roll like diamonds down his face.

"We're here," he whispers, but I already know.

A strong gravitational pull is tugging me toward the lake's floor. As I swim against it, my body feels drawn out like a sniper's patience. Out here, the wind no longer touches my face; the air is stale, and the water is unnaturally still.

"What's your plan?" Ravi asks.

"I am going to bring Leigh back," I say firmly. "Find Jax and the others. Tell them to set up a blockade around the lake in case any daemons come through. Inform him that no one is to enter the portal. There's no telling what is waiting on the other side. If Leigh and I are not back before sunrise, you close the gate."

Ravi stares, pupils blown wide. "With you still inside? Leigh needs to come back."

I nod. If Leigh and I aren't out by sunrise, it means we're gone for good. I refuse to endanger another child—or let those daemons claim anyone else—by keeping the rift open.

"Then, you'd better wish me luck."

"The B-Blades will take the news better if it comes from you," Ravi sputters.

He's right, but they can't depend on me anymore. Leigh is my priority. The rift is theirs. "If I don't see you, take care of yourself and this kingdom."

I inhale a deep breath before delving beneath the water's surface. As I let my body become an anchor, I sink to the bottom of the lake. There, nestled among the dark sediment, I spot a giant tear, resembling a crack in the earth's foundation, glowing a pale purple. I swim straight for it, praying that Leigh is okay and that, by some miracle, she's already found the boy taken by the Dullahan.

All at once, the world dissolves into havoc. Suddenly, I'm not just falling; I'm tumbling through an endless prison with no end and no beginning. The air isn't just seeping from my lungs; invisible hands are yanking it out.

I gasp at the emptiness. I clutch my chest. Is this what death feels like? This sensation of my soul being ripped away from my flesh, layer by excruciating layer?

Heaven above, what the hell have I done?

CHAPTER FOURTEEN

LEIGH

IF I FALL from this height, all the bones in my body will shatter.

The harpy's talons dig deep into my arms. They are sharp enough to make me wince while somehow not breaking skin. We soar through the dense clouds, slicing through thick thunderheads that hover like mourners above the gray wasteland. We veer right, moving away from the castle. My heart plummets. That's where I need to find Fynn.

"Where are you taking me?" I shout, but the unsteady drum of my captor's giant, feathered wings against the storm drowns out my question.

Lightning strikes. It's too close. I scream.

The wind pushes us off course, and my harpy captor struggles to redirect herself.

"We can't fly in this!" I don't even know if the harpy can understand me.

The treetops below grow closer as we descend. The harpy cries as she brings us closer to the green canopy beneath us. The scent of pine and petrichor overwhelms me. A massive nest appears, and my limbs prick with pins and needles.

Oh gods, I'm about to be harpy food.

We hover above the nest, and I shut my eyes, refusing to see my end. When her talons release me, I cry out, plummeting before landing in the center of an empty nest surrounded by wet, scattered feathers. However, it's not filled with ravenous chicks.

The harpy lands beside me seconds later, her powerful wings knocking me backward toward the edge. I manage to catch myself before falling. I look down and gasp. We are at least one hundred feet above the ground, high up in the trees.

Now what?

Slowly, I turn to face the harpy. Her clawed feet grip the nest as she fixes me with a glare that suggests I am responsible for all the world's suffering.

"*Please*," I try to reason. "Let me go."

The harpy's scarred human face, red with fury, studies me. I step closer with open palms.

"I need to go to the castle. I'm ..." I'm wasting my breath. It's never going to let me go.

The harpy cocks her head, its tangled hair falling to the side.

Overhead, a pained cry penetrates the sky. I peer into the clouds as the wails grow louder and more painful. It sounds like another harpy could be in trouble.

My captor answers with a panicked screech of her own before launching skyward. Moments later, her gigantic, otherworldly form is swallowed by mist and rain.

I hurry toward the other side of the nest. If I want to escape whatever fate the harpy has planned, I need to leave now.

Below me, branches thick enough to support my weight extend from the tree's massive trunk. Two more large nests are nestled in the nearby trees. The forest must stretch for miles. I can't see the castle. Thunder rumbles overhead, and lightning flashes. For a moment, it illuminates the dreary landscape.

There! The castle is closer than I thought.

No time to waste. Kosac and his Dullahan could be torturing Fynn right now.

I swing my legs over the edge of the nest and crouch onto a nearby branch. My pulse pounds in my throat as I inch closer to the trunk.

Don't fall, don't fall, don't fucking *fall.*

CHAPTER FIFTEEN
SOTER

OUR TRAIL HAS GONE COLD. We search the forest for the Dullahan's hoofprints, none of us wanting to admit they may no longer exist. Inhaling a lungful of pine-scented air, I hate how alien it is after a life of concrete and brine back in Borealis. A knight on horseback can't just disappear, can he? The gateway must be close by. We shouldn't be chasing our tails.

I can't stop replaying that footage of the creature snatching the child, terror carved into the young boy's face. My first case as commander and I'm already neck-deep in daemons—and now a missing boy. Life really has a sick sense of humor.

If my father saw me wandering lost and mud-splattered, he'd sneer. He'd say a real Blade doesn't miss signs or fall behind. Wendy and the other Blades are probably closing in on the rift already. I can hear my father's derisive voice: *Second best, as always.*

I catch Isolde's eye as she shoves her blue hair out of her face.

No. Wendy isn't beating me. Not now. My girl's watching.

"Who are you texting?" I ask, eyeing Jax. I'd wanted Ry for backup, but Wendy insisted on Jax, claiming he knows these woods. Too bad he also knows me, and every unforgivable thing I've ever done. "Is Wendy checking in again?"

Jax doesn't answer, his phone's glow highlighting his glowering face. I narrow my eyes. "Jax."

He jumps. I raise an eyebrow. Something is going on with him that has nothing to do with me, even if he wants everyone to think so.

"Are you getting updates from Wendy about the search?"

He folds his arms, angling the phone away. "She hasn't found anything."

"But your phone's been buzzing every minute for the last five. If it's not Wendy, who is it?"

"She hasn't found anything," he repeats in a flat, stubborn tone.

Annoyance prickles up my spine. Maybe he isn't texting Wendy. Perhaps he's sending Wilder a play-by-play or just chatting with Desiree instead of helping me. But he doesn't want me here. He'd rather have Wilder leading.

"Get off your phone and focus," I snap, reaching for the device. "We need to be on the lookout for more hoofprints."

Jax pulls back. "Back off, Soter. I am hanging on by a thread, and I don't want to take my anger out on you."

"You already are. Not to mention, you're undermining my authority by texting rather than helping your team with the Dullahan." I gesture wildly at his phone.

"You have no idea what I'm—"

"Quit it! We've been going in circles," Isolde snaps. Flames hover over her palm, casting jagged shadows across her angry face. "I swear, we've passed that tree already. Until we have a real plan, no one's moving."

I groan. We wouldn't be lost if our tracker were actually *tracking*.

"Stop whining and keep moving, *Faez*," I snap. Not Sol. Not after Jax said we weren't even friends, and she just let it hang there without saying anything. Amazing, right? It's fine to tear my clothes off when no one's watching, but gods forbid someone calls us friends in daylight.

I turn to Jax. "Put the phone away. That's an order."

Hurt flashes in Isolde's eyes. "Seriously?"

Jax scoffs. "Forget about him, Sol. He's just pissed because he's failing as a commander. The job is harder than you gave Wilder credit for, huh?"

Isolde sighs, saying nothing. The cold between us settles in for good.

I push through a wall of branches, heat burning in my palm. If she didn't whisper she loved me, I'd swear I was just a distraction to her, good for a secret fuck and nothing more. When we aren't naked, I'm invisible.

Love shouldn't be another thing I have to hide. Maybe I'm an asshole, but at least I own it. She pretends not to be, which is worse.

A branch snaps somewhere ahead. All of us freeze, our magical flames guttering down. My hand goes straight to my gun.

What was that?

Before I can move, Ravi jogs into the clearing. He's dripping wet, waving his arms, face set with determination.

"I'm so glad I found you," he pants, hands braced on his thighs.

"We're in the middle of nowhere, Ravi," I say. "What are you doing out here?"

He glances at Jaxson. "Didn't you see Wilder's text?"

Heat creeps up my neck. "Wilder isn't part of this case."

"I got a text from him, but I didn't read it," Jax mutters, defensive.

Ravi frowns. "The gateway. Wilder sent you the coordinates."

Jax's head snaps down to his phone. The screen flares bright as he scrolls, then— "Shit."

Unbelievable. I snatch Jaxson's phone from his hand. Wilder's thread is open, coordinates right there.

I tap the numbers, and the GPS springs to life. "This spot is close," I manage to say, biting back rage. Why the hell would Wilder send Jaxson the coords and not me? Jaxson might be his best friend, but I'm the goddamn Borealis Commander now. Jax is just Glaucus Domna.

"It is," Ravi agrees.

Isolde grins. "Way to go, Wilder."

How did Wilder find the gateway before I did? The thought alone makes me grind my teeth. "Did he just take a walk and stumble upon the rift everyone's been searching for months?"

Ravi hesitates. "It's a long story. But he wants you to set up a blockade. He said nothing goes in or out—unless it's him and Leigh."

"Is that right?" He's not even in charge, but he still expects everyone to jump when he barks.

"Wait"—Isolde's gasp is sharp—"does that mean Wilder and Leigh went through the gate?"

I remind myself that her panic is for both of them, not just her ex.

Ravi nods. "Leigh went after the boy and the Dullahan."

"And Wilder went after her," Isolde whispers, clutching her chest.

My pulse stutters. A child has been snatched, the queen is missing, and now Wilder is off playing hero while Isolde gazes after him as if he hung the moon. I can't even get her to look at me in public, but one grand gesture from Wilder and she's ready to write sonnets.

Enough. There's no room for jealousy while three people are missing on my watch.

I need to establish that blockade. Now. No one else vanishes tonight. Not while I'm in charge.

A little competition with Wilder can be good for the soul, but not if he's dead.

"Follow me," I bark, leading the charge toward the lake.

"Wait, give me my phone," Jax shouts. "I need to update my commander."

I halt, temper barely leashed. Jax is already wasting time. "I'll call Wendy. You're heading to the castle."

Jax scowls. "Why?"

"Wilder is missing. Someone needs to alert Desiree and wake their mother. If—*when* they return, Wilder and Leigh may need medical attention."

"I can update Wilder's family," Isolde volunteers.

"No." My eyes stay locked on Jax, my hands tensing at my sides. He needs to talk to Desiree and face whatever's got him so angry and distracted. "Jax is going."

He meets my gaze, lips thinned, then glances at Isolde and forces a smile. "Yeah. Sure. I'll go."

Good riddance.

He starts to leave, but I call out, "Only speak to Desiree and Doctor Dunn. No one else."

Until I know the whole story, no one else gets looped in. I'll brief the president after speaking to Wendy.

Jax nods, shoulders reaching his ears, then disappears into the trees.

CHAPTER SIXTEEN
WILDER

I DRAG myself to the lake's edge, coughing up water. It feels like I swallowed an entire ocean to get here. Liquid burns like bleach in my throat as I realize where I am. Rain falls from a sky that resembles a fresh bruise. The droplets hitting my skin are heavier than usual, as if weighted with regret. The dark clouds swirling overhead remind me of a diluted, murky paint mixture.

The scenery surrounding me lacks vitality. The first thought that comes to mind is that all the joy has been drained from this place, leaving behind only hollow echoes of what should be. Even the air tastes stale, metallic, like rust on my tongue.

Is this Mictlan?

This looks like a fucked-up version of our world.

My fingers sink into the bank. Mud crumbles like ash between my fingers, delicate as talcum powder but gray like spent coal. The water behind me sits obediently still. It's obsidian glass that refuses to reflect the stormy night sky above.

The trees surrounding the lake stand like petrified sentinels, their bark the color of weathered bones. My skin crawls as silence presses against my eardrums.

It's quieter than my father's confined cell in Kratos. At least there, distant sounds of life are present, like the guards' footsteps, prisoners' voices, and the hum of fluorescent lights. Here, there's nothing but the sound of my heartbeat thundering in my ears.

Where the hell are all the ghosts?

"Leigh?" Her name leaves my lips as barely a whisper at first, like a prayer. Then louder, desperation bleeding into my voice. "*LEIGH.*"

The silence swallows my cry, offering nothing in return. No echo. No response. Just that suffocating quiet that makes me wonder if sound itself can die.

Where is she? Taking deep breaths that taste of decay, I force myself to think logically. I didn't expect to find Leigh just waiting here—that's not who she is. She will do everything in her power to find Fynn. She'll probably try to bring Aradia home, too.

Lightning crashes, sounding like crunching cartilage. Misty clouds in the distance part as if torn by angry spirits, revealing the twisted spires of what appears to be Traum Castle on the hill. But this version feels like a fever dream: ancient stone blackened as if scorched by hellfire, thorny vines writhing up the walls like claws. The architecture itself seems off; towers bent at impossible angles that hurt my eyes to look at directly.

That's the first place Leigh would go. She wants to find the boy, so she'd march straight into that nightmare, demanding answers from the overlord there. I head into the trees. I'll find her. I'll bring her home. The Blades can handle everything else back home.

A noise like rattling chains startles me, and I duck behind a tree as a group of daemons weaves through the overgrowth up ahead. Keeping out of sight, I watch their serpentine bodies slither across the forest floor. They are heading straight for the lake. They hiss as they enter the chilly water and disappear, passing through the portal.

I don't recognize these daemons. Although they are small, they are quick, suggesting they are potentially dangerous.

Dammit. Jax better have received my text.

I take a step toward the castle but pause. What if he didn't?

"I never thought I'd see you again," a voice says from behind me.

I freeze. The silence was oppressive, but somehow, this was worse.

"I know you can hear me, Wilder."

Each word circles me like a predator, the sound simultaneously distant and so close it could be whispering in my ear. My breath comes in sharp bursts, visible in the cold air. I twist toward the sound, peering through dense trees.

"No." I rear back. "Impossible."

A woman with purple hair steps into the clearing. She crosses her arms, wearing an annoyed expression on a face that sends shock waves through my body. She hasn't aged a day.

Selene Mhoon.

The Lunar Witch worked for Chiron Lyra and the Nyx terrorist group. She was the same witch Leigh's uncle, Don Raelyn, had burned at the stake. But she has no burns; her clothes, a loose pair of jeans and a cropped shirt, are in perfect condition. A disturbing image of her burned body from her case file flashes in my mind, conflicting with the image of her standing before me.

"How did you know I was here?" I demand.

She releases a huff of breath. "Are you accusing me of stalking you?"

All breath leaves my lungs in a hurry. It really is her. The same haughty tone and look of indignation, as if the world is out to get her.

Reality tilts sideways. Selene didn't move on. What unfinished business does she have?

"Why are you here?"

Selene shrugs. "I was going to ask you the same thing. You don't belong here, Wilder. Go home."

I stare, manners be damned.

Selene pokes me in the chest. "Did you hear me? I said leave."

"Why didn't you cross over?"

She lifts an eyebrow—as purple as her hair—and folds her arms over her chest once more. "Nothing gets by you, does it, Blade Boy? And why I didn't cross over is none of your fucking business."

"Where are the other souls?"

"Around. This is like a hotel lobby—there are several levels below where most souls get sent." She rolls her eyes. "You have no idea what you're doing, do you?"

I keep quiet. As horrific as her death was, Selene isn't a friend. When she was alive, I trusted her about as much as I trusted Chiron Lyra when he claimed he wanted the War Letters to help the Nebula. And look how well that turned out. I should reveal as little as possible.

"Have you seen Leigh?" I ask. She hasn't questioned why I'm here, which suggests she knows something. She could help me find her.

Through the canopy, the sky darkens further. Rain strikes my skin like tiny needles. I shield my face while keeping my eyes on Selene.

"Wilder, go home," she says again, more insistent.

"I'm not leaving without Leigh."

Selene's fists clench at her sides. "Leigh isn't here. If she were, I'd know. We don't get many visitors—not of the living persuasion, at least. Especially not the queen."

She's lying. Ravi watched Leigh go through the portal. "You're a shit liar, Selene."

She blinks through the rain. "I bet you say that to all the Lunar Witches you used to arrest. What if I told you Leigh is a Lunar Witch? Would you leave her here?"

I ignore the barb. "Selene. I've been with Leigh for years. I'm aware who and what she is. Now, where is she?"

"She's not your concern right now, but you know what is?" Selene's tone shifts, becoming urgent. "Those daemons that just went through the portal back to your world. Do you know what they are?"

My eye twitches. She's deflecting, but curiosity wins. "What?"

She smiles—even in death, she's still manipulative. "Flesh-eating daemons. They behave like vampires, licking their victims to suck out their life force. They mainly target children and babies, spending their days in cemeteries and hunting the living at night." Her voice takes on false sympathy. "Just one lick completely paralyzes their prey."

I glance back toward the lake, thinking of the wedding guests, of innocent people.

"How do I stop them?"

"Cut off the head, shoot them in the skull—like any snake, you need to sever the nervous system." She steps closer. "Seriously, you're going to leave your friends to die. Damn, I had you pegged wrong. Guess you aren't the hero type after all."

She's trying to guilt me into leaving. "I'm not abandoning Leigh in this place."

Selene opens her mouth, then closes it, her expression drifting as if she's calculating something. She jerks slightly and forces a smile. "Mictlan isn't that bad. Sure, it's gray and dull, but there are plenty of places in the world with crappy weather."

"You don't expect me to believe that this place is some sort of paradise."

"Why wouldn't you? I have no reason to lie." But her eyes avoid mine.

"What about the Dullahan? Kosac? They're reason enough to stay and find Leigh."

"The Dullahan are horsemen with a flair for theatrics. As for Kosac, he's just another bored god—we hardly see him." She is still refusing to meet my eyes.

"Selene." I approach slowly. "I'm not leaving without Leigh."

She laughs, flat and humorlessly. "I forgot how stubborn you were." Then her tone sharpens. "Fine, stay. Doom your friends back home while you chase shadows. Leigh's probably with them right now, fighting off those daemons. She could use your help."

Guilt hits like a physical blow. I think of Leigh in danger, being held captive by a Dullahan, or worse.

When I woke up this morning, I did not intend to be climbing fucking trees in the endless rain ...

I spin. Leigh's voice—I swear I just heard Leigh's voice.

"What is it?" Selene asks warily.

Seriously. When will it stop fucking raining?

"I think I hear her voice. Leigh." She's in my head, her voice clearer than my own thoughts.

Selene doesn't breathe. "That's crazy. You're not a Lunar Witch. Only ghosts can communicate telepathically."

Telepathically? Can this place connect us spiritually because we are both alive? Feeling moronic, I project my thoughts. *Leigh, if you're there, answer me.*

Leigh.

Leigh.

Leigh.

Each mental call echoes unanswered into the void. But I know one thing: I'm staying no matter what game Selene is playing.

CHAPTER SEVENTEEN
LEIGH

I AM NOT DRESSED APPROPRIATELY to scale a tree. The bark is rough yet slick beneath my bare feet, and the rain doesn't make it any easier to hold on. Every movement is a calculated risk. My pulse refuses to slow as I search for something to hold on to. The harpies will come back eventually, and who knows how they'll react to finding me gone.

Still, I force myself to move deliberately. One slip, and it's over. Everyone's counting on me to close this rift. What time is it back home? Is Ravi telling the Blades where I've gone? Has he found the spell we need?

I need to find Fynn to get back to Wilder. Wilder's probably sleeping peacefully, thinking the Blades have the daemons under control, and that tomorrow, Fynn will be safe at the orphanage, and we can finally say *I do*, like we've wanted for years.

Lightning turns the world bright white for a heartbeat, then thunder booms like cannon fire. The rain intensifies, becoming sheets of frigid water that cling to my hair and clothes like a burial shroud.

"Just a little bit farther," I whisper to myself through chattering teeth. The ground inches closer with each careful motion. Twelve feet left. I can do this. I am almost—

Leigh.

I freeze. Did someone just say my name?

Leigh.

There it is again—inside my head, just like the ghosts of my ancestors. Except, it almost sounds like ... "Wilder?" I gasp. It can't be him.

Silence answers. Great, now I'm losing my mind on top of everything else.

Leigh! Goddammit, answer me.

At the force of his voice, I lose my grip on the branch I'm holding onto for balance. I gasp again, barely managing to hang on. "Wilder."

Still no audible response, but his presence is stronger now, like when one of the ghosts takes up residence in my thoughts. Wait.

Wilder? I project the thought this time, hugging the trunk tight as a gust of wind tries to pry me loose.

Leigh. Holy shit. It worked.

I blink water from my eyes, heart pounding. *How is it you are talking to me right now?*

I thought magic didn't exist in this world, but maybe this is a different kind of magic?

There's no time for that, he says. *Where are you? I'm coming to take you home.*

A slightly hysterical laugh bubbles up in my chest. Yeah, that's going to be a little hard to explain. *Don't get mad. I'm in Mictlan. I went after the Dullahan. I—*

I'm here, too.

I nearly fall. My painted nails dig into the wet bark.

He's here? Does that mean it's dawn back home? Or did Ravi break his promise to me? Damn him. I didn't want Wilder to know anything about this place. He was supposed to stay safe. I have everything under control.

Are you here with the Blades? Please tell me he isn't alone, that he has backup.

No.

I frown, though I'm not surprised.

Now that he's here, he'll bring me home. He'll demand we let the Blades handle this situation without us. Except the Blades aren't equipped to deal with supernatural forces like this. I'm a Lunar Witch. Bridging the gap between the living and the dead is my job.

Please tell me where you are.

I shake my head, even though he can't see me. I'm not going home, at least not yet. But he should. It's safer there; he could help the Blades protect the rift. Knowing that he'll be waiting for me and that he's safe will give me the strength I need to carry out this mission. If he gets hurt here ... if he's not at the altar when I return ... The thoughts cinch around my heart like a vice. I gasp.

I'm not leaving, I protest.

A familiar screech splits the sky above me. My blood runs cold. The harpies are returning. Fuck. I slide off the branch, my toes dangling as I try to find the next one.

What does that mean? Wilder asks.

I exhale. He came all this way for me, and I love him endlessly for it, but I can't go home with him right now. I need to do this, to make things right.

Go home, Wilder. I'll be right behind you.

The silence between us is charged with his anger.

Help the Blades, I add when he doesn't answer. I get that he's worried about me and can't sit still when he's scared, but he could funnel that energy into helping the Blades stop daemons from escaping the rift while I'm in here.

You need me more than they do.

I stop moving, heat rising up my neck as I hug a tree for dear life.

Fynn is here. That little boy needs me, too.

What about us and our wedding?

I'll be back on time, I promise.

Wilder's condescending laughter echoes through our connection. *You shouldn't make promises you can't keep, Leigh.*

My muscles lock up.

Wilder. That's not what's happening—

Why didn't you tell me about Aradia and the rift?

Limbs trembling, I keep descending. Ravi must've told him everything.

You were busy with Soter; you would have been disappointed.

That's bullshit. I always have time for you.

He does, but I am doing this for him. For us and our happy future.

Wilder, I need to do this.

I don't like the idea of you traipsing around this world alone.

I roll my eyes. I'm no damsel. *I will be fine. Besides—*

The branch beneath me splinters with a sharp *crack*. Everything happens so fast, I have no time to scream. There is the sickening lurch of free-fall and the knowledge that this is going to hurt, and nothing more.

I hit the ground with enough force to knock all the air out of my lungs. My vision flickers in and out like a weak heartbeat. I can't tell if my limbs are broken, but everything hurts. The pain makes my stomach turn with nausea.

Wilder's voice screams my name, calling for me repeatedly. He grows more desperate the longer I don't answer. I can barely focus on him. A cloaked figure looms over me. Its presence is somehow darker than the shadows around it.

"Hello, Leigh," a voice like midwinter midnight says.

The world doesn't fade to black, it collapses into darkness.

CHAPTER EIGHTEEN
WILDER

MY PSYCHIC CONNECTION with Leigh snaps like a severed wire. The hollowness in my mind hurts worse than an open wound.

I can't feel her at all.

Is she ignoring me? Or worse …?

Each of my breaths ends up shallower than the last. She wants me to leave without her. To help the Blades. Does she think I'd rather work with them than her? Soter has my job, and I gave it to him freely. Haven't I proven that she's my priority?

We are supposed to get married tomorrow. Being with her is the only certainty I have.

She's my pulse. The reason I get up in the morning. How doesn't she see that?

The future I've built—everything I've worked and sacrificed for—means absolutely nothing without her in it.

"What happened?" I ask Selene. She stands across from me beneath the trees. The lake is behind us, beckoning me back, while my heart pushes me toward Leigh. "Our connection just snapped."

Selene pokes her tongue against her inner cheek. Is she ignoring me, too?

If I had my magic, fire would be crackling anxiously at my fingers, but it doesn't seem to work in this realm. Without the constant heat coursing through my veins, I feel exposed, vulnerable. But worse is this icy emptiness seizing my heart, screaming that something terrible has happened to Leigh. Something I could have prevented if she had just been honest with me from the start.

My muscles tighten. "Did you not hear me?"

Selene fidgets. "I heard you, but I don't know what you expect me to do about it. I didn't know you could communicate with her telepathically. You're probably linked because you're both still alive, much like the ghosts are bound by death. What did she tell you?"

I narrow my eyes at her. "You said she wasn't here."

Selene frowns. "I didn't know."

Liar. Her nonverbal cues speak louder than her words. "What are you keeping from me?"

Selene rolls her eyes. "You haven't seen me in ages, and the first thing you do is call me a liar?" She laughs as if she's offended. "I'm trying to help you. This realm isn't meant for the living. Leave, help your friends while you still can. If Leigh is here, she must have a reason. Last I checked, she could take care of herself. Why don't you listen to her?"

I survey the surrounding darkness. Each breath is a struggle, as if a weighted vest is cinched too tight across my chest.

"Please," I beg. Selene cringes. "I need to know she's safe."

"Maybe she fell asleep," she offers, but her tone tells me she doesn't believe that.

"Selene, we've had our differences in the past, but I'm asking you for help." The words tear from my throat. "Can you just ask the other ghosts if they've seen her? You mentioned the ghosts here have a psychic connection."

Selene examines her nails. Each finger is painted a different color, though like everything else in this realm, they're muted, as if viewed through frosted glass. "You aren't going to make this easy—" She cuts herself off with a deep breath she shouldn't need. "If I do this one thing, will you leave? It's for your own good."

Selene doesn't have to look out for me. I can handle myself. "I'll go. But only if Leigh's safe." Which I doubt.

Selene closes her eyes, going preternaturally still. I begin pacing, eyes closed. Worst-case scenarios flash through my mind like a bad horror movie: Leigh hurt, Leigh crying out for me, Leigh unconscious, Leigh—

"Oh!"

I skid to a halt. "You found her?"

"Leigh is fine. She's with Kosac."

Kosac. "How do you know she's fine if she's with *him*?"

Selene clasps her hands together. "I've already told you that Kosac is harmless. This realm is also safe, which means you should go home. Leigh is a Lunar Witch; she doesn't need you to babysit her. She is fully capable of accomplishing whatever she came here to do. Trust me."

My head spins. If Kosac has Leigh, I'm not going anywhere.

"Where are they?"

Selene studies me. "How should I know?"

I've encountered people like Selene many times on the job. She won't share any information unless there's something in it for her. But she's dead. What motivates a ghost? I don't have time to figure it out. If she's not going to help me, I'll handle it myself.

"The castle. What's the fastest way there?" I ask. "This way through the trees?"

Her lips flatten. "Wilder, listen to me. Leave. Leave while you still can. Please."

"Leigh doesn't belong here either," I spit. "I promise, once I find her, we'll both go."

Her lavender eyes narrow, a muscle ticking beneath one brow.

I will bring Leigh back. Even if I have to tear this realm apart by hand, I will find her. Selene can either help or sit back and watch her new world burn.

CHAPTER NINETEEN
LEIGH

I WAR WITH CONSCIOUSNESS.

It's as if my eyelids are made of steel. Sleep tries to hold me in its grasp. Usually, sleep doesn't scare me. Not when I can walk through people's dreams as easily as passing through doorways. Right now, though, no dreams welcome me. No familiar paths open. It feels like I'm back inside the rift, endlessly tumbling through nothingness.

I manage to crack one eyelid open. The effort is like trying to lift a bus with my bare hands. The world swims into focus in fragments: shadows, shapes, movement. Through the haze, one fact becomes clear. I'm being carried. Rough, black fabric scratches against my cheek. But something's wrong. Something's missing. No heartbeat drums against my ear where I'm pressed against my carrier. No warmth radiates from the body holding me.

"W-who are you?"

Only silence answers. I struggle to move. Pain radiates through my body as if I were injected with it. My head pounds relentlessly. Sleep beckons, but I need to make sure Wilder's safe. He needs to be there when I return home with Fynn. Being here must be worth it if I get to spend my life with him.

I attempt to move again, but darkness's greedy fingers yank me back into the void. The last thought that crosses my mind before unconsciousness claims me is that whatever carries me through this realm of shadows isn't my friend.

Chapter Twenty

VANE

I AWAKEN WITH A JOLT.

A troubled mind lingers outside the door. I wince. Their thoughts are so loud and clear, it's as if they are screaming into my ear. Seriously?

I rub my eyes with a groan. I *just* fell asleep. Vampires are not used to sleeping at night, but we need to be awake for tomorrow's wedding.

Seriously, does he have to think so loudly? Usually, I have to actively use my gift to compel people to open their minds to me, but there are times, like now, when someone accidentally directs their thoughts at me like they're using a megaphone.

There's no point ignoring him; he's already made it clear he is here to stay.

Witches and their fucking egos.

I shift to get up, and Desiree stirs beside me. Her naked body presses against me. The thin sheet barely hides her delicious curves. Burying her face into my side, Desiree inhales as if she can never get enough of me, awake or asleep. Her arousal has the sweetest scent. It fills my nostrils, tempting me to stay in bed. Is she dreaming of me? Of us? Her unconscious desire sends heat scorching through my veins. She's my perfect match— her darkness, her insatiable hunger for me, the way she tastes like sin and feels like home.

It takes all my strength to distance myself from her weblike embrace.

I yank the door open. "As a lawman, you should know that loitering is a punishable offense."

Jaxson frowns. "I wasn't loitering."

I say nothing, and he squirms beneath my stare. His discomfort is satisfying. I fight back a smile.

Jaxson inhales a deep breath. His thoughts are a jumbled mess, all focused on me—how insufferable I am, how I could have had the decency to put on a shirt before answering the door, and whether vampires need to exercise to stay in shape.

"Can you stop staring at me?" he finally says. "Or at least blink? It's creepy."

"Jaxson, say what you came here to say, or leave," I reply, but his attention drifts past me to the sleeping beauty in bed. His thoughts instantly soften. Beneath the surface, however, there's a pungent taste of fear.

It's not fear of me, but Desiree. He has things he wants to say to her. Things that could change the course of their friendship. I get why he's hesitant to speak up; I know all his secrets, but it's not my place to intervene. This matter is between them, even if what I'm seeing sets my nerves on edge.

I block his view of Desiree with a low growl. "She deserves to know," I say.

Jaxson narrows his eyes at me. "Stay out of my head, Vane."

I laugh. He's about as much of a threat to me as a blind basilisk. "If you stopped projecting your thoughts so loudly, I wouldn't have a front-row seat to the melodrama of your life."

Jaxson crosses his arms over his chest, and the metal buckles on his Blade uniform glint in the dim overhead lights like cat's eyes protruding from darkness. "I've been trying to tell her."

I lift a brow. "Don't try. *Do.*"

"It hasn't been the right time."

"Make time. She deserves to hear it from you, not someone else."

"Is that someone else you?" he challenges.

I maintain a neutral expression. "Believe it or not, Jaxson, I don't sit around talking about you all night and day. I am an immortal king, and you are just a minor detail in my very long life. I tolerate your presence because you mean something to Desiree."

Jaxson shifts uncomfortably in the doorway, and my annoyance fades. He is caught between the joy of having it all and the fear of loss. What a conundrum.

"Whatever, you don't have to be such a jerk," Jaxson responds, his citrus scent souring. "I just came to tell Desi that Wilder's missing."

I run my tongue over one of my fangs, waiting for him to continue. I already know Wilder is gone, and so is Leigh. It's all been playing out in his mind like a film reel.

Jaxson takes a deep breath. "Wilder and Leigh went through the portal to Mictlan after—"

"I know about the child." Shock ripples through me. Having the gift of foresight usually means nothing surprises me, but this is disturbing. Desiree is not going to handle this well.

"We set up a blockade around the lake and are watching for their return."

"I know that, too."

Jaxson groans. "Is there an off switch with you, or are you always this insufferable?"

Gritting my teeth, I remind myself that Jaxson is important to Desiree. She'd be angry if I disposed of him like a common pest. "Jaxson, thank you for your time. I will inform Desiree about her brother. And I'll get the doctor—"

Jaxson's phone dings. He holds up a finger and checks his messages. I frown at the offensive gesture. What would he taste like if I bit it off?

"You should hurry," he says while reading. "More daemons have come through the portal."

Seeing what he sees, I nod, then begin closing the door.

Jaxson stops me, gripping the edge. "Excuse you."

"Jaxson, I'm doing what you want, but I need to get dressed, and so does Desiree."

Blood rushes to his cheeks, and the scent is sweet and alluring. Slowly, he backs away.

"Talk to her, Jaxson."

"I will," he mutters.

"You're trying to fit both your happiness and hers into a box that doesn't need to conform to your restrictions. There is a reality where things could be different."

Jaxson's eyes snap to mine. "Did you have a premonition?"

"No. But I know Desiree, and unfortunately, because you keep projecting your thoughts and feelings—concerning my *wife*—onto me, I know you. Now, if you'll excuse me, we'll meet you at the lake. Your teammates need you."

I close the door in Jaxson's face. Once his hurried footsteps retreat, I quietly approach Desiree. The last thing I want to do is leave this bed—the oasis we've turned it into—but Desiree will want to be there when Wilder returns. I gently slide the sheets off her. Positioning myself between her thighs, she gasps as I glide my tongue up her center. Eyes fluttering open, she squirms.

"Good," I murmur, flicking my tongue against her sensitive bundle. "You're awake."

Desiree moans, "Is it morning already?"

If only.

I bury my tongue inside her as blood rushes to my groin. The need to fuck her is a sweet agony. Desiree slides her fingers through my hair, holding me against her as she grinds her hips into my face, greedy for release. I give her what she wants, my mouth sealing around her clit, drinking in her taste and the shudder she gives in return, only for a couple of seconds.

"Fuck," she pants. "I love waking up like this."

I chuckle. Nothing makes me happier than watching her spiral from the pleasure I give her, but we'll have to finish this later.

"Desiree, darling," I say bracingly, "it's your brother."

She opens her eyes, and they fill with concern. Her arousal fades like light after sunset. "Is he okay?"

"Get dressed. We'll finish this later."

Unwillingly, I pull myself away from her. Still naked, with my saliva on her skin, Desiree quickly moves around the room, opening drawers. She steps into her underwear, puts on her loose-fitting jeans, and slips into a faded T-shirt. As she ties her shoes, she says, "Tell me everything."

"I will after we wake your mom."

CHAPTER TWENTY-ONE
SOTER

THE SERPENTINE DAEMON LUNGES, fangs bared, jaw unnaturally wide. I've seen what that mouth can do—several paralyzed Blades will need to be rushed to the hospital across the river.

I aim my pistol, sunstone bullet already chambered, and squeeze the trigger. There's no bang thanks to the silencer. The bullet punches straight through the daemon's skull, leaving a smoking hole. The creature drops onto the muddy beach with a wet *thud*.

Thirteen daemon bodies litter the shore around me. Small but lightning fast. If more come through that rift, we need to be ready.

"Good aim, Commander," Wendy notes, lowering her weapon. "You handled that better than any rookie I've met."

I attempt a smile, but the praise feels hollow. I'm not used to compliments. I glance at Isolde, who's gathering corpses with Ry, preparing them for the acid vats back at the precinct. If she heard Wendy's praise, she doesn't acknowledge it.

My frown deepens.

"Thank you."

Wendy nods. "What do you think—should we defy Wilder and send a team after them?"

I glare at the lake's black water, still as death, taunting me like my father's silence whenever we're in the same room. Would my father praise me now, or ignore this victory like all the others?

These weren't Dullahan, but that doesn't mean they won't return. The real threat could be waiting on the other side. It could be suicide.

I hate admitting it, but Wilder might be right. He can handle Leigh. We need to protect this city.

"Wait it out," I order. "If they're not back by dawn, we seal the gate. That's what's safest, and it's the queen's standing order, according to Ravi. It's what Wilder wants, too."

Wendy nods. "Understood."

"Wait," Jaxson shouts nearby. "I didn't think we were seriously going to listen to Wilder. We are trained soldiers; we can easily send a retrieval team after them. It'll be simple."

I exhale. He isn't going to make this easy, and he's thinking too much like a best friend than a Domna. "It's what Wilder and Leigh want. They are being rational, so should you."

"Screw what they want," Jax snaps. "If you're too scared to go, I'll fucking do it myself."

"Stand down, Domna," Wendy cuts in, her voice razor-sharp. "Soter's your superior, act like it."

"But, Commander ..." Jax's protest dies under Wendy's hardened stare.

"Go cool off," I say, my patience wearing thin. I get it. Our choices suck, but I don't need Jax undermining my commands. "We'll talk when you're ready to listen. Remember that your personal problems aren't what's important right now. You swore an oath to protect this city and its people. Right now, that doesn't include Leigh or Wilder."

"They aren't the only ones missing. Fynn is, too, and—"

Wendy produces her credit card with a flick and thrusts it into Jax's hand. "Coffee. Now. If we're going to survive this night, we need caffeine, and you need to calm down."

"A coffee run? Seriously?" Jax stares, incredulous.

Wendy doesn't miss a beat, her tone cold enough to freeze the blood still pooling beneath the dead daemon at her feet. "What's with you tonight? You're not usually this ornery."

Jax's jaw tightens. "I'm fine." He turns to leave but shoots me a glare that could kill.

Years apart, and he still hates my guts. Not even my new title can change that.

I shove my hands into my jacket pockets. Maybe a walk isn't a bad idea.

"I'll be right back," I say.

My boots sink into the wet sediment as I patrol along the moonlit beach. I keep my eyes on the center of the lake, willing Wilder and Leigh to surface. It's infuriating to stand here, keeping guard, not able to do anything because Wilder *said so*. It pains me more to agree to his terms because we don't know what awaits us in Mictlan. Dooming the city isn't worth finding out.

How could he go through that portal without consulting me first?

"Nothing is getting past our perimeter, Soter. I think you can chill."

I glance over my shoulder. Isolde stands with her arms crossed over her chest, her uniform stained with mud and daemon blood. She looks so distant. I want nothing more than to reach out and pull her close, but I keep my arms at my sides. She's beautiful, almost unattainably so. I've longed for her since we broke up all those years ago. I've tried every trick I know to earn her forgiveness for putting my family first, but nothing seems to work. I have her body, but what I truly want is her heart.

I was a jerk at the Academy when I pursued her to get under Wilder's skin. After getting to know her, though, I realized she was the one for me. She's smart, sassy, and brave as hell, and more importantly, she doesn't put up with my shit. I thought I had it all with her. Wilder found out about us, and she chose me, until my father issued his ultimatum: break up with her or lose my place in his family.

Desperate for my father's approval, I pushed Isolde away. Too bad I had already fallen for the blue-haired girl who could no longer stand the sight of me. I destroyed any chance I had with her after that. My father? He respects me about as much as a thief respects a locked door.

I was ready to give up on Isolde. Nine months ago, I confessed my love for her, told her I understood why she could never feel the same, and promised I was done chasing her and trying to force something that was no longer between us.

That's when she finally agreed to give us another shot—so long as we kept it secret.

I agreed, even though I want to shout that she's mine to every asshole who looks at her. But that would mean losing her for good. It's unfair, and I'm done being everyone's shameful secret. I'm the commander now—the title I spent years trying to earn, hoping it would prove to her and my father that I'm enough.

So why aren't I?

"Wilder's a real idiot for going after Leigh alone," I mutter. Isolde's gaze pins me, sharp and unreadable. Silence stretches. My heart wavers. "Who does he think he is, anyway? I swear, he can't last a day without playing the hero. Golden Boy Dunn—guess some things never change."

Isolde crosses her arms, canvas jacket crinkling. "Maybe he went after Leigh because he *loves* her."

"Maybe he can't stand to rely on me for anything."

"Yeah, I am sure he was thinking of you when he heard Leigh had disappeared."

"Abandoning your post to lecture me, Faez? Maybe I should send you away like Jaxson." My voice sounds colder than I mean it to.

Sol bristles. "We've got two cities' worth of Blades backing us up. Nothing's getting through that portal except Leigh and Wilder." She shoots me a glare. "And swear to the gods, if you call me Faez again, I'll slap sense into you. Call me Isolde or Sol, like you always do. Seriously, you're starting to weird me out."

I laugh darkly. "I thought only friends called you Sol. And if I am your commanding officer, can I also be your friend?"

"Stop."

"Stop what?"

"You're being bitter for no reason."

I straighten. "No reason? You let Jaxson treat me like shit because—"

"Not here." Isolde vanishes into the tree line.

A muscle in my jaw twitches. Jax has been a dick all night; the party was just the start. I breathe in, count to five, and head for the shadows between the trees. This talk is long overdue.

The forest eats the light, and sudden blindness makes my skin crawl. "Sol?" I call out.

No answer. Not even a crunch of leaves.

"Come on, where are you? Enough with the games." My voice snakes between the pines.

She's messing with me. She knew I'd follow, and she's making a point by staying silent. I can't stop obsessing over Wilder—about us. About how Wilder always gets everything, including her.

"*Boo!*" Isolde slips out from behind a thick trunk.

I yelp and instinctively reach for my gun. She doubles over in laughter.

Dammit, why can't all her smiles be for me?

"You scream like a terrified recruit," she teases.

I clear my throat. "I do not."

She arches a brow. "You scream so manly, like a bear or a lion. Better?"

I scowl, folding my arms. "You're talking down to me again."

"Am I, Commander?"

"Insubordination has consequences."

She grins. "Didn't peg you for a delicate flower, but if the combat boot fits ..."

"Just—"

She shuts me up with a kiss. It's urgent and fierce, no room for hesitation. Her lips are hot against mine, making every protest crumble. I cave, pulling her tight, wrapping my arms around her like manacles. I'm shackling her to me, not out of control, but out of terror that if I let go, I'll lose her forever.

Her tongue presses against the seam of my lips, and I push her away. "No."

Isolde blinks. I never stop her; she usually brings our time together to an end. We are working right now, and this is my first major case. I'm doing everything in my power to impress her, to be the guy she wants me to be, yet she'd risk me getting fired for a few minutes of fun.

"What's wrong?" she asks.

We aren't together, that's what's wrong. I'm in charge, yet she's calling the shots.

First, it was Wilder keeping us apart, then it was my mistreatment of her, then it was public perception. Now I am her superior. Being the commander should make her proud to be with me, but she's not. We are constantly battling with our hands tied behind our backs.

"What are we doing, Sol?" I ask.

Isolde's lips curve with wicked confidence. "Well, if you'd stop pussyfooting around, I'm trying to kiss you. Maybe something more—if you think we can be away for twenty minutes."

The image of Isolde bent over, hands braced against a tree as I pull her pants down just enough to take her from behind, ambushes my mind. She would have her palms flat on the bark, desperate moans slipping out even though the others are less than a hundred yards away. The risk of being caught. The twisted thrill of almost wanting them to find us—to see how she'd still gasp my name even with their horrified faces because she's too lost in what I do to her to care, brings a sick smile to my lips.

Only that's not how I want them to know about us.

I close my eyes, dragging myself out of the fantasy. No more secrets. No more hiding.

"Why? What's the point?"

She gasps. "Soter. Why are you doing this? Because of Jaxson? You know why I didn't say anything at the party. We are friends. More than that."

"Yeah, I get it." But I wish I didn't.

"Then why are you pushing me away?"

I sigh. "Maybe I'm just over it."

Isolde balks. I'm saying all the wrong things, but I can't help it. I'm angry not only with her, but with myself.

I'm sick. Sick in the head. Sick of all this shit. Not to mention, sickeningly turned on after one small kiss. There are a thousand things I want to do with Isolde in these woods, but I'm tired of hiding in the shadows. I want to hold her and kiss her in front of everyone. I make the rules; she won't break them. Not for me, at least.

"You don't have to be such a jerk." Isolde shakes her head.

I step back. "I thought that's all you liked about me. There's nothing else about me you deem worthy of your love. Or did you lie? Because if you loved me, you'd want to be with me."

"I'm no liar."

Could have fooled me. "Do you not want anyone to know about us because you still love your ex?"

I can't believe I just asked that. I feel like a fucking idiot. Isolde doesn't care for Wilder anymore, not in that way, at least. But I want to make her mad. I want a reason to be angry.

Isolde glares at me as if she wants to punch me, and I step closer, almost inviting her to do it. *Make me bleed, baby.* Hate me; it might help me stop loving you because that's what I need to do. You'll never choose me.

"Are you being serious?" Isolde hisses.

I nod once. "As a trip wire in tall grass."

"I am *not* in love with Wilder; I am in love with *you*. Although I am wondering why that is right now because you're horrible."

There it is. "If that were true, you wouldn't keep us a secret."

"You are my boss."

"What if I wasn't?"

Sol huffs a breath. "You are, so that's a moot point. Don't you think?"

The ground under my feet feels unstable. Somehow, I manage to stay upright despite knowing there's no future for us. "Then let's end things now."

I turn to head back to Wendy and the others.

"Why can't you just be happy with the way things are?" she quietly calls after me.

Because it's not enough; just like I am never enough. I can't control Isolde, but I can control how I manage the Blades. With my head held high and my heart bleeding outside of my chest, I walk away, leaving Isolde alone as I should have done years ago.

CHAPTER TWENTY-TWO

LEIGH

I WAKE up to hushed whispers, which is nothing new for a Lunar Witch whose mind often fills with the chaos of others' thoughts. The voices flutter like moth wings against my awareness. I briefly wonder if the ghosts are back, but these voices are too loud to be in my head.

I roll over, heart racing, chasing my fading dream and the happy look on Wilder's face. *Wilder.* Wilder was there, giving me that look that makes me feel like I'm the only person in the universe. That look makes my heart explode with happiness. We were on the beach. On our honeymoon. The sun shone overhead as he looked irresistible in his beachwear, just like when I dreamwalked with him in Aurora all those years ago. It was the trip I planned for us after the wedding, after I closed the portal.

The portal. The balloon of desperate yearning bursts in my chest, filling me with a bone-deep chill. *Fynn.*

I sit up too quickly. The room with its soaring ceilings, rich plasterwork, and four-poster bed spins like a carnival ride gone wrong. What time is it? Gripping my head between my hands, I squeeze my eyes shut, willing the world to go still.

As soon as it does, I'm out of bed and across the room, gray sunlight spilling in through the nearby window. The door isn't locked. I open it slowly and peek into the candlelit hallway. A figure dressed in black disappears around a corner. Other than them, I'm alone, and I know where I am. I've walked these halls many times since I was a kid.

Traum Castle.

Or at least, the nightmare version of it.

Somehow, after the harpy nest, Wilder contacted me, which might have been a figment of my imagination, and I took a fall, ending up here. How?

Wilder? I try to reach him telepathically, but all I get is static, like he's out of range.

Maybe he took my advice and left. I need to get Fynn back and get the hell home before it's time to put on my wedding dress.

I leave the room, not bothering to close my door. I'm not coming back.

Barefoot, I wince with every step my raw feet take. While the layout resembles Traum Castle back in my world, the interior is a throwback to another time. There's no electricity, and the furniture and paintings are exquisite. They are antiques, but with hardly any wear.

I approach a nearby door. I hold my breath as I twist the brass knob; it still cries like a banshee. There are sheets draped over the furniture as if it were in perpetual mourning. No one has set foot in here in months, maybe years. It's the last place the Dullahan would hide a little boy.

"Careful," a voice warns, sending frost crawling up my spine. "You shouldn't be up walking around. You could be concussed."

A hooded figure stands behind me. It is backlit by flickering candlelight, and my breath lodges in my throat like claws are crushing my trachea.

"W-who are you?" The question comes out smaller than I intended.

"You wander into my realm, and yet you don't know my name?" The voice is undeniably masculine. Thick robes cover his body. Even his hands are hidden in the folds.

If this is his realm ... "Kosac?"

Even without being able to see his face, I can feel him smile. The temperature plummets, chilling me to the marrow. If this creature has Fynn, I'll make him tell me where he is with my bare hands if necessary.

"Your Majesty, welcome to Mictlan," Kosac says. He doesn't bow.

I stiffen. He knows who I am?

I take an involuntary step back into the guest room behind me, where the air is still, and unease courses through my veins.

Before I can ask how I got here or about Fynn, a woman in black rounds the corner. She's carrying a bundle of cloth in her arms. She wears a simple old-fashioned uniform, like palace attendants wore during my great-great-grandfather's reign, but with a shroud over her face. I recognize her simple black dress. I saw her when I left my room earlier.

She freezes the moment she spots Kosac, chin dropping to the floor.

Kosac beckons her closer with one hand, and I hold back my gasp. His fingers are skeletal, literal bones without flesh. Is this how the rest of him looks beneath that dark robe? Is he entirely a walking skeleton, or just partially decayed?

"Please escort our guest back to her room, Henrietta." His chasm-deep voice echoes.

I frown. "Am I a prisoner?"

"On the contrary, you are my guest. I am pleased you are here."

I hesitate before replying with, "I'm not staying. I'm looking for a boy. One of your rangers stole him. He's about four years old. I want to take him back to the land of the living with me."

Kosac begins walking back in the direction I came from. "Let's continue this conversation inside," he says.

Inside where? Reluctantly, I follow the Death God and his ghostly servant.

I suspect she might be a ghost. However, here in Mictlan, she appears in flesh and blood, solid beneath her clothing. Strangely, she is the only ghost I've encountered since I arrived. I know Mictlan has many layers, but I expected there to be more ghosts on this first level. Have all of them descended to the other levels? Where is Aradia?

"Henrietta," Kosac addresses the ghost walking behind him, "prepare our guest's bath. She must be freezing."

Henrietta performs a small, albeit shaky, curtsy before entering the room I woke up in.

Kosac gestures for me to follow her. I consider disobeying him, but he's standing between Fynn and me.

With a huff, I step inside. He is right behind me.

"Where is he?" I question.

Kosac shifts. "Who?"

I bristle. "The boy." He doesn't answer, and I cross my arms. "Why did you take him? And what do you want from me to get him back?" Maybe I'm wrong and the Dullahan took Fynn without Kosac knowing. I shake off the thought. I doubt anything happens in this realm without their ruler's knowledge.

Kosac's laughter is a thundering grumble.

"You want money? Jewels?" I ask, but he says nothing.

"All I want is the pleasure of your company," Kosac finally says, inadvertently confirming he does have Fynn.

I purse my lips.

"I'm having a party, and I'd like you to attend as my guest," Kosac says. "Please, it would mean so much to me. It has been so long since we've entertained the living in this realm. Your vibrance is such a wonder to us who live in perpetual stagnation."

A party? "I don't have time for that."

"Then you must not care about the child."

A sinking feeling grips me. "That's not fair."

"It's unfair to deny the ghosts and me your company—the company of the queen."

Henrietta, whom I've determined must be Kosac's obedient servant, returns from the bathing chamber, still carrying that bundle in her arms. She presents it to me. It's a red dress. One with a low neckline, a dropped waistline, and a heavy skirt. I stare at the ancient garment through slitted lids.

"I'm not wearing that," I say.

Henrietta says nothing. Her gray eyes are filled with sorrow behind her lace shroud. Not gray like mine—gray like they once were a different color but lost all their brightness and cheer. I look away, my own eyes stinging with tears. I don't know her, yet something about her breaks my heart. How long has she been here?

"Is the dress not fine enough for you?" Kosac asks.

"I have my own clothes."

"Henrietta threw out those filthy rags. So, unless you want to wear your nightgown all day, I suggest you accept my offer."

I look down at my white nightdress, which is as archaic as everything else here. "I'll wear the dress." I reach for it. It feels expensive, like silk.

"I'll leave you to change." Kosac turns away. "I look forward to introducing you to the rest of my court and the realm we are in. I promise it isn't as macabre as the stories suggest."

Yeah, maybe because it's worse …

"Wait," I say. Kosac pauses, twists toward me, face still hidden in shadow. "My ancestor, Aradia Graves, is here. Will she be at the party?" Hope expands like helium in my chest.

Silence stretches like a rubber band about to snap. Then, there's an otherworldly screech rattling the ancient windows. Kosac straightens. Henrietta glances toward the window.

"No more questions. Be downstairs in an hour."

Fear seizes my chest. "Wait."

"Someone is stirring up trouble with my Dullahan," Kosac replies with an edge to his voice before vanishing like smoke.

Henrietta frowns at me before storming out. I toss the medieval garment on the bed, chasing after her. Maybe she knows where Fynn is.

"Stop! Where is he keeping that little boy?"

Henrietta disappears around another corner.

I stand in the hallway, a restlessness twitching my limbs.

Wilder? I test our connection one more time. He doesn't respond.

Unease wraps around my throat like cold fingers and squeezes. What if that's him with the Dullahan?

Henrietta comes back before I can go check, holding a glass bottle. She pushes me toward the bath.

CHAPTER TWENTY-THREE
WILDER

SELENE HASN'T CHANGED at all. She refused to help me, telling me it was my funeral and muttering about how I was a nuisance before walking back into the woods. But I'm not dying today.

The castle is a fortress with heavy chains hanging from the wooden doors and bars covering all the large windows. There's no way I'm getting inside to find Leigh, unless someone lets me in.

Which means I need to get caught.

I circle the property, heading toward the stable. If I can rile up the Dullahan's horses, I can lure out the Dullahan themselves. I'd ignite a fire, but that's not an option right now. I can't start a fire without magic either, since everything is so wet.

The musky scent of hay and animals hits me when I enter the stable. The horses, standing about fifteen hands tall and likely weighing around twenty-six hundred pounds, snort upon seeing me. I unlatch each of their dwellings and stand back, expecting them to rush from the barn. They don't move. Nothing can ever be easy, can it? Entering the nearest stall, I carefully maneuver around one of the giant beasts.

"You better not trample me." I slap its wet hide.

The horse whinnies, then takes off in a gallop. I target the next few horses, and they take off out of the barn. Following them, I see the horses running around the castle grounds. Wherever their daemon owners are, I know they'll come for me, and at least they will be on foot.

They can take me to Kosac.

It takes less than a minute before a Dullahan appears from the castle to inspect the noise. The rider spots me, and upon seeing me, lets out an earsplitting screech, likely alerting the entire kingdom that there's an intruder.

I clutch my ears. Pain radiates through my body, and I feel like I'm about to be sick when I notice the Dullahan unsheathing a sword. *Shit.* I figured they'd bring me to Kosac before straight up killing me. Rainwater drips down the formidable blade, and I swallow the bile creeping up my throat.

I'd run, but the plan was for them to capture me.

Despite the heavy armor, the Dullahan pursues me with incredible agility. I barely have time to lift my arms in surrender before more Dullahan appear, their weapons drawn. I'm outnumbered, and with no magic, this isn't a fair fight.

"I surrender—" One blade slices through the air, and I jump back just in time to avoid it.

Another blade arches overhead, and I twist to avoid that, too, only to align myself perfectly with the third Dullahan's weapon. I jerk out of the way, narrowly escaping being skewered.

"Stop!"

Frustrated shrieks escape from behind their armored masks, and I know I can't outlast all of them. My fingers grip the wet blades of grass as I stare into the chasm-like eyes of my attackers.

I'm unable to move as one sword crests above me. But the expected pain never comes.

As if held back by invisible strings, the Dullahan freezes in place. I blink as the other two Dullahan sheathe their weapons. Have they been ordered to stop? I glance at the castle as they reach for me, their grip strong enough to make me wince, but I don't cry for mercy. I am dragged toward the exit they used to come out here, where an open door beckons me into the dark abyss with open arms.

I smile.

I POUND on the bedroom door. I'm trapped inside the castle in a random room on one of the lower floors. One Dullahan discarded me here, nowhere near its master.

Fifteen minutes have gone by. And I've spent every one of them thinking about Jax and the others lying unmoving on the muddy beach. Did they catch all the daemons, or did some slip past? I shove back those thoughts to focus on Leigh.

They are both somewhere in this castle, possibly hurt, certainly afraid. They could be together and in a room like this one.

Either way—no matter what—I'm not leaving without them.

"Let me out!" I rattle the door on its ancient hinges. I'm seconds away from turning it into splinters. "You can't just keep me in here."

The brass doorknob turns. The mechanism clicks, and I prepare to bolt, but a large creature blocks my exit. It drifts closer, forcing me deeper into the bedroom. Its hood nearly grazes the ceiling. The air curdles around the tall figure. What the hell is it?

"I see you've come to wage war against me and my castle," the creature says in a voice that reminds me of mourning bells, of grave dirt falling on coffin lids.

The hair on my arms stands at attention. "Who the hell are you?"

The long dark robes conceal the creature's face and body. Though it talks like a man, it isn't human. It isn't a witch, vampire, or werewolf. It is something else. Something otherworldly.

There's something wrong with it, as if he's encased in shadow, his body entirely comprised of sorrow. My eyes prick with tears I can't explain, a burden of grief pressing against my chest that isn't mine.

"You already know me, seeing as you stumbled into my lands, attempted to break into my house by picking a fight with my rangers, who would have had no qualms about killing you if I hadn't intervened."

I narrow my eyes. "You're Kosac."

The name springs to the forefront of my mind, and everything Leigh said about the creature back at Traum Castle follows. I should have guessed she had something to do with the rift right then. She failed to mention that this reaper-like creature was over eight feet tall. Its robes are blacker than an abyss, which is saying something, because everything else in this realm is a lifeless gray.

"You need to leave," Kosac says. "Only the dead are welcome here."

I refuse to move. "I want to see Leigh. And the boy, Fynn—light hair, blue eyes—disappeared last night. One of your rangers took him. I'll leave when I get them both back."

Kosac drifts closer. The adrenaline pumping through my veins tells me to run, but I stay still. The only thing in this room I could put between us is a bed and an old trunk. There's no use trying to hide.

"Leigh is attending a party I am hosting. You, however, are not invited."

Kosac has a plan. I don't know him well enough to guess what it is, but I suspect it's dangerous and involves my fiancée and a little boy who is somehow linked to all of this.

"What fucking party?" We have our own party to attend back home. One we've been excited about for years.

"It doesn't matter. You do not have an invitation, and last I checked, Leigh told you to leave."

"How do you know that?" I ask. Did Leigh tell him?

"I have direct access to all the ghosts here. Selene's mind is mine to rifle through at any time I want. And you two had quite the conversation down by the water."

I suppress the chill skittering across my skin. He had been listening to my conversation with Selene. He might have been talking to her the entire time.

"Leigh is coming with me. So is Fynn."

"No."

"Yes."

"She does not *wish* to leave with you."

My eyes drop to the floor. Leigh wouldn't willingly stay here because she's trying to get out of marrying me, would she?

"You don't know the first thing about Leigh or what she wants," I bite out.

"If Leigh were in such a hurry to marry you, then why would she agree to stay?" Kosac asks.

"For Fynn."

"Go back, Wilder. You will soon feel the effects this realm has on your mortal body. Leave or regret it." Kosac turns on an invisible wind, floating out the door. The temperature drops another ten degrees in his wake.

It takes me several solid seconds to regain my composure before I hurry after him, reaching for the door handle. I twist. It opens.

To hell with Kosac and his threats. I came here for Leigh and Fynn.

I step into the hall just as a woman—or rather, a ghost—wearing a mourning veil and with ice-covered eyes rushes toward me. She has a bundle of clothes and a creepy mask in her hands. Without a word, she shoves them into my arms. I stare at them, ready to ask a thousand questions, but she turns on her heel and walks away.

What was that?

Returning to my room, I drop the clothes on the bed. I pick up the black leather plague doctor mask, then set it aside. I unfold the garment next. It's a tuxedo—old-fashioned with a white bow tie and pleated shirt, but it's not dusty. The black fabric is cold, as if it had been stored in a crypt for two hundred years. Is the ghost working for or against Kosac? If she defies his orders, does that mean I can trust her?

There's no time to overthink. If Leigh's going to a party, then so am I.

I shrug off my wet jacket and pull off my shirt.

CHAPTER TWENTY-FOUR
LEIGH

THE GOWN REMINDS me of a costume from a gothic opera, with bloodred silk that evokes the image of spilled gore. It has a plunging neckline and the corset that cinches my waist so small I should be in organ failure. When I looked in the mirror, I saw Death's favorite concubine staring back at me.

"Why won't you speak to me?" I've been trying to get Henrietta to talk since she forced me into a bath that felt like snowmelt. She'd scrubbed my skin until it turned pink before wrestling me into a corset. Each shallow breath is a battle, but she nodded in approval at my suffering, as if pleased with her antiquated form of female torture. I can't determine if she follows Kosac's rules out of respect or necessity.

She styled my hair with cold fingers that sent shivers down my spine, pinning it in intricate twists while leaving long tendrils to frame my face. I look beautiful in a haunting way; it's nothing like the warm, happy glow I'd imagined for my wedding day. Instead of getting ready to marry the man I love, I'm being dressed up like a sacrifice. But if playing dress-up gets Kosac to tell me what he wants in exchange for Fynn, I'll be his doll. Then I can get back to Wilder, and the first day of the rest of the life we deserve.

I'm willing to negotiate if it means getting what I want.

I still haven't been able to reach Wilder, and I'm clinging to hope that he's home with our families and the Blades. That Kosac's disappearance earlier had nothing to do with him.

"Did Kosac tell you where Fynn is?" I ask Henrietta as she escorts me to the party. If she's willing to defy Kosac's orders, maybe she'll help me. "You can tell me. Maybe I can help you. Are you a prisoner here?"

If she is, I'll figure out a way to free her.

"Tell me," I urge with a grip of Henrietta's shoulder. Her soft features harden into a death mask. "I'm sorry," I add, releasing her. "I just need to know if Fynn is safe before I go in there. What am I walking into?" Worry makes my hands tremble.

Henrietta scowls. "You shouldn't have come here."

Aha, so she can speak, but she's choosing not to. "I had no choice."

"Nothing good comes from you being here." Is that a warning or a threat?

"If saving a little boy is a crime, then lock me up and throw away the key."

"He will. You should leave while you still can."

My stomach tightens. "Why do you work in the castle if you don't like him?"

Henrietta curls inward. "I made—"

"That's enough, Henrietta." Kosac's voice resembles a venomous hiss.

Henrietta cowers as Kosac approaches, seemingly out of nowhere. He has replaced his midnight robes with ones that have faded gold embroidery. The hood still cloaks his face in shadow. Every step he takes makes the air grow colder. I plant my feet to resist the urge to run.

"My realm suits you," he says.

I don't smile. I don't belong here or in this dress.

"Is this party really necessary?" I place a hand on my hip.

Kosac slips his skeletal arm around the flesh of mine, bones clicking as he pulls me along. I stumble in my stupid satin slippers.

Henrietta stays behind.

"I've heard stories about you, Leigh," Kosac says. "No one described you as rude. So why disrespect me when I've gone out of my way to be hospitable to you?"

My attention snaps to his. Who told him about me? "Have you been speaking with Aradia? Please, tell me where she is."

We stop before the ballroom's massive double doors. Otherworldly music bleeds through the cracks. It sounds like a funeral dirge.

"Here we are. Now, do enjoy yourself. Remember, everyone's been dying to meet you." He chuckles at his joke.

"I did what you wanted; I came to your party—now release Fynn."

"Getting here was the easy part. Now it's time to have some fun," Kosac replies.

"Please. I can't stay here ..."

"This is where I leave you."

"You aren't going inside?" This party was his idea. If he doesn't join me, should we agree on a proper time for him to hand over Fynn? Is an hour of mingling enough?

"I will soon."

"I'm begging you, just bring me Fynn, and I will go home. No one will bother you or your ghosts again."

Kosac steps back, his form seeming to blur at the edges.

"Kosac!"

He dissolves into shadow, leaving me alone in the hallway. I go to inhale a long breath, but the corset immediately punishes me for it. Kosac is a pain in my royal ass. He begs me to go to this party, then vanishes the moment I arrive. Why?

Whatever the reason, I won't find answers standing out here.

Inside the ballroom, a masquerade is in full swing. I sigh. I'm at the wrong party, wrong place, and wrong time. Hundreds of floating candles cast twisting shadows along the walls, and the crowd pulses with unearthly life. Couples dressed in elaborate period costumes twirl across the dance floor, their feet hardly touching the floor.

So, this is where all the ghosts in this level of Mictlan hang out? Do they live here? Do they work here? I wonder if Kosac forced them to attend this party, just as he forced Henrietta to dress me and avoid speaking to me. The instruments play themselves, as if by cosmic magic—a haunted waltz I recognize from my grandmother's collection.

"So, it's true, the mortal queen has indeed honored us with her presence." A man in a moth-eaten wool suit appears before me, extending a hand that looks too pale, too perfect to be real. "Would you do me the extraordinary honor of a dance, my lady?"

"I—" I have no excuse. Kosac holds the answers in his hands. Until he arrives, I might as well question the guests. Henrietta made it seem as though she were a prisoner. Are all these guests here against their will? If that's the case, maybe they'll tell me where to find Fynn, and in return, I will work on finding a way to free them.

Taking my hand in his cold one, the ghost smiles. His teeth gleam like polished ivory.

The ghost leads as we waltz. Forward, side, close; back, side, close. Growing up, my mother insisted that I take ballroom dance lessons. At least I am not making a fool of myself.

Everyone except me is wearing a mask, and they all stare at me unblinkingly. Not the delicate lace ones like at Little Death. These masks cover most of their faces, are white, and have large noses and strong jawlines, as if Kosac wants to hide their identities. Some wear colorful clown-like masks, while the women wear black velvet ones.

"Can I ask you a question?" I ask the ghost guiding me around the dance floor.

"Your countenance is so very like hers," the ghost tells me.

"Who?"

"Hecate."

My great-grandmother's name was Hecate. "You knew Hecate Graves?"

The ghost grins again. "Hecate was my queen, but she was also my childhood playmate."

Ah, I see. "And when you got older, did you stay in touch?"

"Indeed. Until she took my closest friend as her husband."

My brows cinch. "That didn't make you closer?"

"Not when I had formed such an unfortunate attachment to my dearest companion."

Oh.

"I never possessed the courage to speak my heart," the ghost continues. "It remains my most profound regret. Though I was quite certain my affections would not be reciprocated, I departed your earthly realm without ever having confessed the true nature of my sentiments. Too worried I'd upset him."

Guilt pricks behind my eyes. That's terrible. "Is that why you are here?"

I instantly regret my words as soon as I speak. Can you ask a ghost about unfinished business, or is that too personal a question?

"I waited until it was too late to pursue what I most desired in my life," the ghost says before another masked dancer taps his shoulder to cut in.

The person I was dancing with releases me and bows before slinking off into the crowd.

"Your Majesty, dare I say I couldn't believe it when I heard the news?" my new dance partner says in an eloquent tone. He is much larger in build than my previous partner and wears a crooked grin beneath his checkered mask.

I yelp as he tugs me closer until our bodies almost touch. He whisks me around the room in a spirited polka. We move so fast that the party becomes a blur of reds, blacks, and whites.

"What news?" I finally ask during a brief pause between musical phrases.

"That you would come to us. Please, tell me of home. Is it truly so that we prevailed in the war?"

"Do you mean the First War?"

A nod.

Goodness, this ghost is as old as Aradia; only after years of lingering in my world has Aradia adapted to more modern speech. My heart races along with the beat. "Do you know Aradia? Is she here?"

"As a member of the Council, naturally I was acquainted with her. And no, I regret to say she is not."

I almost miss a step. Is he talking about the *First* Council? All those witches were killed, bombed by the Nebula over a hundred and fifty years ago. These spirits aren't just any ghosts; they are the very souls who shaped our history. Most of them have been here for centuries. But if that's true, shouldn't they have moved to the other levels of Mictlan? Is there a lottery system I didn't know about?

"I suspect I know your thoughts," the ghost says. "If we are ghosts indeed, why are we not mourning in the wilderness or seeking oblivion in the river's flow?"

"River?" My voice trembles. Does he mean the Acheron? "Is that the portal to the next level of despair? Did you make a deal with Kosac not to go into it?"

"Kosac proves most gracious in his divine nature, should you possess the courage to strike a bargain with him."

"What sort of bargain?"

The ghost grips my hand tighter. The pressure feels like dry ice on my skin. "Servitude."

I drop my hands, refusing to move as the rest of the dancers continue to circle us in a whirlwind of masks and silks. Some inch closer, but I keep my focus on my companion.

"Are you saying that you are a prisoner, but willingly?"

The ghost opens his mouth, but suddenly, a new partner sweeps me away, and the temperature around me shifts from deathly cold to wonderfully warm. The contrast is so stark it makes me gasp.

"Did I interrupt something important?"

That voice. I peer up at my new dance partner, and my heart nearly stops. The eyes staring back at me behind a black plague mask are green. Green and bright and dazzling with life. Surrounded by so much death, the vitality in them is almost shocking.

Tears brim in my eyes. "You're here."

Peering out at me under a leather plague mask is the man I love. The corners of his eyes are pinched in that way I know means he's terrified, but he doesn't want me to see it. It's him. It's *really* him. I grip his strong shoulders. He's not just a figment of my imagination.

Despite the craziness of this situation, I find myself leaning into him, breathing in his scent, resting against his heartbeat as we dance. I need to get back to finding Fynn, but for some reason, I can't stop myself from dancing a few more steps. A few more beats. When I close my eyes, I can almost imagine we're dancing at our reception.

My eyes burn, and I grit my teeth. We should be wrapped in each other's arms, gearing up for the best day of our lives. Instead, we're here. Because of my damn mistake. I take a deep breath and force the feelings down, burying them. If I let myself sink into the violent sea of what should be, we won't get out of here in time to get married. And I will. This wedding will happen, and it will be perfect.

I start to smile. But if he's here, in Mictlan, then he's in danger.

"You can't get rid of me so easily."

"It isn't safe for you here." It's not safe for any living being.

"You're here," Wilder replies, his voice tinged with an edge that makes my heart ache. It's a vulnerability I've rarely heard from him. "Are you saying it's safe for you but not for me? Did I miss the part of your past where you also had Blade training?"

I swallow hard. No. But I am a Lunar Witch. This realm affects me differently. "That's where you should be. With them. The Blades. They need your help. I can handle things here. Ravi is looking for a way to close the portal. I'm close to finding Fynn and getting back."

"Jax and Soter have it under control." Wilder looks side to side. "And if you were so close, what's with this party?"

I sigh. "Kosac didn't give me details, but I am playing along. It's my leverage to get Fynn back."

"Kosac told me you didn't want me here." His hand tightens on my waist, as if he expects me to push him away. Once I save Fynn and close the portal, I plan to never let him go.

"I don't." My tone is unconvincing, even though I desperately need to handle things on my own. I caused this mess. I put us in danger. I wish he'd let me fix it. If something were to happen to him, I would never recover.

Hurt flashes behind his eyes. "Ouch."

"I can't risk something happening to you."

"Can we talk somewhere more private?" Wilder asks. "I feel like art in a museum."

I search for Kosac. He's still not here.

Taking Wilder's hand, we slip out of the ballroom, through the double doors, and back into the deserted hallway.

"Wilder, you need to listen to me—"

He rips off his mask. Relief and desperation flicker across his face before he cups my cheeks with both hands and kisses me as if he's been starving for it. I melt into him, gripping his shirt. Despite everything with the portal and the Dullahan, he came for me. A tear rolls down my face.

If our roles were reversed, I wouldn't hesitate either.

"You lied to me," he says breathlessly.

I shake my head. "I know. I'm sorry, but you weren't supposed to find out this way. If there's any consolation, I have it handled. Fynn is somewhere close by, and as soon as I find him, I'm coming home. Ravi is working overtime to find the spell to close the portal. I didn't want to tell you because I wanted this weekend to be perfect."

Wilder laughs, but the sound is shaky. "You can't sneak away in the middle of the night and claim you have it handled. All I've done is worry since Ravi told me you went through the portal after Fynn. A portal you opened *months* ago. What would have made this weekend perfect is if my fiancée had trusted me with the truth. Lying isn't protection, it's omission."

I wince. It sounds even worse when he says it.

"Aradia is here because of me," I say. "I was trying to get her back. Opening the rift wasn't supposed to happen. I didn't tell you because I didn't want to cause unnecessary stress. Marrying you was the light at the end of a very dark tunnel, and I didn't want anything to change that."

Wilder pulls me close, wrapping his arms around me like a life preserver. I cling to him as if I'm lost at sea. We're being reckless for staying out in the open for so long; Kosac might come looking for me. But everything in this world feels cold and distant, while Wilder is warm and real. He's my reminder that I have so much waiting for me at home.

"Leigh, Aradia is dead. I know you blame yourself, but her fear of what was waiting for her on the other side is not on you."

I sniff. "I had to try to save her."

"How did you even plan to do that?"

"A story I read. There was this prince who got permission from the gods to tether the soul of his dead bride to him for all eternity by calling on the gods. I could bargain for her, since the gods legitimized my family's right to rule."

Wilder releases me, and I want to beg him to touch me again—to hold me as he would if we were back home, sneaking into each other's rooms because we couldn't stay apart before the ceremony.

"That's just a story," he says.

My heart stutters at his tone—the doubt.

"I had to try."

"You risked everything by coming here. What if something happened to you?"

"What if something happens to Fynn?"

"I get it, okay? This whole situation is a nightmare. But you should have come to us—Jaxson, Soter, me, anyone. We were working on a plan, and if we'd known about the portal's location, we could have prepared for this."

I grip his lapels and push him away. "It's my fuck-up, Wilder. Which means it's my responsibility. The peace we've fought so hard for could have been at risk if Janus caught wind of how irresponsible I'd been trying to bring back Aradia. She might have tried to push me out again."

"She'll be angrier that you didn't consult her. When we're home, you can talk—"

I glare at him. "I'm not leaving without Fynn."

Wilder sighs. "I had a feeling you'd say that, so tell me your plan. How are we saving Fynn and getting the hell out of here?"

My heart flutters and sinks at the same time.

"Kosac has Fynn and wants something from me," I say, and he nods. "If I can figure out what it is—"

"You've made enough deals with devils to last a lifetime. What else?"

I exhale. "The guests in the ballroom are trapped here, just like Fynn. They might know where he is, and with the right leverage, they could tell us."

Wilder frowns. "Considering you came here with nothing, I'd say you don't have much to bargain with. So maybe we start by talking to them. Ask them leading questions to get them to trip up and reveal something they otherwise would have kept secret."

"Or you could go back home and wait for me at the altar? I'll be the one in white."

"Leigh."

"You win. Let's question them."

CHAPTER TWENTY-FIVE
DESIREE

"WHY THE HELL is everyone just standing around?"

It's still dark outside as I run through the trees behind the castle, but daylight isn't far off. We might have another hour or two of darkness, then I'll want to head back inside to escape the sun. Mom and Vane are several yards behind me. Judging by the somber mood among the Blades present at the lake, Leigh and Wilder haven't returned. I scan the serious faces but don't see Jaxson.

"What are you all waiting for?" I shout, pointing toward the lake. "My brother is in there." I rip off my jacket. Wilder is my twin—my flesh and blood. I will not stand by and wait to see if he'll make it back like these jerks. I run toward the water's edge, but two uniformed Blades step in front of me.

One grabs my shoulders and plants his feet wide, while the other snags me around the waist.

"Let go," I shout, squirming against them. "Please. What if he's in trouble?"

"It's not safe," one Blade says to me, voice strained.

If the Blades had discovered the rift sooner, or gone in after the little boy themselves, Leigh and Wilder would be getting ready for their wedding—scheduled to occur in about twelve hours—instead of battling through who-knows-what horrors.

It's moments like these that I wish my dad were here and still in control. He wouldn't be passive like these assholes.

"Do you hate my brother so much that you'd rather he was dead?" I ask Soter.

He grits his teeth. "Desiree, you are blaming the wrong person. I didn't ask him to go through the damn portal."

Yeah, I'd rather yell at my brother, but Wilder isn't fucking here.

"You should be chasing after them, you should be doing something."

The Glaucus Blade Commander, Wendy, frowns. "Mrs. Bathory, I assure you, we are doing everything we can. We've secured the perimeter. Daemons have been shot. But we can't go inside; we could get ambushed—"

"You are being cowards," I sneer.

"We are following orders," Soter adds next.

"Whose?" I ask, still wriggling. "I thought you called the shots now?"

Soter looks toward the water, then back at me. Unease swirls in his mismatched eyes. "Wilder's."

I stop struggling. One Blade restraining me exhales in relief. "What did he say?"

Soter runs his tongue over one of the two symmetrical snake bite piercings in his lower lip. "If they aren't back by daybreak, Ravi should use the spell to close them in it."

"No," I whisper. That's an instant death sentence.

Sunrise is too soon.

Loose strands of hair blow into my eyes, and I struggle to breathe. If Wilder doesn't come back, I'll never get to laugh with my brother again. I faked my death once, thinking I'd have to live an eternity never seeing him, but fate had other plans. We didn't get a second chance to be torn apart again.

No. I swallow back tears. I refuse to accept this.

"Where's Jaxson?" I ask Soter. "He would never let you do this."

"Jax is running an errand," Wendy replies softly.

I shake my head. They sent him away on purpose.

I jerk against my captors, lurching toward the lake again. If I can reach the portal, I'll be in Mictlan before they can stop me. The Blades grunt, and their muscles strain as they try to hold me back. I manage to free one hand and punch one of them in the face, cartilage crunches under my knuckles. The other officer yanks me back, and I land flat on my back with a grunt.

"You bitch," the one I just hit exclaims, blood running down his chin.

"Better a bitch than a doormat," I wheeze.

"That's enough," Soter warns. Neither Blade hears him. One of them comes down on top of me. I growl, hiss, and do everything I can to buck him off. Mud cakes my clothes, my face, and my hair. In my frenzy, I rake my nails across one of their faces.

"I said that's enough," Soter growls, prying one officer off me.

"What the fuck?" Jaxson's voice rings through the air like a shotgun blast.

A moment later, Wendy pulls the remaining officer to his feet. I rush toward the water. But Jax catches me before I can dive in.

"Desiree, stop."

"Let me go." A Styrofoam cup crunches beneath my shoes as I shuffle my feet. There are several more discarded cups lying nearby. Coffee stains the mud a milky brown.

"Don't! Desiree, look at me." All I can see is my desperate need to take action. "Desiree. You're leaving me no choice. If you won't listen to me, I will need to remove you from the situation."

"I won't leave them in there—"

Jax hauls me over his shoulder. "I'm sorry, don't hate me," Jaxson says as he carries me away from the lake.

I stop fighting because he'll listen to me and see reason once he has space from the others. I need to hear from him that he wasn't going to give up on Wilder and Leigh, along with that defenseless child in Mictlan. He has a plan.

Still, I flip off the two Blades with both hands. Soter does a poor job of hiding his smile before smacking them both upside the head. He scolds them a second later, but I can't hear him over the pounding in my temples.

"Desiree?"

A moment later, Vane and my mom appear from the trees. Mom's green eyes bulge.

"It's not what it looks like," Jax mutters to Vane, who folds his arms. "She and I need to talk."

Vane steps aside and allows Jaxson to whisk me away, a brittle smile on his face.

WHEN JAX finally sets me on my feet, I whirl on him, pushing both hands into his solid chest. "What the hell, Jaxson?"

"Have you lost your damn mind, Desi?" Jax fires back. "You were beating up two armed men."

I release a long breath through my nose. "They want to trap Wilder and Leigh in Mictlan," I screech, desperately searching his face. "We can't let them."

Jax frowns as I put distance between us. "It's what Wilder wants."

"How could you say that?"

"I didn't say I was going to let it happen—"

"Then why did you take me away?"

"We need a plan. Soter and Wendy won't—"

"You're a Blade. Fight them off!"

"Wendy is my boss. I need to handle this rationally. I think I can convince some of the other Blades to join our side. Wendy and Soter will have to listen if the majority of us want to carry out a rescue mission."

I scoff. "By the time you get enough people on your side, it'll be too late."

"We can't just jump through the portal with guns blazing," Jax says. "If we do, we could put Wilder, Leigh, and Fynn's lives in more jeopardy. My plan is solid."

"Who the hell are you? You aren't you right now. My Jax wouldn't stand around and play by the rules if a child got taken. He wouldn't let them trap my brother and his fiancée in a realm of sorrow. My Jax would lose his shit and fight back if he saw two men attacking me—"

"I'm not *your* Jaxson anymore." He exhales loudly.

I wince. "I just meant, you are my *best friend*."

Jax wipes his hand down his face. "Desi ..."

"You've been on edge all night, not acting like yourself. I thought it was because of me, but maybe I was wrong."

He groans. "I failed, Desi. I failed to tell you and everyone the truth, and now everything is ruined."

Truth about what? "What's ruined?"

He laughs, but it lacks his usual warmth. "My future."

I blink, still confused.

"I should have been honest with you and everyone else, but I was afraid you all would tell me I was making a big mistake—that I wasn't mature or responsible enough. Now, Fynn is missing, and it's my fault." He closes his eyes and takes a trembling breath.

"Jax, what the hell are you talking about?"

"Fynn is my responsibility."

"You sound like a concerned parent rather than a Blade," I joke, but the words turn his expression raw.

"Jax?" His scent sours—determination mixing with fear. Dread coils in my stomach. What isn't he saying?

He stands taller. "The missing boy. Fynn. I'm adopting him."

His admission is a syringe of adrenaline. "*What?*"

"Anselm and I decided six months ago. It started with supervised visits, and we completed the final paperwork this week. I wanted to tell you immediately, but I was afraid you'd talk me out of it. You know me better than anyone. If you said I was making a mistake, I would believe you. So, instead of being upfront and sharing the big news, I kept it to myself, and it really messed with my head. I even asked Anselm not to come tonight so I could break the news without him there in case you all reacted badly."

Oh my gods. How did I think Jaxson was upset because Anselm dumped him? I thought he was going to confess he was still in love with me. How self-centered am I? Vane must have known about Fynn. Is that why he was so determined Jax and I talk? I want to bury my head in the mud.

"I'm sorry," I manage past my fangs. "I'm sorry you would even think I would tell you that adopting a child with your boyfriend is a mistake. That's not how I feel at all."

"You always said I ran from responsibility." His heart rate spikes. "After seeing you all tonight, I started worrying that I'm not fit to be a dad. My parents divorced when I was fifteen. My brothers are lucky they didn't end up on milk cartons."

A hollow ache expands in my belly. "Jax, anyone can see you've grown up."

"Tell that to Wilder and the others."

"Wilder sees it, too." My chest tightens. "Come with me to Mictlan. Save Fynn. Be his hero."

Jax pauses, then shakes his head. "There's power in numbers. If we can persuade the others to go against Wendy and Soter—"

"Jaxson!" Soter's voice cuts through the trees.

Jax frowns. "Trust me, Desiree. This will work. I'm not risking their lives. We do this right."

I get it. He's trying to be responsible for Fynn. I need to respect that.

"*Jaxson*," Soter screams again.

"Go," I tell him, needing a moment alone. "I'll be right behind you."

Jax hesitates. "I'm sorry I didn't tell you sooner, Desi. I hope this doesn't change things between us."

"It won't."

My vampire heart swells for him as I watch him walk away, fully knowing he will be every bit of the father he strives to be. I'm barely alone a minute before I sense Vane's presence. The hairs on the back of my neck stand up, as they always do when he's nearby.

"I know you're there."

Vane steps into the moonlight, his dark brows furrowing with worry. "Are you okay?"

I inhale a deep breath. "Yes."

"I know when you are lying."

Shaking my head, I say, "I'm fine. I am just embarrassed. I thought Jaxson was acting weird because he was going to tell me he still had feelings for me. I never expected he was going to tell me he was adopting a child."

"He's growing up."

I rub my chest. My heart hurts. "He is, and it's without me."

"It was bound to happen eventually."

"I didn't expect it to happen so soon, and with Wilder missing, I feel like I've lost them both."

Vane takes my arm, turning me to face him. "Look at me."

I refuse to meet his eyes. I'm embarrassed. I wanted him to tone down his affection for me because I thought it would spare Jaxson's feelings. Vane's my mate; I never should have asked him to do that.

"Desiree, please."

I lift my gaze. "What?"

Vane stares down at me, and I strain my neck to meet his eyes.

"Vyvyan had this same conversation with me a long time ago," he begins. "It may sound harsh, but I'm not trying to be."

"Okay," I whisper.

"You are a vampire now. Your mortal life is over. Yes, it wasn't that long ago, and it holds wonderful memories—memories I want you to hold onto with all your heart, because one day, you will wake up and immortality will feel different. The people you love, your friends, your family, will grow old and die. Their time will be brief; yours is eternal. Missing them will be painful but promise me you won't let the fear of losing them stop you from being happy. You deserve to be happy."

He pauses before adding, "Jaxson is your first lesson in letting go. He was your first love, and saying goodbye hurts—that pain may last forever. But it will ebb with time, and I will be here to ensure you stay standing. Wilder is your brother; nothing will ever change that. You didn't lose either of them; they are making their own choices, and those choices have consequences. Now, it is your choice on how you will move forward. With one foot in front of the other, or will you let them dictate your future?"

Something inside me splits—the new vampire part that understands precisely what he means, and the still-human part that wants to scream in denial.

"How do you do it?" I ask. "How do you watch them all slip away and not go mad?"

Vane studies me for a long moment, and I see decades of loss in his eyes. When he speaks, his voice is still soft. "You're strong, Desiree. You know yourself better than I knew myself at your age. You've grown and adapted, refusing to let your vampirism define you. It'll prevent you from hardening into a monster. Every loved one becomes an integral part of who you are, and that part remains with you forever. The gift of immortality isn't surviving; it's carrying that love through time."

Fresh tears trickle down my face. "Your wisdom betrays your age, old man."

Vane frowns. "I was trying to be nice."

"Maybe I don't want you to be nice," I reply with a weak smile, failing to lighten the mood.

"Desiree."

I squeeze him tighter when his grip on me loosens. "Hold me."

"Forever, if you let me."

We cling to each other in the dark. I cry into Vane's chest; he never tells me to stop.

Silently, I wish Jaxson and his growing family all the best. I remind myself that Wilder will be fine. I'm not saying goodbye to him today or anytime soon, even if I might have to someday. And on that day, it'll hurt like hell, but I won't be alone. I won't ever be again.

CHAPTER TWENTY-SIX
WILDER

LEIGH and I go back to the party. She mingles with the spirits, trying to gather information about Fynn's whereabouts. Kosac probably has him locked away somewhere. But where and why? Does he have some sinister reason for wanting an orphan boy? We need to find Fynn before anything happens to him.

While Leigh works the room, I keep a low profile. Kosac still hasn't arrived, but when he does, I don't want him to see me. He told me to leave Mictlan. I'm sure he'll have zero remorse when he has his Dullahan finish what they started earlier.

Talk to that one, I say to Leigh through our strange telepathic bond, indicating to a blonde ghost with a tan complexion. She wears a black domino mask and flicks her frayed fan in sharp, restless motions. Unlike the others, she stands a little apart, shoulders tense, on edge. Her eyes behind the mask are restless, constantly scanning the room like a thief choosing her target.

Why her? Leigh asks, unconvinced.

Trust me.

Leigh saunters over to the ghost. "You look familiar," she says.

The ghost smiles. It's guarded yet interested. "Do I? I assure you we've never met, Your Majesty, but I do have a face that's hard to forget."

Leigh's smile wavers. She clearly doesn't recognize the ghost and is searching for the right words, her hesitation lingering a moment too long. I can see her trying to come up with questions that won't send the ghost straight to Kosac. The ghost's eyes flick toward the empty throne, impatience showing in her rigid posture.

Say something, I urge.

"Are you famous? How do you seem so familiar?" Leigh asks.

Good, now work Fynn into the conversation.

Easier said than done is Leigh's bratty reply.

"Not famous for anything good," the ghost replies darkly.

"So, infamous then?" Leigh asks. I drift to the side, pretending to inspect the food spread, which I suspect is meant more for Leigh than for the ghosts. He wants her fed and happy. For what?

Leigh hesitates, then tries again. "Did you do something you shouldn't have?"

The ghost chuckles. "If spending five years robbing banks to give the money to the Nebula in the BOD counts as bad, then I suppose I'm guilty."

Ha—I knew she was a thief, even if she stole for a worthy cause.

I clear my throat and catch Leigh's eye.

Keep the conversation going, I tell Leigh. *You need to connect with this ghost. Talk about your work on repealing the Labor Laws. Your common ground is that you're both fighters for the Nebula, then you can steer the conversation toward Fynn. If Kosac brought you here, chances are Fynn is here, too. She may bring you to him if she thinks you are an ally.*

Leigh's jaw tightens as the woman shifts uneasily. Leigh can't let her slip away—this bank robber and dedicated Nebula supporter could be the ally we need to find Fynn. She has morals and cares about justice, which sets her apart from the aristocrats in the room.

How do I even start a conversation like that without it seeming fishy? Leigh huffs.

You're not talking to her at all, which isn't helping.

Feel free to step in at any time.

Leigh. You've got this.

The woman looks back and forth between us. "You two seem busy. Enjoy the party, Your Majesty. We'll meet again soon." She slips into the crowd.

With a groan, Leigh joins me at the concession table. She idly examines the food while I pretend to watch the dancers. "You're better at interrogations than I am," she mutters. "You could have had her talking faster than me. Maybe you should talk while I coach from the sidelines."

"You were doing fine," I lie.

She gives a wry smile. "Hardly. What would you have said to her?"

I keep my eyes on our surroundings; Kosac isn't here, but other ghosts hover with predatory curiosity. "She stole from the rich to help the poor. She knows how to bend the rules. All the ghosts here are Kosac's lackeys. And they share a psychic connection, like we do, which means that if a mortal boy were being held prisoner somewhere, it would be hard to keep it a secret. We have to find her angle, appeal to her curiosity, or get her to trust us."

Leigh groans. "This is why you should be doing the talking. You do this professionally."

I frown. "No, I don't." Not anymore.

She snorts. "Denial is the first stage of grief. I bet if you went home right now, Soter would give you your job back."

"I don't want it back."

"Why? You love it, and you're good at it, too. I don't want you to quit something because of me. I want you to have everything you want."

Longing tightens my stomach. "I want you," I mutter.

Leigh's gaze lingers on me. "I think you miss it."

I've never been able to lie well to Leigh. I *do* miss it. I loved being a Blade, but my parents ... "Desiree and I paid the price for my parents' selfishness. I don't want that for you."

A flush rises in Leigh's cheeks. "Wilder, I think you're making a mistake."

No. Losing her would be a mistake.

"Come on, princess, let's try someone else—" My words die as I see Leigh lift a glass of sparkling liquid. Starlight flickers in the drink. Before I can stop her, she takes a sip.

"What are you doing?" I hiss.

She shrugs. "I'm thirsty."

I scan her for any signs she's been enchanted or worse. Stories about people losing their minds to fairy wine or spirit drinks flash through my mind. Why should Mictlan be any different?

"How do you feel?"

She smiles, unbothered. "You worry too much."

"You shouldn't be so careless."

Leigh takes another sip, keeping her eyes locked on mine.

"Don't," I warn softly.

She groans. "We're no closer to finding Fynn. Aradia isn't here—what else am I supposed to do?" She lifts her glass. "I had something profound and meaningful to say at our wedding, but all I can say right now is 'bottoms up.'"

"That sounds a hell of a lot like giving up," I say under my breath.

With heavy shoulders, Leigh sets her drink down. "I don't know what else to do."

Neither do I but getting drunk will only weaken us. Fynn is somewhere in this realm—maybe even this castle. "You said you tried exploring earlier. What did you find?"

"Empty rooms."

"Upstairs?"

She nods, catching my urgency. "What are you thinking?"

"Does this place have a dungeon? Kosac doesn't want us to find Fynn. I say we tear this castle apart until we do, starting from the ground up."

A gleam of resolve sparks in Leigh's eyes. "Then we'd better hurry before he gets here."

CHAPTER TWENTY-SEVEN
RAVI

EVERYTHING IS A MESS.

Aradia's journals are scattered throughout the Traum Castle library, opened to random pages that contain pieces of information that may or may not be useful. However, I haven't found anything concrete about how to close the rift. Aradia was a powerful Lunar Witch, but her journals mostly focus on her life at court and her early days as queen, especially after the First War and her sister's "death." While many believed her sister Ivah was killed, she was actually banished. Sama and I are living proof of that.

I flip to another page in the journal where Aradia writes about a meeting with the Council. They proposed new laws aimed at punishing the Nebula who supported Ivah with Labor Laws. I pause briefly on the entry. These are her accounts of the birth of the Labor Laws—the laws that Leigh abolished and laws Felicity wants restored. My stomach knots.

The library door swings open, and I slam the journal shut. I twist in my seat. I still have two hours to figure this out. The Blades can't be here already.

"There you are."

Sama smiles at me. She steps into the room, and the moonlight shining through the windows threads through her shimmering pink aura, illuminating her oval-shaped face.

I exhale. "What are you doing awake?"

Sama takes a seat at the table beside me, still dressed in her navy party dress. "I couldn't sleep. There was too much sugar in the wine." She laughs. "I went to your room, but you weren't there. You weren't at the party earlier, either."

I keep my voice quiet. I've spent my whole life trying to keep her safe, moving her from place to place under the cover of darkness. I'd hoped we could finally settle down and make a permanent home with Leigh, but it might be time to leave again. And this time, it's my fault. I never should have helped Leigh open the rift. If she doesn't come back, we're all in serious trouble. Especially if Felicity follows through on her promise to get rid of my sister and me for threatening her throne.

"I made a terrible mistake," I mutter, rubbing my eyes.

Sama sits quietly, unmoving.

"I-I've been trying to fix it." My voice cracks. If she knew Leigh was in Mictlan, she'd insist on going inside after her. I can't lose them both. "If I don't, they'll blame me. If I don't, everything will fall apart."

The Council, Queen Jorina, and Cynthia will want a scapegoat to justify their grief. I'm new to this family and disposable, like I've always been. They might even align with Felicity if she takes the throne.

Sama's breath is steady as she presses her hand against mine. It's so small and delicate. She's always been tiny—so I nicknamed her Tiny Whisper when we were kids. I can never hear or see her coming, just the whisper announcing her presence. She was destined to be a Lunar Witch from birth.

"I'm sorry, but what are you talking about?" she whispers, as if the question is a secret.

Come dawn, everyone will know Leigh and Wilder are missing. When I close the gate, they'll be stuck in another realm. Felicity Graves will become queen, and it'll be entirely my fault. Sama would freak out if I told her what Felicity said about us and the Nebula. She may start a civil war by insisting we tell Queen Jorina. It'll be Felicity's word against ours.

My stomach hardens into a cold stone. "Be glad you don't."

Sama purses her lips, studying me, then picks up a leather-bound book. She flips it open. Her eyes scan the pages. "Whose journals are these?"

"Aradia's."

Sama continues to flip through the handwritten pages. "Wow, I'd love to spend a week or more reading these. What are you looking for? Maybe I can help."

I refuse to implicate her. If I have to lock Leigh in Mictlan, I will take Sama, and we will leave right after first light.

"You should rest," I say. "Tomorrow's going to be a long day."

I'm so tired of running, but it might be our only option.

A blanket of shadow, calm and comforting, drapes over my shoulders a second later. It's Sama's magic. She offers a small smile, her long black hair glowing in the firelight.

"You should rest, too. All your problems will still be there in the morning."

I groan and bury my face in my hands. My sister has no clue how serious our situation is.

"Well, this is interesting," Sama says, eyes on a particular passage. "Could it be about Leigh?"

"Huh?"

Carefully, with both hands, Sama hands me the journal she's reading. "I think it's some sort of prophecy," Sama says, reading over my shoulder.

From darkness, she shall rise: the one chosen by the gods. This queen alone maintains the balance between shadow and light. As long as she lives, peace and harmony will persist. If her life ends too soon, chaos will spread across the world. Protect her fiercely, for without her, all hope of balance vanishes...

I stare at the passage unblinkingly. It does sound like Leigh, but as far as I know, Aradia never mentioned anything to Leigh about being a harbinger of peace. Did she? If it referred to Leigh, wouldn't Aradia have wanted her to know? Then again, perhaps the weight of that knowledge was something Aradia wished to spare her from. Maybe she believed Leigh would be better off not living with such a burden.

"You have that look. What are you thinking?" Sama presses.

"That I need to find what I am looking for sooner rather than later," I say.

Sama frowns. "You're being strangely vague, brother."

"Let's just say there's a rift to Mictlan, and I need to close it."

She tilts her head. "The ghost realm? Who opened it? And why not ask them to close it?"

I suppress a groan. Sometimes my sister can't see past the immediate problem; she's always been this way, as shown by her trusting Alden's brother Zeus with our secrets and telling him we're Ivah's descendants. She was blinded by his supposed affection and trusting the wolves' invasion plans from years ago. But now isn't the time for that lesson.

"That person isn't here anymore. So, if we don't close it, anything could get through it. The Dullahan are not the only nightmares trapped in that realm. There's a god named Kosac ... who knows what terror could unfold if he got out."

"Kosac can't leave Mictlan; if he does, he'll wither away since he is sustained by the souls trapped there," Sama says, her gaze steady. "The Dullahan can leave because they are his creations. But none of that matters, because I can close it."

I lean back in my seat. "You know how to close the gate?"

Sama stands taller. "You sound surprised. When I was Zeus's prisoner, I had many conversations with our ancestors. I learned a thing or two." There's pride in her voice. "It's simple, really. There's a tear in reality, and we must stitch it back together."

"With what, a magical needle?" I joke.

"Sure. But we can also try encircling the rift with condemning symbols and divine names that have protective powers," she says, rolling her big brown eyes as if explaining something painfully obvious. "We could try a daemon-trapping bowl."

"What if the rift is inside a lake?" My fingers drum against the wooden arm of my chair.

Sama considers my question, then grins. "We write what we need in the dirt surrounding the lake."

"The rain will just wash it away."

"Then we get a Green Witch to reinforce the land against the elements."

"Yeah, who? The Council wants this to stay a secret."

She shrugs. "The Council knows?"

I don't answer. I've said too much already. I push to my feet. Sama's shadows retreat to her like obedient pets.

"Where are you going?" Her question follows me as I hurry toward the tall shelves.

"To find a book on what symbols to use." My voice is steadier than it has been since October.

Sama's smile stops me in my tracks. "What?" I ask.

"I'm just happy you are letting me help," she says. "I didn't want to go back to bed and stare at the ceiling."

I study her. She seems so happy here. For the first time in her life, she appears content and rooted. I can't take that away from her, but if Leigh doesn't return, we'll go down together.

CHAPTER TWENTY-EIGHT
WILDER

LIGHT DOESN'T PENETRATE this deep within the catacombs of Kosac's castle. Leigh breathes heavily behind me as we shuffle across the weathered stone floor, checking inside cells for Fynn. A set of old-fashioned keys I found dangling from the wall when we first entered hangs from my hands, along with my mask.

No one is supervising the dungeon, which implies the cells are empty, but I refuse to leave any stone unturned. In our world, the castle's dungeons were converted into storage facilities. But in Mictlan, they are still designed with heavy bars and bare cots to hold prisoners. Except, none are here. If Fynn is being held in this dreadful castle, I pray it isn't here. The atmosphere is enough to give any child nightmares for the rest of their life.

"Fynn?" Leigh calls. No one responds.

"What about this one?" I ask, pointing to the only closed door in a long line of barred cells.

Leigh shrugs. "Is it some kind of office?"

"Guards quarters, if I had to guess, which usually has a prisoner log."

Leigh nods. "Hurry. Kosac has probably realized I'm gone and has Henrietta looking for me."

"Henrietta?"

"The female ghost dressed as a lady's maid."

Maybe it's the same ghost who gave me my party clothes? If Kosac has her hunting Leigh, that would mean she's not an ally. If that's true, though, then why give me the clothes and the mask? It felt as if she wanted me to go to the party to find Leigh.

I reach for the handle; it groans like a drunkard as the hinges rub. We step inside the inky blackness.

I cough as Leigh swats spiderwebs away from her face.

"Another dead end?" Leigh asks, her voice small in the vast darkness.

I stay silent because I'm not entirely sure if it is yet. The room is small, with wooden beams and a tiny desk cluttered with dusty logbooks. Leigh has her hand resting on my lower back as she leans forward, eyes focused intently on an open booklet, its fragile pages yellowed with age.

"What's this?" she asks.

Drawn by her focus, I lean forward. "The latest log."

I read the old-fashioned names on the pages, starting with A and ending with Z. Aradia and Fynn are not names found on the list.

"Goddammit." I shove the books off the desk and watch them clatter to the floor, dust billowing up in a cloud. Leigh stills. "Where is he. I'm starting to doubt he is even here because what the hell?"

Every second we spend searching for Fynn is another moment slipping away, bringing us closer to being trapped here forever. I'm not leaving the boy, but I can't help but think about how Leigh and I should be at home, waking up as joyful as can be on our wedding day. It's also another moment where the rift remains open, possibly allowing more nightmares to enter our realm. If the number of daemons coming through cannot be controlled, the Blades and the Council won't be able to keep the rift a secret for much longer. There'll be widespread panic.

My chest tightens with each shallow gasp.

"Wilder, it's okay," Leigh reassures me. "Fynn isn't down here, but that doesn't mean we should give up." She wraps her arms around me from behind, resting her cheek against my back. "We still have options."

I squeeze my eyes closed. "You sound so sure."

Leigh tightens her grip. "I am."

We are out of our depth. Neither of us knows enough about this realm; the ghosts only answer to Kosac, who wanted Leigh to attend his party, but for what purpose? Why is he celebrating? And what does Leigh have to do with it? Nothing good.

"Leigh. Maybe we should come back—"

She releases me. "No."

I frown at the loss of her comforting touch.

"Fynn isn't staying here. He's probably scared and confused. Besides, he has no one—no family waiting for him. He deserves to know he isn't alone."

Leigh's shaking. She must be tired, yet she refuses to acknowledge her needs over others'. This lack of self-care will ultimately be her downfall; she works herself to the bone, ignoring the signs of exhaustion.

"We'll come back," I say again as I extend my hand to her. She looks at it with hesitation evident in every line of her body. I let out a sigh. "Please. You need to rest. We can regroup—"

"You'll have them close the rift the second we step through it."

I keep my hand outstretched. "We don't belong here."

"No, *you* don't belong here."

I drop my hand. "Back to that, are we?"

"You shouldn't have chased after me, you—"

"What did you expect me to do, just sit around and wait for you to come back? When have I ever done that?"

She frowns. "You wouldn't be sitting around if you were working with the Blades."

"I don't want to work with them," I yell. Why won't she accept that?

Her scowl deepens. "Liar."

"Takes one to know one."

Leigh's jaw drops, and I instantly regret my retort. But then she smiles. "Are you ten?"

"No."

"Could have fooled me."

We both glare at each other, but after several tense breaths, we burst into laughter. Our brains no longer able to process our bleak reality. Leigh doubles over. The situation isn't funny, but laughing is a better alternative than crying.

Mirthful tears stream down Leigh's face. "We are so screwed."

I laugh even harder in disbelief. "And we might get stuck here."

We keep laughing as I reach for her. She presses her face against my chest. At least, if we get stuck in this terrible place, we'll be together. It's not the life I imagined for us—no kids or summer vacations with our families—but at least we are still together. Leigh takes a deep breath, and I finally manage to regain my composure, ignoring the feverish chills running through my body. Like a parasite, this realm is already feeding on me, stealing my vitality moment by moment.

A heavy silence blankets us.

I run my hand down her back. My fingers get caught in curled tendrils of her hair.

She tenses. "Ow."

"Sorry," I murmur.

"Are you mad at me?" Leigh whispers.

Technically, I am furious, but that's the last thing she wants to hear. What she's done is foolish and reckless. But have I acted any differently? I chased after her into this unknown realm without backup or a full-fledged plan.

"Hey." Leigh touches my cheek. I open my eyes. Hers are full of concern. "Are you okay?"

Sweat glues my shirt to my skin, but I'm not hot. I'm freezing.

"It's this place," I say. "It's as if the very air is stealing my joy."

"I know. I am a Lunar—"

"Shh." Leigh frowns at how I cut her off. But I hear voices. "We aren't alone."

"Kosac?"

I race across the room to close the door. We don't want him to catch us snooping.

I flip the lock and put my finger to my lips, silently warning Leigh to stay quiet. She nods and presses her ear against the door. I have the urge to pull her back, needing as much space as possible between her and Kosac.

"I don't hear anything. Do you—"

I draw Leigh closer. He can't take her if I don't let her go.

"Quiet," I whisper.

She nods, pupils expanded with fear.

We are now just centimeters apart. Her parted lips just inches from mine.

I'm scared, she tells me through our strange telepathy.

I know. I am scared, too.

"I don't see anyone down here. Are you sure they came this way?" Comes Kosac's chasm-like drawl.

"I'm sure," replies a second voice. It sounds familiar.

"Keep moving," Kosac demands. "This way."

Their footsteps recede, likely heading deeper into the cells. Leigh reaches for the latch. I grab her hand. "Don't."

"We are wasting time down here."

I shake my head. "They'll be back. We have to be patient."

Leigh groans. "I don't like being confined to dark, enclosed spaces." She peers up at me, her eyes steady with her lips slightly parted. Then she slowly and deliberately runs her tongue over her lips. My pulse quickens. She laughs.

"Stay quiet," I murmur. "Not a sound."

Leigh nods, but she's already restless in my grip—a voltage racing through my fingers.

"*Leigh*," I warn.

"Distract me."

She rises onto her toes and her lips crash into mine, urgent and reckless in movement.

I kiss her back, hesitant, every nerve on edge. Half of my brain is focused on the not-so-far-away ghost and its overlord, while the sensations of Leigh consume the other half—her fingers tangled in my shirt, her body pressed against mine. She nips at my bottom lip, tugging gently, and I'm about to lose it. My self-control is a bunker taking heavy fire. The cracks are spreading under the relentless assault of her touch.

"Take off your pants," she whispers against my mouth.

I freeze, just having hallucinated. *What?*

I'll be quieter if you keep my mouth busy.

Heat spears through me. She rubs against the swelling in my pants, teasing me beyond reason. I know we shouldn't, but her touch drowns out every warning. We could get caught, but I'm more focused on how her lips feel against my skin.

Slowly and deliberately, Leigh drops to her knees. Her eyes lock on mine.

She undoes my pants with nimble fingers. I should stop this. I have more willpower than this … but when it comes to Leigh, restraint has never been my strong suit.

Tell me this is a bad idea and I'll stop, she says.

It's a terrible idea, but don't you dare.

Her laugh is low and breathless, sending a jolt straight to my groin. I'm aching for her. She wets her lips, eyes wide and determined, a mix of fear of being caught and excitement. Leigh's breasts strain against her low-cut dress as she inhales deeply. She knows exactly what she's doing, and I am mesmerized by it.

Delicate fingers grip me, then slide up and down my shaft with maddening confidence. I tell myself I can keep it together, that I can enjoy this and still listen for footsteps in the hall. Her mouth ghosts over me, and I'm already close to losing it. Heat boils low in my gut at the way she drags her tongue along the underside of me. Her mouth closes around me. She hollows out her cheeks, and I bite back a moan.

Open your mouth wider, Leigh.

Obedient, she sinks back on her heels, looking up at me, lips parted, wide-eyed and sinful. She's an angel and a menace.

My dick slides past her lips, and her nails dig into my hips, urging me forward. She takes me deep, silent except for the wet sounds and her barely-there moan as I brush the back of her throat. I give a shallow nod.

Take over, I urge, unable to speak otherwise.

Her hand grips tighter, her tongue swirling, messy, merciless.

I tilt my head back and squeeze my eyes shut. Fuck. It's too much.

I want to beg her to slow down, but we don't have the luxury of dragging this out. A moan slips free, and I curse myself under my breath. I'm shamelessly hers.

She takes me deeper, swallowing every inch of my self-control.

I thread my fingers through her hair. The silk strands slide over my knuckles, anchoring me. Beyond the door, I hear something. Are they back already?

"Hold still," I say in a strained whisper. "No hands."

With her hands folded neatly in her lap, Leigh's eyes burn with mischief.

I thrust, slow at first, but then passion burns away caution, and I can't help but thrust harder. Tears glisten on her cheeks, like splinters of crystal. I feel monstrous in this moment—raw, desperate—but Leigh doesn't shy away. She never does.

My grip tightens in her hair. She blinks once, a signal. *Do it.*

I stifle a groan, and my every muscle locks as release slams through me. I empty myself down her throat, helpless to the bliss. She doesn't spill an ounce of my cum, just licks her lips clean when I pull free, greedy for every last drop of me.

I sag against the door, spent. *You have no idea how much power you have over me.*

She smiles; it's my whole universe, right there in the curve of her lips. *I have an idea.*

Leigh stands while I fumble to fix my clothes, both of us still trembling, wrapped in the high mix of danger and pleasure. Then she straightens. Her gaze shifts to the door, and her every muscle coils. The voices are right outside.

I force myself to listen.

"You owe me," a woman says.

"Owe you?" Kosac drawls.

"Yes, we had a deal."

"I recall that your side of the bargain only happens if you manage to get—" Kosac cuts off abruptly as if he was about to say something he shouldn't.

A groan from the female ghost rumbles through the silence, prickling my skin with goose bumps.

"I told you *everything*," she complains. "The longer we argue, the more likely she is to escape."

Leigh goes rigid.

"Not without the boy. No one saw her leave the grounds."

A wooden laugh comes from the female ghost. "You didn't see her leave the party? I bet they're already at the river. She's figured it out, I'm telling you."

"Then I suppose we need to go see."

CHAPTER TWENTY-NINE
JAXSON

A WEIGHT HAS BEEN LIFTED from my shoulders. I should have told Desiree the truth a long time ago. She responded better than I expected. But her reassurance, along with my peers', means nothing unless I can bring Fynn home from Mictlan safely.

My *son*. The word still feels foreign, terrifying.

Here's what I need to do: convince at least three Blades to disobey Soter and Wendy's orders. Isolde is already wavering. I heard her when Janus wanted to keep Fynn's kidnapping a secret; she's not happy with lying, just as I am sure she's opposed to leaving Wilder and Leigh in Mictlan. Ry will follow if I can make him see reason. Maybe Pallas, too, since he's always questioning authority.

We'll tell the other Blades and our commanders we're conducting a standard perimeter sweep, then slip through the rift as a group. It's risky since none of us are Lunar Witches; we have no idea what we're walking into, and we could all die in that realm. But we are out of time and left with a single option.

I'm still figuring out how to be a father, but I know it starts with trying to rescue him.

I've been acting hostile and insecure all night. I imagined false scenarios where my friends told me adopting Fynn was a mistake. In the end, my only mistake was not trusting my choices. I've grown up since leaving Borealis. I now have responsibilities, and my family is one of them.

Two years ago, when Anselm consulted on a case for Wendy and me, I fell for him. He's a former orderly who is now a counselor at Psyche Psychiatric, and we needed him to assess a suspect's mental state.

Throughout our meetings, he maintained perfect professionalism despite my subtle attempts to get his attention—bringing him coffee every morning, lingering after briefings, and finding excuses to ask his opinion on matters far outside his expertise.

I memorized his order—a caramel latte with light ice. Sweet, just like him. For weeks, I watched him sip that coffee while discussing patient psychology, his gentle voice explaining complex diagnoses with a patience I've never seen in anyone. He treated even the most difficult cases with compassion, never judging, always trying to understand.

He's nothing like Desiree. Where she's fire, passion, and chaos, Anselm is steady warmth and quiet strength. When I first moved to Glaucus, I couldn't stop thinking about her, couldn't shake that final fight at Chiara's house. It ate at me, knowing she didn't want to be with me romantically anymore.

The hardest conversation of my life was telling Anselm about that pain. It was a blow to my ego—having to admit I was hurting over my ex while still falling for him. Most people would have walked away, but he listened. Really listened. Then he said something I'll never forget: *Your feelings are valid, and maybe it is time to love someone who will love you back.*

That someone was him.

We moved in together a year ago, and I've never been happier. Things moved quickly when Anselm shared his dream of becoming a father. After practically raising my two younger brothers since my parents' divorce, I thought I was done with kids. I spent my teenage years fighting to keep my loved ones safe, helping with homework I hardly understood myself, and acting as the parent while our real parents were doing everything they could to put food on our table.

Maybe all those years of stumbling through life and raising my brothers weren't just to help my mom and dad. It was practice.

When we met Fynn during a supervised visit six months ago, I knew we were meant to be a family. He was a tiny four-year-old who barely spoke, but the way his turquoise eyes lit up when Anselm read to him, I was a goner. We signed the final paperwork earlier this week and were told that once everything cleared, we could bring him home this Sunday. It gave me the perfect opportunity to break the news to my friends while they were all in town for the wedding.

That's why tonight matters so much. I'm not just trying to save some random child—I'm trying to save my son. The child Anselm and I chose, who chose us back in his own quiet way.

I see the lake coming into view, Soter pacing its edge while Wendy talks on the phone. They are the last people I want to deal with, but I have no choice.

"Jaxson?"

I pause, spotting Isolde sitting at the base of a tree, almost obscured by darkness.

"Hey," I say, approaching. "Taking a break?"

"More like hiding." Her voice carries sadness.

"From Soter?"

She exhales. "Who else?"

"Can I join you? I'd love to avoid him, too." Soter and I have never gotten along and having him in charge when my son's life hangs in the balance broke something inside me tonight. Wilder might have forgiven him for all the terrible things he's done, but that doesn't mean I have. More than just commiserating about our mutual hatred for Soter, I need Sol's help.

"I doubt I'll be good company."

I sit beside her, noticing mascara smudges beneath her eyes. Whatever Soter did to her, he'll pay for it later. Right now, I need her on my side.

"Do you ever wonder if you're making a mistake," she says, "but the thought of not continuing makes you feel empty inside?"

I nod, thinking of every doubt I've had about becoming a father. "All the time."

"Gods, I hate him."

"Soter?" We're still talking about him?

She nods.

"Sol, what's going on between you two—"

Her eyes go wide. "Did he say something?"

"About you? No."

Her shoulders sag. "Oh."

Before I can press further, she tilts her head. "Do you hear that?"

"Probably just an owl." I need to focus her, convince her to help me save Fynn.

"That's not it." She rises, dusting off her fatigues. She disappears behind a tree. "Wait. There it is again. It sounds like …"

She vanishes into the darkness.

I frown, following. Then I hear it, too—a sound that stops my heart.

Crying.

"Is someone crying?" I call after her, pushing through low-hanging branches.

Isolde gasps. "It's the missing boy," she calls, voice catching with disbelief.

"Fynn?"

I break into a run, ignoring the sting of twigs raking my skin. Nothing matters except reaching him.

Please let it be him. Please let my son be safe.

MY HEART POUNDS against my ribs. I think I've found Fynn, and Kosac is going to lead us to him. He's somewhere near the river, and if we go now, we'll see him, rescue him, and go home.

I reach for the door handle of the guard's office, but Wilder grips my wrist.

"What are you doing?"

"Fynn! We need to follow them to the river. They think I've found him."

Anticipation sings through my veins. I grab for the latch again.

Wilder shakes his head. "We're not going anywhere with a half-cocked plan."

I can't help but smirk. "I don't recall anything ever being half-cocked between us."

He frowns, gravely. "I'm serious, Leigh. Let's think this through for a second. Why would Kosac have Fynn at the river?"

I groan, the need to act burning inside me like a fever. Wilder is too suspicious. Kosac didn't know we were down here, and he let it slip that Fynn would be at the river. His mistake is our gain. "Wilder, I want to go home. I want to bring Fynn back safely, put on my dream dress, and marry you in front of everyone. Today has been a nightmare, but it's almost over." I'm desperate to get him on my side. We are debating the wrong things. "Please, don't fight me on this."

It doesn't matter why Kosac has Fynn at the river. What matters is that Fynn is there.

"I want that, too, but we also need to take precautions. What are we going to find when we get there? Will Kosac have Fynn alone, or will the Dullahan be with them?"

The words nearly undo me, but I force myself to stay focused. "There's no time to overthink. We can hatch a plan on the way."

He still doesn't budge. I meet his gaze; the green of his eyes looks duller. So does his skin.

"Are you feeling okay?" I ask.

Wilder wipes the light sheen of sweat from his brow as if this conversation were exhausting him. He's fading, and fast. Wilder can't stay in Mictlan much longer. "I'm fine."

"We should go. Please, trust me."

"I'm trying," he says, voice rough.

I push the door open. If Fynn isn't at the river, I'll have to convince Wilder that he can't stay. I pray to whatever gods can hear me that Fynn is there because Wilder needs to go home. It's for his own good. But if Fynn isn't there, I know he'll still refuse to leave without me, which means I will have to force him to go or watch him die.

WILDER AND I walk along the crumbling cobblestone path that leads from the castle down to the river. The Acheron flows through Glaucus like blood pumping through an artery, but it lies silent, no rushing water, just a smooth surface glimmering beneath the peculiar half-light of Mictlan's sky.

I don't see Kosac or Henrietta anywhere, but the castle's impending presence presses against my back.

Wilder trails behind me, moving slower than usual along the river's edge. He keeps his eyes fixed on the trees lining the opposite side of the path.

"Leigh, wait," Wilder calls after me, several paces behind. "He's not here, and even if he were, I doubt Kosac would just hand him over. You said you'd convince him, but that doesn't sit right with me. He could demand anything from you, and you'd just agree willingly?"

I frantically glance left and right. Fynn has to be here … Kosac made it sound like he was. If I'm wrong, I don't know what to do. Should I go back to the castle? Wait around for Kosac to appear? We are running out of time. Wilder is out of time.

He looks ghostly. Each breath takes an effort.

I'm close to solving this mystery and can stay here a little longer. But Wilder needs to leave. It's for his own good, and I'll do anything—say anything—to save his life.

He is in danger, and I refuse to watch him die.

I turn to face Wilder just as he jogs up to me. Our breath fogs in the cool air. Sweat beads on his temples despite the chill. My heart pounds. I'm prepared to fight to get him to see reason and go back home.

"Fynn isn't here, and we are running out of time before Ravi closes the portal. You should go back, tell him to wait a little longer. Hold off any daemons so that it is safe for Fynn and me to come through," I say, letting determination ooze into my voice.

"Leave now?" Wilder asks.

I nod. "I'll be right behind you."

"Leigh, stop," he says. "For the thousandth time, I'm not leaving you here. What if something happens to both of you? We either go home together, or we don't go at all. End of story."

I frown. When it's time to leave, he might not have enough strength to get home. "You don't have any faith in me, do you?"

"Kosac is messing with you. Can't you see that? First the party, and now this? If Fynn were here, we would have already found him. I know this realm doesn't affect you the way it does me, but Leigh, I know you can feel that something is very, very wrong here."

Yeah, I understand, but that's my burden to carry, not his.

"You're right; this realm affects me differently, which is why *you* should go. Fynn is here somewhere, and I am going to find him. I'd be able to if you weren't stopping to warn me about the dangers of this place me every five seconds. I see them, feel them, but you don't have to."

Nostrils flaring, Wilder says, "Kosac is playing with you like a puppet."

"Maybe, but I'm not giving up."

"We can't trust anything he says. He wants you to believe this realm is different from the stories, but look around, Leigh—it's worse."

I laugh dryly. "I'm not an idiot. Those ghosts at the party are all in Kosac's service. They work for him, and in return, he gives them something—eternal comfort, power over the unworthy ghosts, or whatever. If Kosac deals in leverage, then so can I. You're right, I'll do whatever it takes to get Fynn back, but I'll do it alone. You're sick. This realm is killing you, and I can't keep searching for Fynn if I am worried about you, too."

"Whatever it takes," Wilder mutters. "I hate the sound of that—"

"What choice do I have?"

"I don't know."

I reach for him, ready to plead for his life. "You can't stay. I'm not giving you a choice. Go home, wait for me there. I refuse to return to a world where you are no longer in it because you wasted away here. I refuse."

Hurt flashes across his face. "That's not fair. I told you I am fine."

My own desperation erupts and overflows. "No, you're not being fair. You aren't listening to me. You are sick, Fynn is still missing, and Ravi could be moments away from sealing us in here for good. Hell, maybe Ravi already locked us in here. Or maybe they are all dead on the beach because daemons killed them."

"Stop it."

"No, you stop. Why can't you let me take care of you? 'Through sickness and health' starts now." My voice cracks. "I won't fail you like I failed Aradia."

Wilder stands his ground. "I love you, that's why I *can't* leave you."

"You have to try," I shout, fists shaking.

He steps closer, a wall of heat in this frozen place. I glare back, refusing to yield. "Leigh, stop, I can handle myself. You need to have more faith in me."

"You are dying."

"No, I'm not."

I need to push him harder if I want to win this argument. "Maybe this was a mistake—us getting married. Look where it has led us?" I gesture wildly around me, while inside my heart is breaking. "If fate wanted us to be together, we wouldn't be here."

"Fate? *You* did this!" Wilder's words cut through the air between us. I flinch. He softens, but it's too late. We are finishing this now. "You should have left Aradia's death alone. You wanted to entangle your soul with hers? Aradia's been gone for over a century—she doesn't belong in our world."

Hysteria brews inside me. He has a right to be angry. I ruined everything, but I won't be the reason his family has to mourn his death back home. "No, *you* don't belong in *my* world. We are too different; we want different things. You are a Blade, and I am the queen. You stick to what you excel at, and I will do the same. Maybe we should be grateful that we've realized we aren't compatible now, rather than three years from now. Go back home, Wilder. Forget about me."

"That's not fair. You don't mean that."

"Life isn't fair. Then you die. Ask Aradia," I say, forcing as much sincerity into my voice as I can when all I want to do is hold him, kiss him, tell him nothing I just said is true.

With a gulp, I stand my ground.

Wilder studies me, searching for signs that I'm lying, but I keep my features statuesque while I'm crumbling inside. "I can't believe you just said that to me."

I shake my head. "Please, just leave. Get out of here while you still can."

He inches closer, and I intentionally step back. If he touches me, I'll fall apart. I need to stay strong. It's safer back in Glaucus. We can work things out between us later. "I'll go."

My chest finally expands fully. "Good."

With his hands clenched into fists, Wilder starts to walk back up the river. Each step is heavy, and his body is hunched, as if he is thoroughly weary.

Somewhere in the distance, just barely audible over the steady rhythm of my pulse, is taunting laughter, as if Mictlan itself is mocking me.

CHAPTER THIRTY-ONE
LEIGH

THE LAUGHTER BUILDS. It starts as a whisper and swells to a crescendo. The ghastly sound reverberates through the vacant streets, bouncing off stone, multiplying until it seems to come from everywhere at once. It vibrates in my chest, rattles my bones, and hollows my ears. It steals what little joy I cling to, leaving me an empty shell.

"Bravo." Kosac appears like a nightmare taking form. "I haven't seen a performance like that in years. Well done."

I stare at him with blank eyes. Wilder took all my fight when he left. I got what I wanted, but part of me fears I may have been too convincing, and he'll never forgive me for my lies. "Where's Fynn?"

I'm done with games, done with riddles. It's time to go home.

"He isn't here." Kosac's voice is as desolate as an abandoned tomb.

I shake my head. Liar. "I'll do it—whatever you want, it is yours. Just free him."

Kosac glides behind me, floating inches above the pavement. He grabs my shoulders, the bones of his hands impossibly frigid against my skin, each fingertip like a shard of ice. The reaper turns me so that I face the river, his grip unyielding.

"I swear on all that is holy and unholy, the child isn't here, but you know who is?"

Kosac urges me forward. I fumble a step.

"Look." The command is a sinister whisper in my ear.

I stare at the unmoving water below. "What am I looking for?"

"You'll see." I'm about to tell him where to shove his cryptic words— but then the water transforms before my eyes. It's not still; it just moves so slowly that it seems motionless. The longer I stare, the more faces I see beneath the glassy surface, eyes open, bodies writhing with silent screams, causing my body to recoil in horror.

"Ghosts?" I gasp. "There are ghosts in the river."

"Yes." The single word carries satisfaction, as if my fright pleases him.

"Why?"

"This river carries souls from this level of Mictlan to the next. Those I deem worthy can stay here unscathed, while the others will weaken through nine levels until the cycle begins anew." Kosac's spindly fingers dig into my skin, marking me. The pain pales in comparison to the despair unfolding below.

"What do they need to do to be considered worthy?" My heart beats madly inside my chest.

"They prove themselves to me by being useful."

I blink. I have millions of questions, but none of them get me what I want.

"What does any of this have to do with Fynn?" I finally ask.

"Nothing," Kosac replies. "But it has everything to do with you."

"What—"

"Don't you see her?"

"Who?"

"Aradia."

There, among dozens of others, Aradia's soul floats upstream. Her eyes are closed, no torment radiating from their depths, but her once-vibrant presence is now reduced to a translucent hue, fading like an old photograph left in the sun.

"Aradia," I scream, but her eyes remain shut. I jerk out of Kosac's hold and clutch the rusted railing, seconds away from jumping over it. "Aradia."

"She can't hear you."

Aradia is stuck here because of me. I failed her, hurt her, just like I've hurt every person I love. "Free her."

"I can't," Kosac says. "But you can."

The air leaves my lungs. "Me?"

Kosac's robes billow in a windless gust. Overhead, a harpy cries. I don't need to look into the sky to know they are circling, waiting to peck at the scraps their master leaves them.

Kosac gets straight to the point. "Your soul for hers."

"My soul?" My back collides with the railing. The biting iron digs into my spine.

Kosac looms closer, the darkness beneath his hood seeming to deepen. "That's the price—an afterlife with me."

My soul? The magnitude rattles my brain. One day, I'll find myself in this realm, destined to enter this river because I will never be deemed worthy of this Death God. I refuse to give him the satisfaction of ruling over me for eternity.

"Why is this the price?" I ask.

"A soul for a soul. Do this, and I will release her. She'll join your father and brother in Heaven. Isn't that what you want?"

My shoulders strengthen with renewed strength. It will be a terrible afterlife, spending eternity in this half-light, but if that means Aradia will find the peace she deserves ...

It'll be years before I need to worry about it. Years to figure out how to undo what I'm about to do.

"I'll do it," I breathe.

Kosac extends his hand. "Shake on it."

I grasp his hand in mine and a surge of heat shoots through my palm. I scream. It's like I'm being cut in half. Split down the middle by one of the Dullahan's swords—white-hot agony burns through every nerve, every cell.

When Kosac finally lets me go, I drop to my knees on the cracked pavement. My stomach convulses violently, and I vomit, my entire body shaking from the force of it.

"What did you do to me?" Saliva drips from my cracked lips.

"I've splintered your soul from your body. Congratulations, Leigh. You are now mine."

I jerk away from him. Cold realization kicks me hard in the teeth. He said my *afterlife*. I thought he meant my soul would return to him after I died. Of course, if he's just taken my soul, maybe I'm dead now.

"I've been planning this for so long, you see, but I never thought it would actually work." Kosac crouches before me. His bones creak like the snap of dry twigs. "You are as selfless as I was led to believe," he says, an evil smile in his voice, "and now, I own you."

"Why me?" I ask as tears slide down my cheeks.

"It's nothing personal, but you were always a means to an end. You see, Leigh, a millennium ago, the gods—the ones you revere—imprisoned me in this agony, while they lounge in the heavens in eternal bliss. But four years ago, fate shifted. Your magic emerged; you were a Lunar Witch with ties to the dead, just like me. When you seized the throne, my plan fell into place. You were always destined for greatness. The gods chose you to bring peace to the world of the living. You are their savior."

A cold wave rushes through me, making my teeth chatter.

"You make me sound like some kind of prophet," I manage to say.

"Without you, the world of the living will descend into chaos and endless suffering. You"—he shifts closer—"are my revenge. By capturing you, I've destroyed their hopes for peace on your planet. You fell into my trap just as I hoped you would." He sneers. "I opened the gate the night you tried to contact the gods and sent my Dullahan after a child with your brother's name to bring you here. It worked perfectly. When your little lover came after you, I worried you might not be willing to bargain with me for Aradia's sake, but I underestimated your need to protect the people you love. When you sent him away, it almost made me shed a tear. And now, you have given me your soul."

My stomach turns again. Oh gods, Kosac has been planning this for years. He was cursed to rule this realm for eternity, and to get revenge on the gods who did it, he's cursed me as well. I knew there was something off about Kosac; I just thought I was one step ahead of him. I played into his skeletal hands by sending Wilder away. "You hurt an innocent boy just to reach me?"

"The child was never harmed or even here. He was never my target, only you."

"You tricked me," I whisper.

Kosac rises to his full height. "And when the gods learn what I've done, they'll rage."

"You're terrible."

"Enough." His voice hits like a blow, silencing me. "Ghosts cannot address me without my consent. You may have been a queen before, but now you are my subject."

He snaps his skeletal fingers, as sharp as the crack of a whip. Metal materializes around my throat, heavy against my skin. An invisible leash stretches out to Kosac's hand. He gives it a savage tug, and I lurch forward.

"No." I tear at the collar, but the stupid thing won't budge. I can't stay here. If what he says is true, and I am part of some prophecy, I've doomed everyone back home. My people will suffer, and my home will be reduced to ruins. I can't let that happen.

"Behave," he warns, yanking the leash again. "You made your choice."

His grip is absolute. With that final verdict, he hauls me to my feet. I stagger after him, terror and regret twisting inside me.

Fynn was never here. At least I freed Aradia.

As Kosac drags me toward the looming castle, I glare at him. "What happens to Aradia?"

"Her soul will go to Heaven," he replies, without breaking stride.

"I can't even speak to her? I deserve to say goodbye."

He chuckles—so wrong for something so inhuman. "That was never part of our arrangement. But if you stop fighting me, maybe I'll let it happen as a reward for your obedience."

It takes everything in me to hold my fucking tongue.

CHAPTER THIRTY-TWO
JAXSON

I CAN'T BELIEVE my eyes. It's Fynn.

Isolde hovers ahead, frozen. I slide past her and stop suddenly. There, huddled among tangled ivy and thorny bushes, is a small boy. I almost pinch myself, fearing it's a dream. But it's him—Fynn—unruly hair, freckled nose, olive skin smeared with blood and dirt. His arms are wrapped tightly around his knees, shoulders shaking with silent sobs.

He recoils, not seeming to recognize me.

For a few seconds, I'm cemented in place—overwhelmed by too many frantic thoughts at once.

Go to him.

Get a healer.

Find Anselm.

Isolde slowly—careful so not to startle him—kneels in front of him. "It's okay. My name is Isolde. This is Jaxson. We're Blades—you're safe now."

It takes every ounce of strength not to pull Isolde back, to take over, tell her I'm Fynn's father. He's terrified enough already. The best thing for him is Isolde's soothing touch. She's in pain. They can comfort each other, and I can update Soter so that he knows Fynn is safe now. He's with me.

"Can you tell me if you're hurt?" Isolde asks in a soft voice, kinder than I've ever heard.

Fynn stays silent. Isolde and I exchange an uneasy glance.

I fumble for my phone, hands shaking, and send a quick message to Soter. He can hear a shout from here, but I don't dare startle Fynn more.

Dropping my location, come quick. We found the missing boy. Bring Chiara Dunn.

When I look up again, Isolde has coaxed Fynn into her arms. He clings to her; tiny fists balled in her shirt. Tears sting my eyes when his eyes meet mine, and they flare with recognition. I give him a reassuring smile that says *I'm here.*

Fucking hell, I thought I'd lost him forever.

But how is Fynn here? We assumed the Dullahan dragged him to Mictlan. Unease trickles down my spine. I scan the shifting darkness among the trees, suddenly hyperaware.

Something left him here. Something—or someone—could still be nearby.

"We shouldn't stay out here," I tell Isolde, my voice low. "We need to get him someplace warm."

"This is a crime scene, Jaxson. We wait for Soter. Until then, no one moves," she says, steady as ever. "We need a healer. Call—"

"Already done."

She nods, adjusting her hold around Fynn.

"I can hold him," I offer.

Fynn only buries himself deeper into Isolde's arms.

"I'm good, thanks," Isolde says, with a little smile. "I didn't know kids were your thing."

I laugh. "That kid is."

Before Sol can question me, Soter, Ry, and Wilder's mom arrive. Chiara beelines to Fynn, evaluating him where he sits rather than prying him from Isolde's grasp. Soter and Ry head my way, but my gaze keeps drifting back to Fynn.

Chiara's voice is calm, soothing, and directed mainly at Isolde since Fynn won't speak. After a few questions, she pulls a kit from her bag.

"I need an update," Soter says, handing a pocket-sized digital notepad to Ry. "Take notes."

Ry raises an eyebrow. He looks more at home with a rifle than a pen.

"I was heading back toward the beach when I found Isolde," I start. Soter nods, but his focus is pinned to Isolde as if she'll disappear.

"What was Officer Faez doing?" Soter asks crisply.

I don't mention the tears I'd seen. "She was on patrol, I assume."

"Are you assuming, or do you know?" Soter's gaze flicks to me, sharp.

"She looked upset. I stopped to see what was wrong, and then we heard it."

"Heard what exactly?" Soter prompts.

"Crying," I say.

He nods to Ry. "Did you get all that?"

"Yes, Commander."

"Ry, we need to update the president," Soter adds. "Inform her that the missing boy has been found. We also need her final decision on the gateway. Ravi texted. He can close the rift, but I need confirmation from the Council—do we seal it permanently? Tell her Wendy and I await her final orders."

Ry gives a brisk nod, but I catch the flash of hurt in his eyes. His friend is trapped in a realm of despair, and all he thinks he can do is relay messages. "Of course."

Chiara approaches, her face serious despite the slight tremor in her hands. I move closer to her, lowering my voice.

"I'm working on a plan to get them out," I tell her quietly. "I can convince some of the other Blades to—"

She shakes her head to cut me off. "Jaxson, he's the most capable Blade any of us know. If anyone can navigate that realm and bring Leigh home safely, it's Wilder." Her voice wavers slightly, but her conviction remains strong. "He'll find a way out in time."

I search her face, seeing the effort it takes her to maintain that faith. "What if—"

"*He will*," she says firmly, then places a hand on my arm. "I need you to have faith, too. The same faith I'm holding onto right now. Can you do that for me?"

The strength in her voice, even though her hands shake, makes something settle in my chest. If Chiara can believe in Wilder's ability to return to us safely, so should I.

But watching her fight to stay strong only makes me more determined to have a backup plan ready.

"Commander Telfour, may I have a word about our patient?" Chiara asks.

Fynn still clutches Isolde like she's his lifeline, so tight his knuckles are white. He trembles in Isolde's hold. Soter straightens.

"Yeah, just give me a sec." Soter aims toward Isolde and Fynn, removing his jacket.

"You can give me the update; I'll tell Soter," I offer.

"Physically, the patient is fine," Chiara says, her tone clinical but gentle. She looks both ready for battle and as though she were just pulled from bed—rain boots, leggings, a plaid coat—sleep traded for adrenaline. "The blood isn't his."

I close my eyes, relief flooding me.

"Why won't he talk?" He's a quiet kid, but not this silent.

"Mute shock. Totally normal at this stage. He doesn't know us, not yet."

As she looks back at Fynn, I notice how intently he watches Isolde, never blinking as she stares at Soter. I smile, feeling happy he is safe and that he trusts Isolde enough to let her comfort him after everything he has been through. I used to give Isolde a hard time because of what she did to Wilder, but she has proven again and again that she is a good person whose past does not define her. Maybe I've been too hard on Soter tonight. He's handling the situation with remarkable professionalism.

"He's formed an attachment to Isolde," Chiara whispers.

I clear my throat, knowing I need to contact Anselm. "So, what's next?"

"You can call Child Protective Services. I'll have Isolde bring him inside and wait until someone from the orphanage can pick him up."

The urge to argue rises. I want to be Fynn's protector, his calm in the storm, his family. But I recall Isolde's tears, the way he holds her, and let it go. They need each other tonight. Separating them would just deepen the wounds. He's safe. That has to be enough for now. I can take care of him for the rest of his life.

"I'll make the call," I say.

Chiara's smile is tired but kind, so like Desi's that it knocks the wind from me. "Let them know he's safe. If they want to speak to me, give them my number. I'll check on him within the hour."

"Thank you, Chiara."

She squeezes my arm before returning to the others. Isolde wraps Soter's jacket around Fynn, cocooning him. Soter hesitates, sharing a silent glance with Isolde before moving away, shoulders stiff. She gazes after him for a moment, then takes a deep breath and turns away.

I can't spare energy for whatever's going on between them. I text Anselm that Fynn is safe, then dial the orphanage, my hands still shaking as the adrenaline fades. Tonight could have ended a hundred ways. But I'll make sure Fynn's story gets a gentler second chapter.

"Hello, this is Domna Foster-Reid, Fynn Cygnus's adoptive father," I say to the woman on the line from Child Services at Lethe Orphanage, loud enough to capture everyone's wide-eyed attention. "I've found him. He's safe."

CHAPTER THIRTY-THREE

ISOLDE

THE SITTING room door inside the castle swings open. Light from the hallway spills into the soot-scented darkness. I sit upright on the leather sofa. Fynn's sleeping weight is a fragile anchor against my chest. Doctor Chiara Dunn walks in, her sharp eyes immediately finding me and the boy.

My thumb hovers over my phone screen, a half-written message to Soter glowing:

ISOLDE

I knew you'd do this again

I delete it, humiliation burning fresh.

I love him—gods help me, I do—but he broke my heart once already. When I chose him over Wilder, Soter's father called me "Nebula trash" and told his son to "loosen the dead weight" if he wanted to make something of himself. I was the dead weight.

He's spent years trying to apologize for his family, whispering promises that I'm the most important person in his life, claiming he'd do anything for me. That he loves me.

But ambition still burns in him—that desperate need to surpass Wilder, to prove himself to his father. Am I just another trophy in his rivalry with my ex?

Chiara approaches, and I quickly lock my screen.

"How's the boy?" She presses her hand against Fynn's forehead.

"Content," I whisper. "Fell asleep about ten minutes ago."

"Has he said anything?"

"No. I'm not very good with words tonight, apparently."

Chiara settles beside me, her presence as comforting as it's always been. I've known her since childhood—not as Wilder's mother initially, but as a doctor, then later as Altum Healer Dunn, who gave me lollipops at the clinic during visits. "Sometimes presence is enough." She studies my face in the firelight. "You look like you're carrying more than just this child."

I adjust Soter's jacket over Fynn's shoulders. Of course, it fucking smells like him. Like palo santo and tobacco. I wouldn't be surprised if his pack of cigarettes were still in the pocket. I wish someone would tell me that I dodged a bullet with Soter, so I can finally let him go. "I did it again. I fell for the wrong guy."

Her expression shifts to understanding. "Again, huh? Are we talking about Soter?"

I'm glad I didn't ruin our relationship when I destroyed what I had with Wilder. I've always been able to talk to her about anything.

"He said he'd changed. It's why I gave him another chance. But he kept pushing me to go public, claimed his family's opinion didn't matter once he became commander." My voice cracks. "But deep down, I knew he'd choose his ambition over me again—choose proving himself over caring about what I want, so I refused."

"You kept the relationship private?"

"I couldn't undergo that humiliation again. The thought of everyone watching me get rejected publicly by the same guy twice was too much to bear." I shake my head. "Momma spent my childhood promising she would be different—no more drugs, no more men, no more cons—but people don't really change, Chiara. They just find prettier ways to break your heart. Soter's no different."

"And he ended things when you told him this?"

I shift Fynn in my arms. "I didn't tell him in so many words. I know how our story ends—he's my boss, not my boyfriend. He got what he wanted: the promotion, the power. That will always be more important than me."

Chiara's smile is sad. "It sounds like you were so afraid he'd choose everything else over you that you never chose him."

I scoff. "I did choose him. Against my better judgment. Then, he dumped me tonight, just like before." Fynn stirs, and I lower my voice. "I'm tired of being second best. When will things finally get better?"

I was raised between right and wrong—my mom and aunt stealing, lying, keeping us afloat with broken promises. When I emerged as a Solar Witch and joined the Blade Academy, they were appalled. They toed the line of crime while I wanted to be better. Then I proved I was worse.

With Wilder, I always felt the disconnect—his hardworking, stable, married parents versus my uncharacteristic upbringing. If he thought I was trash, I'd have believed it. But with Soter, I wasn't embarrassed about my past. We were the same—both forgotten and using each other to feel better about ourselves. Until feelings muddled everything, and I realized I liked being with him. I was free.

"You should tell him," Chiara encourages.

"That he's an ass?" I laugh darkly. "Oh, he knows."

"Allow Soter to choose you. How is he supposed to give you what you want if he doesn't know what it is? Maybe he thinks he's being the person you want." I stare sideways toward the window. No way. "Look, Isolde, I'm not your mom, but as a mom and wife of a former commander, I will say that I may understand a thing or two about Soter. He will never know how you feel unless you tell him. Don't wait until it's too late, like I did."

I chew on the inside of my cheek. "What didn't you say to your family that you wish you had?"

"I thought that pursuing the Altum Healer position would make me a better mom, but instead, I ended up neglecting my kids. I assumed they would be happy growing up with more money and parents who held titles." Chiara clenches her hands. "I had no idea Moran was involved with Nyx and had killed the president for Eos to protect our family. Now, he's in prison. As for Wilder, if he had told me he wanted to quit his job, I would have advised him against it. He and Leigh are made of stronger stuff than Moran and me. I wish I had fostered more open communication in our family."

I shake my head. "Do you really think you were a neglectful parent?" I had looked up to her as a kid. She was so thoughtful that I looked forward to going to the doctor. Chiara was the mom I wish I had. She had the stable, ideal life I had always dreamed of. She inspired me to be a better person. Hearing her say this now makes me question everything I thought I knew.

"I make mistakes, but I also make a difference, which I will never regret," Chiara says. "However, I can't help but think that if Moran and I had wanted each other as much as we wanted our careers, we wouldn't have to settle for one face-to-face meeting a month."

"Does Moran feel this way?" I doubt it. Moran always pushed Wilder to do better; he believed I was a distraction. When Wilder and I broke up, I'm sure he would have celebrated, if not for the world falling apart the night Prince Gwyn and Fynn died. I've often wondered if Moran and Chiara blamed me for Wilder moving to Aurora. I've never been brave enough to ask.

"Moran has his own regrets, yet he loved us in the best way he knew how."

"Momma always said love was just another transaction."

Chiara drifts toward the exit. "Maybe. People can surprise you. They can change. Look at Wilder. He went from hating the world and the people in it, especially the Epsilon, to marrying one. Go figure."

"Wilder and Soter couldn't be more different."

She pauses at the threshold. "You think so?" Chiara glances one last time at Fynn. "A representative from Lethe Orphanage should arrive soon."

After she leaves, I look down at Fynn's cherub face. "What do you think, little guy? Can people change? I'm not convinced Soter can, at least."

His small hand curls around mine, and something solid inside me cracks.

I unlock my screen and type a message that feels like asking too much.

ISOLDE

Choose me, and I'm yours …

My finger hovers over the send button. Gods, I wish I were braver. Wouldn't it be more daring to say those words to Soter's face?

CHAPTER THIRTY-FOUR
WILDER

I WALK THROUGH MICTLAN, holding onto whatever remaining dignity I have. How dare she? I left Leigh by the river to clear my head. She doesn't have to marry me, but I'm not leaving her here. I need a moment to gather my thoughts before I face her again. She's upset about the whole situation. Hell, I am, too. I just don't take it out on her like she does on me. If she meant to hurt me, she damn well succeeded.

I know Leigh is trying to protect me; she doesn't have a malicious bone in her body. But it's not her responsibility to fix everything at the expense of her own well-being. When will she realize that?

You are a Blade, and I am the queen. You stick to what you excel at, and I will do the same.

Her words sting. I served as Blade Commander longer than I needed to. I claimed it was for her, but really, it was for me. Soter was ready a year ago. Why did I hang on? Because I wanted to. The command, the purpose, and the excitement that came with closing a case. Am I just like my parents—cold and power hungry? I gave everything up for Leigh, but if it was the right thing to do, then why does it still feel like I lost a piece of myself? The piece that made me who I am. Leigh fell for me as a Blade; she knew what that meant and chose me anyway.

Despite my limbs feeling heavy as lead, I turn around, wanting to confront her and face our fears. We need to clear the air between us and make one last effort to find Fynn. We cannot give up on ourselves or each other in this world. It will break us if we let it. My body is already fighting the effects this land has on the living. I feel like a living corpse, and I know

Leigh can see what I'm feeling. I love her for trying to help me, but she doesn't need to sacrifice herself or our relationship to do it.

"You're going the wrong way," a voice calls behind me.

Selene emerges from the mist, purple hair and rain-slicked shadows materializing with her. I keep walking. I'm not dealing with her right now.

She hurries beside me, water running down her jeans and spectral face. Her grip on my arm is as cold as plunging into winter. I jerk away.

"Did you hear me?"

"I did."

"So why aren't you going home?" she presses.

"You know why."

"You won't find her there." Her smile is glass, cracked and sharp.

I stop. "Where is she?"

"Kosac has her. She's his now."

Her words stab deep. "What is that supposed to mean?"

"She sold her soul for Aradia's freedom," Selene responds, satisfaction coloring her words, while dread crushes my insides into dust. She's lying. Leigh would never ... but who am I kidding? Of course, she would. "She'll be Kosac's prisoner for eternity. You should have listened to me. There's nothing left for you here. And if you don't leave, you'll be stuck here, too."

Rain pours down my face, sticking hair to my skin. Selene's delight in this misery only deepens my dread. "Did you do this?"

Everything clicks. The voice in the cell. The smile. She pretended to be ambivalent about the dangers of this world, but that's because she's been working with Kosac all along.

"Why Selene?" I ask.

"I did what I had to—always have," she says, chin high. "I survived."

"Survived?" My voice is acidic. "You're dead, Selene."

She throws her arms wide, laughing bitterly. "Exactly. Just when I found a family with Pallas and Chiron, my life was taken from me. Leigh's cowardice got me *killed*, and now I'm trapped here. Pardon me for trying to make my afterlife bearable! Leigh ... meeting her was my undoing, but now, she is my ticket to making the most of this misery."

"Leigh isn't a coward. She's always been brave," I reply. If she traded her soul, there must be a way to get it back. We can't give up. Selene can help me.

She blinks. "Leigh hid her powers and cowered behind her family's name when she could have changed things for Lunar Witches. She's a terrible person."

"You're wrong." My voice cuts through the storm. "She closed the asylums and turned them into centers for rehabilitation." Selene's silence suggests she hasn't been paying attention to the living since her death. Leigh has made the world a better place. She's made significant strides toward peace. We've both come a long way from the day we met Selene. "When you met her, she was in denial, just like you are now. But she changed."

"I am not in denial. Leigh is why I'm dead. That's a fact."

"You're blaming the wrong person," I spit. "*Don Raelyn* killed you. *Eos* put you here."

She stiffens, but her expression stays tight. Selene's mistaken about Leigh and holding on to her remaining resolve.

"Chiron wasn't your savior," I say, removing my soaked jacket and letting it hit the ground with a splat. "You traded freedom for scraps. He tricked Leigh, locked her in a vault, and tried to use her to spark another civil war. Leigh didn't kill you. But you are condemning her out of spite."

She clenches her jaw. "Kosac and I struck a deal. I told him everything I knew about Leigh, and in return, he'll let me spend the rest of my days on this level of Mictlan, never experiencing the other levels of sorrow. He sent the Dullahan to kidnap the boy named after Leigh's brother, knowing she'd act to save him out of guilt."

My heart skips an uneasy beat. "But Leigh opened the rift. How could you predict that?"

"*Kosac* opened the rift the night Leigh tried to call the gods for Aradia. He blocked her signal and made his move. She agreed to his terms: her soul for Aradia's. Your leaving gave him the opening. She fell right into his trap." Her hands fall limply to her sides.

White-hot guilt floods my chest. I shouldn't have left. By leaving, I let Kosac fulfill his wish. "She made a mistake. Mistakes can be unmade."

Selene frowns. "No, Wilder. She's stuck here, forever."

No. The word repeats—booms—throughout my entire being. I refuse to believe that. I can fix this; I'm a Blade, and I solve tough cases in my line of work. Leigh is going to be my wife, in this life and the next. I'm not giving up on her.

Selene lets out a strangled sound. "You never liked me, Wilder. Admit it. You probably felt relief when I died. The Lunar Witch got what she deserved."

Heat flushes my cheeks. She isn't entirely wrong. I was raised to hate her kind. But when she died, all I felt was disappointment in the system and myself for believing in it. Leigh changed my views—as well as the world's views—on Lunar Witches with Aradia's help. She abolished the Labor Laws, freeing the Nebula from being forced into jobs dictated by their respective magic sectors. For the first time in my life, I had a choice about my future. However, I still chose to remain a Blade. It was never my dream, but gradually, it became my calling. By dooming Leigh, she has put all of us at risk of repeating the past.

"You're right," I admit. "How I treated you was wrong. I'm sorry."

Selene's jaw drops.

"Leigh changed my life." My fear eases. "The world's different now. Pallas works for the Blades, Chiron is serving a life sentence, and Leigh is queen. Things are better. Why undo all that now? For petty revenge?"

A shadow crosses her face. "Because I—" She cuts herself off, pain in her eyes.

Guilt is probably eating at her, but it's not too late for her to fix what's broken. She can help me. Help Leigh.

"What happened to you is unforgivable, Selene. But Don is in prison; he stood trial for his actions. While his crimes can't be undone, Leigh made sure he faced the consequences. You still have a chance to make things right. You deserve peace. Let her have hers, too. Help me, please."

She shudders, rain and ghostly tears mixing together. "I wanted happiness. Thought revenge would give me that. I thought you, of all people, might understand after what Chiron did to you by recruiting your dad into Nyx."

I shrug, water running off my arms. "Eos corrupted my dad, and ultimately, justice prevailed. He made his choice. He faces that regret every day, but you don't have to follow the same path. There's still time for you to change course."

Something softens in the haunted depths of her face. She whispers, "Oh."

"Where is she?"

"The castle."

I don't hesitate. Heart pounding, I run toward Leigh. She's my heart, my anchor, my home. I'll steal her back right from under Kosac's nose. Each sprint brings me closer to her, to whatever madness, hope, or heartbreak lies ahead.

As I run, the rain steadies, echoing my determination. For the first time since I arrived, Mictlan's storm seems to part, clearing a pathway just for me.

I want it all, and I'm done waiting.

CHAPTER THIRTY-FIVE
LEIGH

IT'S IRONIC.

The prison cells beneath the castle—the same ones that once held rebels and political prisoners during my ancestors' reign—now only hold a single occupant: me. What was meant to break the spirits of many now targets only my isolation. The dungeons should be haunted after centuries of suffering, yet even the ghosts seem to have abandoned this place, leaving me in a silence so complete it becomes its own form of torture.

I researched this realm to rescue Aradia and came here for Fynn. I succeeded in saving one but failed with the other. Fynn was never here. The little boy might have been taken from his bed by one of the Dullahan, but he was never dragged beneath the lake's surface or brought into this gray scale realm of the dead. He was just bait—bait I swallowed whole.

Is the prophecy true? If it is, without me, the peace I have fought so hard to achieve will crumble into dust. My people will suffer, and everything will be worse than ever.

I pushed Wilder away.

I sold my soul.

Now look at me. Trapped, soulless, and alone.

"Hey." I rattle the bars of my cage. "How can I trust your word that Aradia is safe if I don't get to talk to her?"

No one answers. Fucking figures.

Trembling, I slowly lower myself to the damp, stone floor. I hug my knees to my chest; my corseted undergarments provide little warmth against the iron-cold surroundings after shedding my borrowed gown. The situation I'm in closely mirrors when Chiron locked me in that vault several years ago. The same claustrophobic walls closing in, the same helplessness tearing at my throat. Only this time, no one is here to save me. Kosac got what he wanted. I'm stuck like a fly in amber, forever trapped in my mistake.

More seconds tick by. I play with the fabric of my silk slip, the fine material now torn and soiled—the perfect metaphor for my ruined plans.

This cannot be my future. I need to escape and ensure that the prophecy—true or not—doesn't fall apart without me.

The bars are reinforced steel, hard and unyielding. The keys hang tantalizingly out of reach, placed there by one of Kosac's cronies, who had locked me in here earlier.

The Dullahan can leave this realm, and so can the daemons. If I can escape this cell, there's a chance I can go as well. I'm not a ghost. If I can break free from this world, I can help Ravi seal it. I'll confront Kosac after my death.

"Leigh?"

I sit straighter.

"Leigh?"

My heart rate increases. It can't be. "Aradia?"

"Where are you?" Aradia calls.

I push to my feet, ignoring the whine of my tired muscles. I stick one hand between the bars, waving her down.

"I'm here!"

Aradia appears before me, and I can hardly believe my eyes. She looks so real, with her dark hair tied back and her light eyes full of life. Her cheeks have color, and tears prick my eyes.

I did that. Although I may be trapped here, seeing her vitality restored makes part of my hasty decision worthwhile.

"Leigh, what the devil did you do?" Aradia asks.

My hands fall to my sides.

"I wanted to help you," I say, though it justifies nothing. I'm a fool.

She frowns. "By trading your soul for mine? Do you have any idea the damage you've done?"

"I have an idea ... Are you going to Heaven?"

"Yes." Aradia sighs. "But you should have left everything alone."

"I did it to help you. It's my fault you're here. If I had crossed you over—"

"No, I am here on my own volition because I was afraid. Afraid that, despite helping you right the wrongs of my life, it would still not be enough to undo the evil I let persist during my reign. I was scared I'd end up in Hell, but all that got me is a one-way ticket to limbo, which is a hell in and of itself."

"See, that's why I couldn't leave you here." Aradia's the reason the world found peace.

She raises a thin brow. "So, it's better you were stuck here instead of me?"

I say nothing, staring at the ground.

"Stop prioritizing others over yourself, Leigh. I know that as a queen, you must be dedicated to your people, but it's essential to take care of yourself first."

I can't meet her eyes. She's right.

"I didn't want to tell you about the prophecy because I couldn't handle seeing that pressure land on your shoulders. But I can see now that you thought your joy didn't matter when, in fact, it does. You were chosen to finally undo my mistakes and lead our people to peace. You deserved to know. Maybe if you did, you wouldn't be imprisoned here."

Emotion clogs my throat. "I'm sorry."

"Even without the prophecy, your life is just as valuable as mine or anyone else's. If you spend your whole life trying to keep everyone else happy, you'll end up failing them all. You *need* to pursue your own happiness as well."

I nod, but she frowns at me. "Use your words. Tell me you understand, because I don't have much time left."

"I understand," I say, and I genuinely mean it. I always put others first. I pushed Wilder away to protect him and traded my soul to free Aradia. By doing these things, I saved the people I love, but now I'm empty inside. Selflessness isn't the same as sacrifice; there's a middle ground I have refused to acknowledge.

Aradia smiles. "Good."

"What does it feel like?" As I ask, her form flickers, like a light about to go out.

"Like open arms welcoming me home."

"I'm glad," I say a tad breathlessly.

"I will beseech the gods for your release from this place," she vows. "I promise—"

She disappears.

The prophecy was real. My people will suffer if I stay here. I'm getting out.

"Let me the fuck out," I scream, my voice echoing. "Kosac, I know damn well you can hear me."

He's probably watching me now, enjoying the show, like how he watched me push Wilder away at the river. He's the eyes and ears of this realm. It probably amuses him that I'm trapped. He has my soul, my future happiness, and all to spite the gods who spited him. Fuck him.

"Kos—"

"Leigh!" Wilder's voice cuts through my rage like scissors through silk.

I freeze. Unable to believe my ears. Wilder didn't leave.

"Leigh. Answer me."

Hope flutters in my chest. "Wilder."

"Where are you?" he calls.

I grip the bars tighter. After I tore him down and pushed him away, he came back for me. He shouldn't be here. This realm is destroying him, and I shouldn't be glad he's here, but gods, I am.

I love him deeply, and I never want to be apart again.

"Here!" I press against the bars, straining to see him through the shadows.

Moments later, he's standing in front of me with the thick bars between us where Aradia previously stood. His clothes are wet, his hair glued to his unnaturally pale skin, water dripping from his chin. Pain and doubt shine from his eyes. Emotions I put there. Seeing him takes my breath away.

"I'm so sorry," I say, the words tumbling out in a rush.

He shakes his head, eyes scanning the cell. "Later."

"I didn't mean what I said." I keep going despite his protests. He's sizing up the bars, not meeting my gaze, his hands testing the lock's strength. "I said those things to get you to go home. You don't belong here. Mictlan is killing you. I wanted to save you. And I do want to marry you. It's the only thing that has brought me joy throughout this entire ordeal."

Wilder's hands wrap around the metal. "Say that last part again."

His grin is contagious. "I want to marry you."

"Then let's go get fucking married."

He makes it sound simple and inevitable.

My smile falters. "Last I checked, I am a prisoner." I tap the bars between us with a fingernail, the slight *clink* underscoring my point.

"Easily remedied," a female voice answers.

A face I didn't think I'd see again materializes from the shadows. Selene looks the same as she did when I last saw her alive. Her long purple hair catches what little light filters into the dungeon, creating a halo effect. I clutch my chest.

"Selene?"

Selene puts a hand on her hip, striking a pose that's so painfully familiar it hurts. "In the flesh." Hesitation flickers across her face, followed by a rueful smile. "Well, sort of. I don't really know what we are, but we aren't alive."

I laugh through my tears. Selene is here. Taken too soon because of my cowardice three years ago. I've changed; I've learned from my mistakes. "I can't believe it's you. Pallas will never—"

"We need to hurry," Wilder tells me. To Selene, he asks, "Did you grab them?"

Selene lifts an old-fashioned key ring into the air.

Wilder takes the keys from her and sticks the largest one into the lock. It turns with a whine of ancient metal. The iron doorway opens. Wilder rushes inside the cell. I throw my arms around him with enough force to nearly knock him backward.

I breathe him in, not caring that he's sopping wet. I cling to him as if he were my salvation. *He is.*

"I'm sorry," we say simultaneously, then laugh.

Wilder pulls back just enough to meet my gaze, his hands still holding me close. I smile up at him as if he were the sun. He's the most vibrant thing in this entire realm. So beautiful. So perfect. So mine.

"We need to hurry," I say. "Ravi needs to close the rift."

"Kosac opened the rift, not you," Wilder replies, causing me to trip.

Kosac opened the rift? That means I've been blaming myself for something that wasn't my fault in the first place. But if he opened the rift, does that mean he can keep doing it to reach me?

"It took an enormous amount of power," Selene comments, as if she's reading my thoughts. "If he tries again, it will only weaken him further."

I nod. If he tries again, we'll know how to stop him. At least that's what I tell myself as I pull Wilder out of my cell.

"You think you can run in those?" His eyes drop to the satin slippers on my feet.

"I have a wedding to get to."

We move swiftly through the castle, choosing speed over stealth.

Soon, we're exiting through a servants' entrance. The damp air hits my skin, chilly but welcome after the stale prison. We traipse across the wet grass toward the forest.

No one stops us. No alarms sound. It's nearly too good to be—

A loud horn blares, the powerful sound sending goose bumps over my skin. The earth vibrates a moment later. I look at Wilder, my heart lodging in my throat. He looks at Selene.

"Hoofbeats," Wilder says.

"Dullahan," Selene confirms. "All of them."

"Run."

I drag Wilder toward the forest. We're running for our lives now. The trees loom ahead, offering potential cover. Behind us, the hoofbeats grow louder—a murderous rhythm that matches the pounding in my chest. If the Dullahan catch us, we're all doomed. My soul already belongs to Kosac. What will he do to Wilder and Selene for helping me?

The air burns in my lungs as we sprint, but I don't slow down. I *can't* slow down. Freedom is ahead, and death rides at our backs.

XXI
THE WORLD

CHAPTER THIRTY-SIX
GIANNA

IT'S WEDDING DAY.

I pull back the curtains, and darkness swallows the room I share with Meg in its navy-blue hue. I'm too anxious to sleep, needing everything to go perfectly today, which is why I'm up just before dawn to take a shower and go over my to-do list again. Meg mutters something incoherent in her sleep, still curled in the sheets, looking cute in her matching pajama set—lavender with whimsical unicorns and ruffles.

I grin at the sight of her all cozy and carefree. She really is something else.

I could crawl back into bed beside her, tuck myself into the warmth, and forget about all the things that need to be done. For a moment, I let myself hover on the edge of that temptation.

Today isn't about me. It's about Leigh and Wilder. If I want to avoid delays, I need to be dressed, fed, and ready to drag Leigh out of bed (her claims of sleeping alone are about as believable as the flying unicorns on Meg's pajamas—everyone knows unicorns are land dwellers).

I'm almost to the bathroom when a sharp knock rattles the wooden door. Not now. The day is scheduled to the minute; anyone not on my itinerary can come back later. Plus, I need to look effortless, and that takes actual effort.

The knock comes again.

I sigh, frustration knotting my shoulders. "Go away."

"It's Cynthia." Leigh's mother's voice has my chest pounding like mad. Why is she here?

Leigh had better be okay, or else there will be hell to pay.

I open the door and smile at Cynthia. Her blonde hair is a mess—frizzy and unkept—and her usually flawless makeup looks rushed and worn out. She's tall, about the same height as Leigh, which usually makes her tower over me, but her shoulders are hunched, and her limbs tremble.

"Heavens, are you all right?" I ask, opening the door wider. I've seen this woman out of sorts only one other time in my life: the night her husband and son died.

Needles pierce my throat, my skin, and my eyes. Oh gods. Leigh?

"How could you?"

I suck in a breath. "I'm sorry?"

"I just had a visit from President Dyer."

"Oh?" My mind races through various scenarios regarding the president's visit with Cynthia and how it might be connected to me. I come up short. Janus hasn't spoken to me directly in ages.

"Leigh is missing," she says, her voice low and urgent. "Janus informed me that she has been unaccounted for since last night. There's something about a rift to another world, daemons, and a lost boy who isn't truly lost, but that's beside the point. My daughter is *missing* and so is Wilder. The president has decided to seal the portal with Leigh still inside, as per my daughter's orders. When I asked when Leigh gave these orders, she told me it was last night, while we were still at the party. She said you knew!"

I gasp. Why would Leigh go through the portal? "I can assure you, Cynthia, I had no idea Leigh was gone. Yes, Ry told me about the daemons last night. He asked on behalf of the Council and Leigh to keep up appearances while they dealt with the threat, but—"

"You didn't think to tell me?" she shrieks.

"I didn't want to worry you or Queen Jorina. When I didn't get an update after the meeting, I assumed the daemons were handled. I thought I was helping."

"Helping my daughter make a reckless decision. If I had known about the rift, I could have stopped her. If I had been made aware, I would have seen the signs." She inhales shakily. "Gods, there were signs. I thought they were just nerves, but she was planning to go into that rift the entire time to rescue a child who happens to share her brother's name."

I stand there, stunned. Why didn't Leigh tell me her plans? I'm supposed to be her best friend, yet I had no idea any of this was going on. My knees feel weak, but I lean against the door frame to keep myself upright.

I've planned a wedding for two people I might never see again. How did this happen?

Cynthia's eye ticks in a tiny spasm—she's more rattled than she lets on. If Leigh doesn't return, she'll have lost her husband, son, and daughter. She will have no one left.

Should I have told Cynthia about the daemons at the party last night? She was so happy there, and I didn't want to take that away from her. Throughout my life, I've made it my goal to keep everyone around me happy, but I always end up making things worse.

Shit. "Cynthia, I am so sorry. What can I do?"

"It's too late. Leigh is gone."

I shake my head. "No, please. I can talk to Ry and the others and get an update; maybe Janus was mistaken."

Tears stream down Cynthia's face, and the urge to make things better between us overwhelms me.

"Does Queen Jorina know about Leigh?" If she doesn't, we need to move fast—talk to the Blades, corroborate Janus's story, and get our facts straight before the queen learns the truth and everything else falls apart.

She laughs harshly. "Of course not. This news will devastate Jorina. Leigh's her only grandchild. That's why you're going to tell her instead of me. Face the consequences of keeping secrets from us." With that, she turns on her designer heels and marches away, leaving behind a cloud of rose-scented perfume and despair.

I close the door. Anything I say will send the already ailing queen into a tailspin.

"Gianna?" Meg's sleepy voice from behind makes me wince.

I hope she heard everything so I don't have to repeat it. I don't have the strength.

Meg sits up, puts on her glasses, and studies me intensely.

"Leigh and Wilder are missing?" she confirms.

I nod, gutted. "Why did they keep this from me all night?" I snap. "I could have helped. Not just with damage control; I could have lent a hand. I could have ... done something."

"Yeah, but maybe they were afraid you'd be upset. You put so much into this wedding." I flinch. "It's been your only focus for quite some time now. Every detail had to be perfect."

I pinch the bridge of my nose. "That's because Leigh's my best friend."

"Is that the only reason?" Meg presses.

A hollow laugh escapes me. "What's that supposed to mean?"

Tears threaten to fall. I want to help. I want to make Leigh happy. She took me in after I got out of rehab and had nowhere else to go. Elio abused me. My mom allowed it. Besides Stellan, Leigh is my family. I didn't want to disappoint her, but maybe I took on too much. Maybe I feared she'd resent me if I didn't go above and beyond to please her. It's what I'm used to, having survived a terrible childhood where being agreeable kept me from endless ridicule. Except Leigh's gone, and none of that matters. I wish she felt like she could have come to me, confided in me.

"You're hurting."

I roll my eyes. "Excellent insight, you must be psychic."

Meg purses her lips. "Gianna. I'm not your enemy. You don't have to hide from me."

"I'm sorry, I'm just scared. And now I have to tell Jorina her granddaughter is gone? She'll blame me."

"Why? You didn't force Leigh through that rift."

I sigh. "Everyone has always thought the worst of me."

Although I try to change, I still seek to please others. I turned down Ry's proposal and prioritized myself. It was a step in the right direction, but it clearly wasn't enough. I'm still trying to make sure everyone around me is happy and content. But what about others doing the same for me?

"Whoever made you think that can go to hell," Meg replies.

I laugh. "Elio's already there."

"Good."

My heart constricts. "I should have told Cynthia about the daemons."

"You didn't have all the facts. How were you supposed to know Leigh would disappear? She asked for help with her wedding, you gave it, and Ry asked you to keep the daemons a secret last night, so you did. You are not at fault here."

I dig my nails into my palms—an old habit to hold back tears, which I should just let fall. Meg isn't going to judge me. She never has.

"I should get dressed." If I'm going to face Queen Jorina, I can't do it in my nightgown.

I trudge toward the bathroom, but Meg stops me before I can barricade myself behind the door. I need to cry—so badly it aches in my chest. Leigh is gone, and she may never come back. She promised me she wouldn't die, but I promised myself that my compulsive need to make others happy ended with Elio's death. I guess we are both liars.

"What is it you want, Gianna?" she asks. "Do you even know what will make you happy?"

HAND IN HAND, Wilder and I tear through the tangled trees with Selene just behind us. Spindly branches whip at my face and arms. Thick roots threaten to pull me down. I clutch Wilder's fingers so tightly I worry I'll break them. We need to reach the lake, make it through the gate, and pray Ravi is ready to close it, if he hasn't already.

"Faster," Wilder shouts.

The trees are thinning. Through the branches, I catch glimpses of dark water. Hope awakens in me, sharp and painful. I gasp. "I see it!"

But behind us, the rumble of hooves grows louder, mixed with grunts and snarls. It's unnatural. Terror clamps my ribs. How can we possibly outrun death?

"I will try to distract them," Selene says. "You two keep going."

Wilder glances at me, determination set in his eyes. I force myself to look away. We've endured worse—we can do this. I have to believe it.

Selene turns back toward the castle. I send a prayer to whatever gods are listening to keep her safe. If we make it out, I swear I will find a way to free all the souls stuck here. They don't deserve to suffer for eternity.

We burst from the trees, lunging for the water.

Wilder kicks his dress shoes off. "You'll swim faster without them," he pants, but my shoes are already soaked. I stagger into the shallows. Water sloshes around my ankles, then my knees.

The water is chillier than I remember. My legs grow heavy; fear drags at my every step.

"Leigh, hurry," Wilder calls. He's supporting the majority of my weight, holding me around my waist as the ground disappears beneath us. I swim, but my body feels impossibly heavy, as if invisible shackles are attached to my feet.

"I'm trying."

Tears sting my eyes, but still, I claw forward through the water, paddling hard toward the center of the lake. Each stroke gets me no closer to the gate.

Behind us, Dullahan rangers on monstrous black steeds burst out of the trees, their burning gazes fixed directly on me.

Kosac appears a moment later, icy fury radiating like seismic waves we can feel even from this distance. The ground shudders with his rage, but it hardly matters now; if he wants me, he'll have to get wet. I flail, struggling to stay afloat as Wilder and I desperately push farther toward the rift, but the harder I swim, the less distance I cover. That invisible force pulls at me—unyielding—steadfast in not letting me go.

"Leigh, stop," Kosac rumbles.

The world seems to freeze; even the harpies overhead vanish from the sky.

I gasp for air and force myself to keep treading water. "To hell with that," I spit out.

"You feel it, don't you?" Kosac calls out. "This realm owns you now—just as I do. My duty is to this world. As my prisoner, your only duty is to me."

"Don't listen." Panic consumes Wilder's expression. "He'll say anything to keep you here."

I keep swimming, but dread settles deep in my bones. I can feel it, a force dragging me under, turning every stroke to lead and every breath into a battle. If Wilder weren't at my side, I'd be underwater already.

"You no longer have a claim to the living," Kosac says. "You must stay."

Wilder kicks harder. "What the hell is he talking about?"

Kosac's voice is flat. "She gave up her soul to save Aradia. She's bound here."

"But she's not dead; she has a whole life ahead of her."

My tears mix with murky lake water. "Just let me leave," I shout, my voice cracked and raw. "I don't belong here! My *soul* doesn't belong here."

My home, my friends, my family, and my kingdom still need me. There's a life waiting with Wilder, one I'm eager to live. I want to get married, have children, and grow old with the person I love.

Kosac doesn't flinch. "It doesn't work that way. Besides, nothing delights me more than infuriating the gods." His voice drops to an unforgiving tone. "If you run from here without your soul, you won't last among the living. You'll wither away, piece by piece, until nothing of you remains."

I shake my head, the truth sinking in like stones. He can't be serious. Can he?

"Leigh, keep moving, don't listen to him," Wilder urges, tugging me. "He's bluffing."

I press my teeth into my trembling bottom lip. "He's not. I thought we could both get out—that I'd have time to fix this. But Kosac won't let me leave, and if he's right—if I force it, maybe I really will disappear. Either way, he wins."

Leigh, please, Wilder urges telepathically. *For me.*

I look at Wilder, forcing calm into my voice. "You have to go. Find Ravi, close the rift. Aradia's begging the gods for mercy. There's a chance they'll listen." My voice trembles, but I force conviction into it. "If I run now, and Kosac's right, I'll fade away. By doing that, I'm helping no one." Wilder's face hardens in disbelief. "I swear I'm not giving up, not on us. That's a promise."

"Do as she says, Wilder." Kosac's tone is a death knell. "Leave. This is your last warning. I'm out of patience."

"Fuck you," Wilder shouts, but Kosac only stares.

I cry harder. "You have to go. *Please.*"

"I won't leave you."

My heart splits wide open, but I shake my head. "You must. Let me figure this out from here. I swear, I won't give up. I'll find a way back to you."

He searches my face, and I let him see everything I feel: my love, my regret, my determination.

Then I make myself release his hand, even though it's the hardest thing I've ever done.

CHAPTER THIRTY-EIGHT
WILDER

IT'S agony to keep treading water, yet I can't stop. The thought of abandoning Leigh in this shadowed world hollows me out until the cold surrounding me is just an afterthought.

"Please don't do this," I manage through chattering teeth.

Leigh's voice trembles. "Wilder, it has to be this way. For now."

"No." I swallow water in my reply. This is no time to be altruistic. "Without you, there is nothing for me back there."

"If you stay, Mictlan will take both of us. I need you to live. Live for me. Go back to our friends, tell our families what happened. Return to your life, live, until I come back to you."

"I can't do life without you. I won't," I whisper, dripping with desperation.

"Listen to her, Wilder," Kosac growls, his shadow threateningly large at the water's edge.

"You should go. I'll stay ..." I say to Leigh, ignoring Kosac. He shouldn't get a say in our future. "I'll trade my soul for yours."

"No." Leigh chokes on a sob. "If you offer up your soul, I'll turn around and do the same for you. We'll trade eternity back and forth, forever lost. That isn't love. That's torment."

She's right; I can't throw myself away if I ever want to be with her. Then it hits me—a memory, sudden and blinding: Leigh told me she bargained with the gods for Aradia's life by linking their souls.

What if I try that very thing now? She risked the wrath of the gods for her friend. How can I do any less for her? There's a chance the gods will ignore me, but I have to try. I'm not royal. I'm not anyone special. Still, my heart refuses to give up. Leigh made me a promise. Our love must mean something.

With the last of my strength, I lift my face to the storm-dark sky and shout, "If you can hear me, I'm no prince, no god—maybe no one at all. But Leigh is. You chose her bloodline to rule. If she matters to you, then bind our souls as one. Let us share our fate. Let my strength be hers. Let us return to life. Entwine us together until the very end. And when our time comes, let us go into the light side by side."

Silence follows, deep and chasm-like. For a moment, all I hear are our splashes and Leigh's breath. The emptiness presses in. Was that all? Just a hopeless plea flung into the shadowed void.

Then the current shifts as the wind picks up. Warmth blooms beneath us, golden light spiraling up through the icy water. My skin tingles all over, no longer from the frigid air.

Thunder crashes overhead as lightning skips across the sky. The water glimmers faintly with more light—something impossibly alive, impossibly kind, is moving through it now.

Kosac screams on the shore. The Dullahans' horses whinny.

"No. Stop—"

Lightning cuts off Kosac's words. The warmth from before seeps into me, filling every part of me, entwining with my very essence. I feel Leigh differently now. Not just her hand in mine, but her soul weaving through me, a connection deeper than flesh or bone. It's like a summer breeze whispering inside me, foreign yet intoxicating. It's as if her soul is filling every empty part of me, as if she were always meant to be here. The suffocating grip of Mictlan fades. The sky brightens gradually, and for a moment, I'm filled with awe.

"It's over," a resonating voice says. I look up at the sky and blink repeatedly. Aradia's spirit is there, surrounded by bright, white light. "Leigh and Wilder may return home; the gods have made their decision. They've answered Wilder's call. As our chosen queen, Leigh will go back to her kingdom, where she will rule with Wilder by her side until the day comes when they both will return to Heaven. So long as nothing happens to Wilder, Leigh will live a long and fruitful life."

Kosac's voice comes through, hollow and defeated. "But he is merely a mortal."

Aradia remains silent. Turning to Leigh, she says, "Your souls are now joined. Unless you turn away from the light, Mictlan will claim neither of you ever again."

I inhale a shuddering breath. "Leigh, we did it."

Leigh stares at me, stunned. Then joy explodes across her face. "It's over."

"Yes," I reply.

We hold each other, breathlessly overwhelmed with relief, gratitude, and pure happiness. I press my forehead to hers. Our hearts beat in perfect sync. Our legs windmilling beneath us. "So long as my heart still beats, I am yours. Nothing can take you from me."

"Let's go home," she whispers through tears.

Holding hands, we swim toward the center of the glowing lake together, the gods' light parting before us. As a current gently pulls us home, I look to the shore once more, where Selene now stands. She throws me one last sad smile, and there's a flicker of peace in her lavender eyes.

Go, she says with her gaze. *I'll be okay.*

It's time. We take a breath, diving underwater, and leave the darkness of Mictlan behind.

CHAPTER THIRTY-NINE
RAVI

IT'S the hour between night and morning, that time when everything merges into the same faded color. I crouch beside the runes Sama and I carved into the dirt surrounding the lake. Pallas stands nearby, his earth magic protecting the runes from the elements. All that's left now is a signal from President Janus Dyer, and Sama and I will speak the final words, and all of this will be over.

That what I want, but I can't move. I keep imagining Leigh trapped somewhere I can't reach—locked behind the rift, crying out for me, banging against an invisible barrier, unable to come through. Sama looks at me, pain in her eyes. She knows Leigh's inside Mictlan now. When she found out, I had to beg her to still help me. She agreed only because I promised her it was what Leigh wanted, but she still doesn't want to do it.

My gut twists. If we close this rift, she'll blame me for Leigh's and Wilder's deaths. And she should. I should have told Leigh to cross Aradia over even though she insisted she didn't have to. I should have stopped her from going into Mictlan. But I didn't because I was afraid she'd hate me, afraid she'd send me away and rip away the only real home I've ever had. I've been running all my life. I don't want to run anymore. If I'm the one who shuts this door, I'll regret it.

Felicity will be queen, and nothing will ever be the same.

But if I don't close this rift when Janus orders me to, what will she do? Will she force me? Will she use Sama against me, just as Zeus did? Maybe I should have run when I had the chance. *No.* Staying was the right choice. Without me and Sama, this rift will never close, and I can't live with that either. But we can't give up on Leigh yet.

We need to buy her a little more time.

With a hesitant look, Janus checks her watch as the other Council members stand beside her, bleary-eyed in the early hour. She appears to be doing what she thinks she needs to do, even if it doesn't seem like what she truly wants.

Beside her, Felicity smiles. They have already started mobilizing succession plans, and Leigh isn't even dead yet. In fact, Felicity might be the only person on this beach who isn't reeling.

"Ravi, it's time," Janus says in a small voice.

I know I need to give Sama the signal, but my limbs refuse to respond. Janus doesn't want this; none of us do. So why are we doing it?

"Just five more minutes," I beg the president.

"Ravi, we discussed this. It's what Leigh wanted," Janus insists.

Fuck this. I'm done listening to her and everyone else's orders.

"The daemons that came through last night paralyzed several Blades. Just imagine the casualties if more daemons like that, or even worse ones, were to come through. You'd be putting an entire city of innocent lives at risk. This is serious. Please, I know it's difficult, but Leigh might already be dead."

"Five minutes!"

Felicity frowns. "Madam President, he's defying your orders—"

"There," Jaxson shouts. "Is that another daemon?"

I freeze at the fear in his voice. He's pointing at something. The Blades reach for their weapons.

"Hold fire," Soter yells. "I think ..."

A hush settles over the group, then a gasp. I follow Jaxson's gaze. Two heads break the water's surface, and I drop to my knees.

It can't be. Leigh gasps, and Wilder waves their hands in the air before swimming to shore. Both are alive, battered but whole, and finally home.

Janus holds a hand over her heart. "Thank the lucky stars."

Felicity stomps her foot and turns toward the castle.

Desi splashes into the lake first. She runs straight to Wilder with her arms open and seizes him. "You stupid idiot—I thought you'd died."

Wilder, too stunned to respond, allows Desi to wrap her arms around his neck. Only then does the tension in his shoulders ease, and he hugs her so tightly that her breath catches in a laugh as they fall back into the water.

Isolde splashes over to Leigh. "What the hell is wrong with you?" Isolde chastises.

Leigh smiles. It's tired but genuine. "Great to see you, too."

Leigh wraps her arms around me next, and I jolt. I'm still unable to believe it's her. If I had listened to Janus, my fears would have been a reality. "You have no idea how happy I am to see you," she breathes.

I bury my face in her shoulder for a moment, struggling to hold back tears. She's real. She's safe. "Leigh, I almost ..." I whisper, ensuring only Leigh can hear me. "Oh gods, I almost trapped you and Wilder there."

Leigh hugs me tighter. "Hey, it's okay. I'm back, but we need to shut the rift now. Do you know how? Kosac was not happy we left."

Sama's gentle hand finds my shoulder, steadying me. "Ravi, let's finish this," she says.

Leigh releases me.

I nod, swallowing hard.

Leigh steps back, returning to Wilder's side, and he immediately links their hands together. With everyone watching, I take my position beside Sama, and together—under the first genuine light of morning—we prepare to speak the words I've dreaded saying all night.

"I call upon the forces that bind reality together, heal this wound, mend this tear, and restore the barrier between realms," I call, mentally focusing on the rift at the bottom of the lake. The ground groans and moves, shifting like tectonic plates before the sections grind together and lock into place.

Sama continues speaking. I silently thank whatever mercy brought Leigh back to me. I don't know what I did to deserve it, but I'll spend forever by her side, eternally grateful.

CHAPTER FORTY
LEIGH

MY HEART IS SO full it could burst. I look like a bride. My hair is perfectly curled, and each golden spiral catches the fading light with every movement I make. The subtle scent of violets rises from my wrists and throat. Jewels dangle from my ears like captured stars. The dress cinches at my waist and then flows outward in waves of fabric, intricately beaded with pearls and crystals that shimmer with every breath I take—a gown fit for royalty.

Felicity will have to wait another day to steal my crown; I'm not going anywhere.

"You look beautiful," Gianna says from the edge of the bridal suite's bed. She fans her immaculately painted face with two manicured hands. Her eyes shine with genuine happiness—a rare, unguarded moment for someone usually so composed. I'm breathless seeing it.

I smile. "Thank you."

"You really look so pretty, Leigh, even though I still want to wring your neck for lying to me last night, never worry me like that again," my mother says, and I cringe at the thick emotion in her voice. Unlike Gianna, her tears carve glistening paths down her defined cheekbones. "Still, I just wish your father were here to walk you down the aisle."

I squeeze my mother's hand. "He's watching us from afar."

My mother nods, but still, her tears fall, catching the light like the jewels in my dress.

"Besides," I add, forcing lightness into my tone, "we wouldn't want to rob me of my solo descent down the aisle. It's my chance to live out my dream of being a runway model."

Gianna snorts inelegantly. "You aren't tall enough to be a model."

I stick my tongue out. "Whatever. Neither are you."

"With this face, it doesn't matter."

My mother finally cracks a smile. My heart warms.

A knock at the door interrupts us, and an attendant steps inside. "Her Royal Highness Queen Jorina would like to speak with you, Your Majesty."

We all fall silent. Great.

My grandmother is about to lecture me on responsibility and royal duties. And I deserve it. I made her worry. Given her condition, I'm lucky she didn't end up back in Hygeia Hospital.

"How was her mood?"

"Uncertain, ma'am."

Damn. She's pissed.

"Well, I'll see you all at the abbey," I say to my companions, smoothing the front of my dress.

"It was nice knowing you, Leigh." Desi laughs from the chaise lounge, where she is elegantly draped like a cat. Her pink bridesmaid dress sharply contrasts with her bone-white skin, red eyes, and ebony hair. "Queen Jorina is likely going to kill you before you can become my sister-in-law."

"That's because someone"—I shoot a glare at Gianna—"told her I was never coming back."

Gianna scoffs. "Well, excuse me, how was I supposed to know you'd return mid-conversation? She deserved to know. We all did."

I fold my arms over my chest, careful not to ruin any part of my dress, while cringing. I never meant to hurt any of them. Though I should have known that was inevitable. I was just trying to make everything better so we could stand here today, smiling like we are now. "You could have waited another hour. Now, I'm going to get lectured. On my wedding day, no less."

"You deserve your grandmother's wrath," says Gi, "after lying and making us all worry."

"I agree," my mother says, dabbing at her eyes with an embroidered handkerchief.

"Does anyone else want more bubbles?" Meg asks from across the room. She looks adorable in her strapless gown. It fits her perfectly, though it does nothing to hide the faded hickey she's trying to cover with a partial updo. I hide a smile. After everything Gianna's been through, I hope it works out between them.

"I do," Isolde says before downing her drink. She gives Meg her glass. She's had two flutes already, as though she's trying to work up the courage to do something big. Whatever it is, I pray she doesn't get too drunk before she can get the words out. I also hope she doesn't trip on her way down the aisle.

I look at my bridesmaids with tears in my eyes. Years ago, if anyone had told me I would become a queen while an openly practicing Lunar Witch and the wife of a former Nebula Blade Commander, I would have thought they were high. The fact that I'd get there by surviving the deaths of my father and brother and a haunting journey through a ghost wasteland would have made it even more unbelievable. Yet here I am. Every trial the gods have sent me has shaped me, making me stronger than I ever imagined. It all began when Wilder saved me from Thayer's earthquake and again after an explosion at a festival. Since then, we have saved each other countless times.

Now he truly is my soulmate. Our lives are linked, and no one will ever be able to tear us apart again. "Til death do us part" now has a whole new meaning since our souls are connected. I am still so overwhelmed by Wilder's selfless act. For me. Not only did he follow me into Mictlan without any warning, but he also risked everything to bring me home. If that's not love, I don't know what is.

"Okay, wish me luck," I say.

I leave the bridal suite, the heavy door closing with a solid *thud* behind me, and I head down the hall toward my grandmother's quarters. The hem of my dress whispers against the carpet, paired with the soft click of my heels. A few royal attendants smile as I pass. I smile back, my confidence growing with each step.

I knock on my grandmother's door.

"Enter," she calls.

My grandmother's rooms here in Glaucus resemble her space back in Borealis. Green dominates every surface—drapery, chair cushions, and bedding—creating a forest-like atmosphere that feels both regal and suffocating. My grandmother, dressed in a stunning sapphire gown that matches her eyes—Fynn's eyes, Don's eyes, Felicity's eyes—sits in a high-backed chair. She looks incredibly poised despite her age, or maybe because of it. At the sight of her, healthy and present, my eyes prick with tears like they have every time I've seen her since I found her unconscious in that hospital bed months ago. I am so grateful she's alive.

"You look hot in that dress," I say before I can stop myself.

My grandmother frowns. "You look *alive.*"

I laugh and take the velvet seat beside her. "Barely."

"What were you thinking, Leigh?" my grandmother chastises.

I sigh. "I thought I could handle it."

"You're lucky you have a devoted fiancé."

Warmth spreads through my chest. My grandmother has no idea.

Wilder and I haven't told anyone about my pact with Kosac to sell my soul in exchange for Aradia's freedom, nor have we revealed his deal with the gods to share his life force with mine. Some things are too outrageous to believe. Everyone knows we barely escaped Kosac's grasp, surviving together by the skin of our teeth, and that's the truth—just not the whole story.

"So, are you going to punish me for being a reckless queen?" I ask.

Her eyes twinkle. "If I did, would you listen?"

I tap one finger against my armchair. "Probably not."

My grandmother sighs, and the sound carries decades of exasperation. "You might be surprised that I called you here, not to chastise you, but to express how happy I am that you are safe."

I balk. Usually, my grandmother is such a stickler.

I shift in my seat to face her directly. "You know, I do have something I want to tell you."

My grandmother sits straighter. "Go on."

"My last name," I begin. My grandmother purses her mauve-colored lips. "I've decided I'm taking Wilder's."

"The last name of a convict? Or have you forgotten Moran Dunn is still in prison?"

"No. The name of the man I love. Wilder can't help who his father is."

Her smile twitches. "Can you at least hyphenate? To honor your father."

"Hmm ... Leigh Amaris Raelyn-Dunn." It's a mouthful, but it doesn't sound half bad. "I'll consider it." My father couldn't be here today, but I can do this for him.

"That's all I can ask. The decision is ultimately yours. I may have my opinions on things, but don't let them influence your choice. Whatever you decide will be the right one."

Who is this agreeable woman, and what has she done with my grandmother?

"Fine," I say, carefully. "There's one more thing ... When Wilder and I decide to have kids, that will be my choice, and neither you nor my mother can interfere. I understand it is my duty, and I take my role as queen very seriously." Especially now that I know I am the prophesied keeper of the peace. But above all, I have to start prioritizing my wants and needs. Wilder and I deserve our peace, too.

"I agree. That's a conversation between you and your intended."

"Seriously?" I ask after a beat. That's it? She's been fighting me tooth and nail about tradition and duty for years. What's changed?

"I want you to be happy," my grandmother replies. "When I realized you were missing, I had an epiphany. Maybe I was too hard on you. I see now that I was forcing my beliefs onto you, and I need to step back and let you make your own choices. You are the queen, and I am here to support you, not to force you."

I smile awkwardly. Wow. Did I leave Mictlan and stumble into another parallel universe?

My grandmother reaches for her cane, the gold fox head handle glinting in the light. "Let's get you to the abbey. After today, you'll be Wilder's problem instead of mine, and I can finally know peace."

"Har-har, you can't get rid of me that easily." I offer my arm to help her stand.

As we leave the room together, I see my reflection in a large mirror—a queen in white, about to marry the love of her life.

CHAPTER FORTY-ONE
WILDER

I'VE NEVER WORN A MORE expensive outfit in my life.

The tailored tuxedo fits perfectly, better than anything I've ever worn. Each pearl button gleams in the sunlight streaming through the tall windows of the groom's suite. The reflection in the mirror shows someone I'm proud to recognize—polished, commanding, fit to stand beside a queen. While I will always feel more at ease in my Blade uniform, this is a close second.

The door to my room swings open, and Jax saunters in carrying two bottles of sparkling wine. Now that the rift is closed and Fynn is safe, Jax looks more like his usual cheerful self again. I still can't believe he's a father, but then again, he was made for such a role.

"Who else is ready to get this party started?" he asks, uncorking the first bottle with a loud *pop*. He overflows the first glass, slurping the fizzy drink as it spills over the sides.

"Barbarian," Pallas mutters, fiddling with his bow tie.

Jax is too high on life to notice or care.

The door opens again, and Desiree slips inside. She stops when she sees me, her pastel dress brighter than anything she has ever worn. Her mouth hangs open.

"Wow. I don't think I've ever seen you look so dapper, little brother. Well done."

Desiree crosses the room and plops down in an empty chair.

Pallas reaches for one of the sparkling wine flutes, but Jax's attention fixes on my sister.

"Tired of the girls already, sunshine?" Jax says to her.

"Leigh finished getting dressed, so I thought I'd crash this party," Desi says with a shrug. "And I hoped to talk to Wilder alone." Our gazes collide. "I have something for you."

"Give us the room, please?" I ask.

Pallas nods. Everyone, aside from Jax, leaves.

"What's wrong?" Jax asks Desi.

She smiles. "Mind your own business. It's twin stuff."

Jax looks at me, and I shrug. "I'll see you at the altar. Don't forget the rings."

Jax rolls his eyes as he leaves, tilting the open bottle to his lips as he goes.

"I have something for you," Desi says.

"A wedding present?"

She shakes her head. "It's from Mom. She thought you wouldn't accept it if it came from her."

I notice the white envelope in her hand for the first time. "What is it?"

"You tell me."

I take the envelope. There's no name or return address. Mom could have told me whatever it says herself. Using my finger, I break the seal. Inside is a piece of white paper folded in half.

With my heart in my throat, I unfold it. The handwriting—sharp letters with little spacing between words—is my dad's. What the hell does he want?

I'm tempted to crumple the letter and pretend it never existed, but curiosity betrays me.

Dear Wilder,

If you're reading this, it means you didn't crumple this letter the moment you realized who it was from. I'll admit, I wouldn't have blamed you if you had. After everything, maybe that's what I deserve. I know I wasn't the father you needed. For too long, I let my expectations and worries get in the way of simply loving you.

I wanted nothing more than for you and your sister to succeed and thrive. However, I've realized that my way of showing support ultimately pushed you away. I should have been honest with you, and I should have listened when you spoke.

But it always felt easier to tell you no. For you, "no" meant a dead end—a final answer. I realize now how many times I shut you out that way. And I'm sorry.

In my effort to keep you safe, I ended up making deals with the wrong people. The Magician blackmailed me into killing the president. Still, I have to smile because I get to look him in the eye at breakfast, knowing that my son married his niece—not just married her but helped her become queen. You achieved Prince Gwyn Raelyn's dream of changing the world with truth and courage. You revealed the letters, changed the laws, and both of you stood up to centuries of tradition.

Your mom mentioned that you quit being a Blade and stepped down as commander. I commend you for that decision; I know I couldn't balance being a good husband and a leader. We are more alike than you might want to admit.

I bet Leigh looked stunning in her wedding dress. I hope your mom brings me pictures on her next visit—unless you want to show them to me yourself.

Proud of you,
Dad

I glare at the letter, ignoring the sting in my eyes. Dad won't get the satisfaction of claiming we are alike. I left my position as a commander to avoid becoming like him—more focused on work than my family. Now he's twisting the story, suggesting that we are the same *because* I quit.

Well, screw that.

Dad has never told me he was proud of me in my life. Not when I graduated from the Blade Academy, not when I accepted a position in Aurora, not when I helped save the Council and hundreds of innocent lives from Nyx's bomb several years ago, and not even when I returned to Borealis after the wolves' failed coup. Of course, he would wait until now, when I am happiest, to worm his way back into my thoughts.

"Selfish bastard," I mutter to myself.

I hate him. I hate that he controls my emotions so much. I hate that Dad should be the one escorting my mom down the aisle to her seat today. I hate that he would have loved to see how pretty my edgy sister looks in her pink bridesmaid dress. But that's where I come in; I get to pick up the pieces where he fell short.

I inhale deeply, stifling the sob threatening to escape.

"What does it say?" Desi asks.

"Dad thinks we are alike."

Desi reaches for the letter. "Show me."

I let her take it. Desi reads, while I pace before her.

"What the hell, Des? I have no idea what to think right now. Dad being nice wasn't the final plot twist I was expecting. And screw him for approving my decision to quit the force instead of giving me reasons to stay. Who does he think he is, really?"

Desi sniffles. "Aw. That was ... sweet."

"He's deranged—that's the only explanation."

Desi sets the letter on the small antique table beside her. "What are you going to do about it? Take back your old job?"

I shake my head. Soter is the commander, but maybe I'll go back to working as a liaison or something. Anything to avoid giving my dad the satisfaction. I don't have to choose between being Leigh's husband and being a Blade. If anything, loving her makes me a better Blade—she gives me something worth fighting for.

The door to my room creaks open, and lo and behold, Soter pokes his head into the suite. "Sorry to interrupt, but, Wilder, do you have a minute?"

I nod, eager for a distraction. Soter steps in, and I frown. My former Domna is in civilian clothes: faded jeans, a studded belt, a loose-fitting long-sleeved shirt, and a backpack slung over his shoulder. Why isn't he dressed for the ceremony? "What's going on?"

"I'm sorry to do this now, but I've been thinking about it a lot. Though I thought this was what I wanted, I've realized that what I truly want is something I can never have. So, consider this my official resignation as Borealis Blade Commander." He hands me the silver pentacle commander's pin.

I stare at the pin. "You're quitting?"

"I'm stepping down. You enjoy giving orders; maybe you should just take up the mantle again." He adjusts his bag.

I observe him closely. He seems the same, yet different. Being a commander is everything he ever wanted. Why has he changed his mind, and why am I more excited than angry? I spent so much time training him, and he holds the title for a weekend, then quits?

But this is the universe telling me I can have it all.

"You'd work under me again?"

He shrugs. "I have bigger issues, trust me."

I laugh, then notice he's eyeing the door. "Going somewhere?"

"Borealis."

"You don't want to stay for the party?"

He grimaces. "Thanks, but we all know everyone will have more fun without me."

I open my mouth to argue, but he gives me a casual salute. "Congratulations, Your Highness. See you back in Borealis. If you decide to give that pin to someone else instead of wearing it yourself, make sure they know what they're doing. I don't have time for idiots."

With that, he leaves.

"Okay, what the hell?" Desi appears beside me. "Tell me that wasn't divine intervention."

"Can you help me put this on?"

I hold out the pin.

My sister grins. "I had a feeling you were going to ask. But shouldn't you talk to Leigh?"

"Leigh will be fine with it. Trust me."

Another knock. This time it's my mom. Her smile is radiant against her fancy silver dress. "It's time."

I STAND at the front of the abbey with its elaborate vaulted ceiling and ornate flying buttresses, facing a nave of nearly two thousand faces. In the first row, I spot my friends and family. My mom dabs her eyes with a well-worn tissue. The bridesmaids have just finished their entrance. Gianna waits at the base of the dais to take Leigh's bouquet, her eyes shining.

I stare at the closed double doors at the back of the room, a lump rising in my throat.

Any second now, Leigh will appear.

Violins croon a haunting, beautiful piece that sounds just like Leigh. As everyone stands, the rustle of fabric momentarily overtakes the melody.

The doors open.

I freeze, utterly transfixed by Leigh as she steps into the golden light wearing a dreamy expression. Her beauty in her white gown nearly brings me to my knees. Her shoulders are bare, her long hair tumbles in soft ribbons down her back beneath a trailing veil. Layers of silk, jeweled and beaded, flow elegantly from her waist. Diamonds glimmer against her glowing skin.

But all I see are her eyes, fixed on mine.

My throat is so dry I can barely swallow. The officiant hides a small smile as I shed a tear.

Leigh walks steadily down the aisle. When she reaches the front, she hands her bouquet to Gianna. I offer my hand. She takes it.

She looks up at me and smiles. "Hi."

"Hi," I manage, my heart pounding madly.

CHAPTER FORTY-TWO
DESIREE

NEON-BLUE TEARS FLOW from my eyes. The stained-glass windows of the abbey project colorful patterns across Leigh's white dress and light up Wilder's face as he gazes at her with pure adoration, like she's the moon and he's the sun, shining only for her.

Vane silently offers me his handkerchief. The silk is incredibly soft, likely centuries old, and smells like Little Death—chocolate, cherries, and Vane himself. I breathe in deeper.

Vane rests a hand on my thigh, then whispers, "Enjoying yourself over there?"

I laugh through my tears, earning a wide-eyed look from Jaxson, seated next to his boyfriend, Anselm—a tall, strawberry-blond, Green Witch with a tidy beard. We met before the ceremony in an awkward but sweet shuffle of introductions. He seems like the nicest guy. He works in town at Psyche Psychiatric and apparently is the one who introduced Leigh to medical-grade suppressants when she was a patient under his care.

In some way, Anselm was always destined to play a role in all our lives. Jaxson's warmth, the way he draws people to him like moths to a flame, is who he is at his core, and I'm so glad he found someone who stands in the light with him. We'll always love each other, but I belong in the darkness. I belong with Vane. He is my heart's match, and I will stand by him until the end of the world. Even then, we will be scattered dust blown by the same wind.

At the altar, Wilder and Leigh kneel before flickering candles and scattered crystals, heads bowed. The royal officiant places a golden chalice on the altar between Leigh and Wilder. My mom's lips move as she mutters blessings under her breath.

Leigh takes the chalice first. She sips, then hands it to Wilder. I look at my brother and my new sister-in-law and am so disgustingly, sincerely happy for them my heart could burst. One day, this moment will become a cherished memory that'll come with a pang of sadness, which is already beginning to develop in my chest. I place my hand on top of Vane's and give it a firm squeeze.

"Now, stand," the robed officiant orders.

Wilder rises and offers his hand to help Leigh rise. Beaded silk shifts and rustles as she stands. They turn to face one another, holding hands and smiling, ready for their vows.

"I love this part," Anselm whispers.

I smile, because so do I.

Honestly, weddings are my favorite. Black may be my signature color, but I've always dreamed of wearing a white dress and exchanging vows with the one I love.

I sigh, lost for a moment.

"Everything okay?" Vane asks quietly.

I nod, but it's a lie. Vane and I are already married. Besides, vampires don't get married in Parthenons, abbeys, or grand ceremonies like this. It feels silly even to want it. Or does it?

"I want to have a wedding ceremony like this one," I finally admit under my breath. "With flowers everywhere. With you."

A slight flush creeps up his neck, but then a slow, delighted smile spreads across his sensual lips. "As you wish."

I gasp. "Seriously?"

His expression is neutral, but his eyes are dancing. "Seriously."

I tune back into the ceremony, warmth spreading in my chest.

CHAPTER FORTY-THREE
LEIGH

WILDER TAKES MY TREMBLING HANDS, his voice calm and confident as he begins his vows, and I can't stop my heart from pounding. I can't stop looking at him. He's beautiful, and not in the classic way; he's no Prince Charming, but he's the handsome hero in my story, and in just a few moments, he'll be mine. Mine to hold, mine to kiss, mine until the end of time. I just hope I can get through my vows without becoming a weeping disaster.

"Leigh, you are my twin flame. You know me better than I know myself, and you have never tried to change me despite our very different backgrounds. Your love helped me see that my flaws are really my strengths. No one will ever compare to you, and nothing will ever come between us. I wouldn't allow it. You are the love of my life. I will cherish you until our dying day."

Oh my gods. This man. My soon-to-be *husband*. He always says the right things to make me fall in love with him all over again. I struggle to wipe the tears from my face fast enough beneath the sheer fabric of my veil.

"Now, Leigh," the officiant says, "it is your turn."

Rising from her seat with the other bridesmaids in the front row, Gianna hands me my printed vows. I hold the expensive stationery, but I can barely read the quotable, queenly words through my tears. The first word is his name. I see that, but dammit, I can't make out the rest. What I wrote is beautiful and eloquent and has the royal stamp of approval, but what I really want to say is messy, raw, and very much me.

I crumple up my vows and toss them back to my maid of honor. Gianna catches them as surprised murmurs reach my ears from our guests. Wilder raises a brow.

I clear my throat. "Wilder, I am so happy to be with you here today and to start living this life of ours together." My voice rings clear and strong, even as emotion vibrates through me from head to foot. "Over the past few years, you've been the best partner I could have asked for. You've loved and supported me, even when my ideas have been—let's admit—questionable." The audience laughs, pleased. "We've loved each other through the good days and the bad, been there for each other when the world seems to be falling apart around us, but most importantly, our values, outlook on life, and of course our love for the arts—and spicy romance books—align. I wouldn't be here today if it weren't for you, and I want to say thank you. Thank you for your love, your friendship, and your commitment to our relationship, even when I don't make it easy. You are my light in the dark, and I will always find my way back to you."

Wilder wipes away tears. He mouths, "I love you," and I silently say it back. Because if there's one thing I am certain of in this upside-down world, it's that I love Wilder with every fiber of my being. My heart beats in tune with his, and we will dance to that beat until we take our last breath.

"Now the rings," the officiant says.

Jaxson rises, straightens his jacket, and hands the officiant our wedding bands. He winks at Wilder before retaking his seat between Anselm and Desi.

After the rings, the officiant calls out, "Now, you may kiss the bride."

Wilder draws me into him. One hand lifts my veil to fully reveal my beaming, tear-stained face, while his other arm sweeps around my waist, gathering me close. He kisses me deeply and I arch into him, decorum be damned. The way he holds me is probably illegal in at least twelve territories. The audience gasps, laughs, and titters. Somewhere in the crowd, Alden's delighted yip rises above the din.

The second Wilder pulls away, I want to yank him back. Still, I'm too breathless, dazed, and incandescently happy to protest when our officiant calls, "May I present Her Majesty, Queen Leigh Amaris Raelyn-Dunn, and His Highness, Commander Wilder McCoy Dunn."

The abbey erupts in applause as, hand in hand, Wilder and I descend the dais. We walk back up the aisle to greet our wild and unpredictable future together, at last.

CHAPTER FORTY-FOUR

GIANNA

"GI, WAIT UP."

Meg nearly topples over in her heels to chase after me, but I'm on the hunt for the missing bride and groom. They have a ballroom full of people waiting eagerly for their first dance. It's on the itinerary, and Leigh better not fuck it up. The band worked hard to learn how to play her favorite song.

"Leigh is being so selfish," I mutter. After everything she put us through ...

"Or maybe she wants to be alone with her husband?" Meg points out.

I glare sidelong at her. "Whose side are you on?"

"You sound like Alec," she says with a laugh, referring to her middle sister.

"I just think it would be nice if they put in a little effort; we were all worried sick this day would never happen," I say.

Meg nods. "Or maybe you should put in less effort."

I scoff. Meg's words from this morning still taunt me. *What do I want?* I haven't had time to consider that—not after my conversation with Queen Jorina was interrupted, not since I rushed to Leigh the second I heard she was back, and not while I sat through hair and makeup to ensure Leigh walked down the aisle on time.

We turn a corner, and we both stop short.

"Looks like we found them." Meg snickers, while my cheeks heat.

Leigh has no idea we're here; she won't stop kissing her husband. The gasping breaths and silent words of love and devotion they whisper to each other make it clear they believe they are alone.

Seeing them in this stolen moment, tucked in a shadowed hallway, the sound of distant music muffled by thick walls, I understand what Meg was trying to say.

They don't care what anyone else thinks. All they care about is each other.

Wilder sits with his back against the thick plastered wall, legs sprawled, pulling Leigh on top of him until she's straddling his lap. Leigh paws hungrily at his shirt, nearly ripping the stubborn buttons from his chest. His bow tie hangs loose, and his jacket must've disappeared ages ago because it is nowhere in sight.

They kiss fervently, greedily, tasting the night and all its possibilities. His hands slip under the layers of her skirt. Shoving the fabric up until it's gathered around her waist, he exposes the garter circling her thigh. When she kisses the sharp line of his throat, he groans deep in his chest, and the sound sends me glancing at my date, whose jaw is hanging open.

By the stars, I've been neglecting her all weekend, focusing more on this wedding than on her needs. Needs that certainly need tending to. Immediately.

I clear my throat pointedly. Leigh wrenches herself off Wilder's lips to find me standing above her with Meg, arms crossed, both of us trying hard not to laugh at the sheer look of horror on both of their faces.

"I hate to ruin the moment," I say, "but two thousand guests are waiting to watch you dance and shove cake in each other's faces."

"Tell them the bride and groom are a little indisposed," Leigh shoots back as a grin slowly spreads across her face.

Wilder laughs, but I'm not letting them off that easily. Ultimately, it's their decision whether to stay or go, but I want them to make an informed choice.

"Fine, go ahead and jump-start the honeymoon, but I won't be the one to break the news to your mother and grandmother, Leigh. Jorina has been looking forward to this day since you were born, so go ahead and risk breaking her fragile heart."

Leigh glares at me. "You're evil."

"You love it," I reply.

"What do you want to do, Leigh?" Wilder asks.

Leigh looks back at him and smiles. "One dance, then we do as Gianna says and jump-start that honeymoon—"

"What about cutting the cake?" I exclaim, then reconsider. "You know what, forget it. Do you, or each other. I don't care." I grab Meg's hand, turning to go. I don't get far before I turn around again. "Oh, and one more thing, I won't be at breakfast tomorrow. Meg and I are leaving after the reception for a camping trip to Lua to see the Northern Lights." I finally stalk off, dragging Meg with me, but I do catch Leigh and Wilder's shocked whispers.

"Did she say camping?" Wilder asks.

"So that wasn't a hallucination?" Leigh answers.

I smile.

"Northern Lights, huh?" Meg asks.

I stop walking, and so does she. "You know how you asked me about what I want?"

She nods, and I lower my eyes to the ornate carpet. No one has ever asked me that question before, except for my counselors at rehab for my VT addiction. If I'm honest, I want to make my own decisions. I'm tired of feeling indebted to others. I thought I had to shed my need to please people after I turned down Ry's proposal, but it turns out that was just the tip of the iceberg. I still genuinely want love—something to nurture rather than trade or run away from. Even if it brings me pain, I want something real. I want Meg.

"I know what I don't want. I never want to feel the kind of loss I experienced when I thought Leigh had died this morning," I murmur, struggling to meet Meg's gaze. But then I remind myself that I'm done hiding. That's why I moved to Aurora two years ago. I'm no longer ashamed of who I am.

"That's good," she teases. "What else?"

"I want to be with you. I want to enjoy each moment together as it comes."

She tilts her head, looking at me from under those enviable lashes.

"And you know I want you, right?" I nod, blushing. "Good. Anything else? Don't hold back. Lay it on me."

"I want to kiss you," I admit in a whisper, my voice curling into the space between us.

She arches an eyebrow. "Just a kiss?"

I step close enough to feel the heat rolling off her skin. My pulse stutters in her presence, and I can barely catch my breath. "For now," I say, and it's a promise. "I'm not an exhibitionist like those two."

"Me neither."

I tilt my chin up. "I'm waiting."

Meg lowers her face to mine, her hands coming up to cradle my jaw. "Blessed relief."

Her lips meet mine—soft as a petal, lush and deliberate. The kiss starts sweet, tentative, but there's no mistaking the craving coiled beneath her lips and their movement. My hands grip her waist, fingers shaking as I pull myself against her solid form.

I refuse to move a muscle, fearing the moment will end before it even truly begins.

CHAPTER FORTY-FIVE
ISOLDE

WILDER SPINS Leigh around the dance floor while the crowd surrounding them claps and cheers. Leigh's mother cries openly while Queen Jorina sways in her seat with regal composure. But I hardly notice any of it. I desperately scan the room, searching every foreign face for one familiar one. Where is Soter?

All the Blades were invited to the ceremony and reception in recognition of our work, so he should be here. I crane my neck.

Jaxson bumps my shoulder, grinning. He's already drunk. "Looking for someone?"

My throat tightens. Honesty has never been my strong suit, especially regarding my relationship with my commanding officer. Still, I'm trying something new: trusting and being brave. If I want it badly enough, maybe it will come true. And I want Soter. I'm going to tell him how I feel, and if he doesn't feel the same, at least I tried. "Soter."

Jaxson groans. "Didn't you get the memo? Work's finished for the night."

I manage a smile.

"Besides," Jax continues as Wilder dips Leigh low, and the crowd hoots and hollers, "whatever you've got to say, you should say to Wilder instead."

I frown. "Why Wilder?"

Jax looks at me sidelong. "He's coming back to the force. Soter stepped down."

My mouth falls open. "Soter did *what*?"

Jax takes another sip of his drink. "He left. Went back to Borealis."

Probably should've stayed—maybe a party would loosen him up. He's wound so tight, I bet he shits diamonds."

A group nearby is laughing, but I don't join in. "You don't have to be so mean."

Jax, with his jokes and carefree personality, will be a fantastic father. Something he never openly said he wanted, but now, I can't see his future any other way. So why can't Soter prove me wrong? Did he step down for me? I won't know unless I ask.

Jax's laughter falters. "Huh?"

I straighten. I'm not here to argue with Jaxson—we're friends—but I am a little pissed about his remark about only friends using my first name. I know what Jax said isn't the reason Soter broke things off, though. I can only blame myself for that. Me and my reluctance to make us public. Enough is enough. I'm tired of feeling like I can't trust the people I love because I am afraid they'll let me down.

"You're all so hard on him," I say. "I know he gives just as good as he gets, but we're a team. You may not live in Borealis anymore, Jax, but you're still one of us—and Soter has been there since the beginning. If I have any say, he's not going anywhere."

I turn, heart pounding, determination burning away the last threads of doubt.

"Where are you going?" Jax calls after me.

"To the train station," I shout. "I'm getting my boyfriend back." I don't care who hears me.

CHAPTER FORTY-SIX
SOTER

I MISSED the last train out of Glaucus. The whole city is celebrating Leigh and Wilder's wedding, with posters of them plastered over every building and bus stop. Someone tried to sell me a ceramic tea set and a matching towel with Wilder's face on it. I just said hell no, and kept walking.

Giving up the commander position was probably the hardest, yet also the easiest, thing I've ever done. My father has already sent multiple messages of disappointment and the usual jabs about how unsurprising it is that I quit. I've always been a letdown, a joke to him. I'll never be like Keris—and honestly, that's a good thing. My brother sucks. I'm over trying to be like them; it won't make me happy, and they don't seem to care about who I am or what matters to me. The one thing that would bring me joy is out of reach now, since there's no way she would look at me twice after I demoted myself. It's time to leave the past behind and start living by my own rules.

Alone at the Weiss Train Station, I lean against a pillar and pull a cigarette from my pocket. I snap my fingers to summon my flame. I take a deep inhale. The familiar burn at the back of my throat fades into the numbness I've been chasing. Bliss from the first drag lasts only a moment, then I'm empty again.

I take another drag.

"Miss, the platform's closed," someone shouts.

"I'm looking for someone."

My heart jolts. I drop my cigarette and grind it under my boot. From the mouth of the corridor, under flickering gas lamps, Isolde strides right onto the platform, radiant in her pink bridesmaid dress, tattoos on display, blue hair falling in loose waves. Those heels are too high, but they make her legs look unfairly long. She's stunning—and she's here.

"The last train left an hour ago," the ticket salesman explains.

"No," Isolde breathes.

My heart wavers. What is Isolde doing here? Surely, she wasn't planning to make the trip back to Borealis wearing that dress and those shoes.

"I'm sorry, miss," the salesman says, his tone softening. "You can buy a ticket for the morning, but nothing leaves until seven."

Isolde nods. "Thanks. Can I have a minute?"

"Five. Then I lock up."

"I'll be gone before then," she promises.

The salesman disappears back into the warm glow of the station interior.

Isolde stands there, hugging herself and staring down the tracks.

She can't be here for me. Maybe she just wanted to leave the wedding early? But there's no luggage, nothing but her and her phone.

She clutches her phone and starts typing. A second later, mine buzzes in my pocket. When I look at the screen, all breath leaves my lungs.

> **ISOLDE**
>
> I'm sorry.

I wait, staring at the screen, heart pounding. Then, more messages come, one after another.

> **ISOLDE**
>
> I made a mistake.

> **ISOLDE**
>
> I was scared.

> **ISOLDE**
>
> I have trust issues.

I freeze. Sol knows I'm here.

She turns, and her eyes find mine.

I step fully out from behind the pillar. "How did you know?"

She glances around the deserted platform. "I sensed someone lurking in the shadows."

I laugh. "You always were good at your job."

"Yeah," she says, taking a breath, "but I wasn't so good at being yours."

I let that hang—painful and true.

"Why are you here, Isolde?"

Her heels click on the old tiles as she draws closer. "You got my texts."

"I did."

"Then you know I came for you."

"Sure, but what does that mean?" I hold her gaze, trying to hold myself together despite my heart pounding a mile a minute in my chest. "I was clear last night. We aren't sneaking around anymore. If I'm not enough, then find someone who is."

She licks her lips, gloss catching the outdoor light. I want nothing more than to taste her.

"You stepped down as commander ... Was that for me?"

I shake my head, an incredulous laugh breaking out. "No? That was for me."

She nods. "You could've told me."

"Was I supposed to?"

She steps closer, raising her chin. "As your girlfriend, I have a right to know. Why'd you do it? I thought you cared more about the title than about me."

Is she for real? I thought she wanted me to have the title so we could be together, and she'd be proud of me. All this time, I thought I had to prove myself to her. To everyone. "My girlfriend?"

She nods, daring me to protest with her intense stare. "Don't tell me you don't want to be my boyfriend. I've already told everyone at the party you are, so if I go back alone, I've got a lot of explaining to do. But if you're going to let me down, please do it gently."

I blink. She told people about us?

"I wasn't ashamed of you; I was ashamed of myself and stuck in the past. Not to mention, selfish with your heart. Will you forgive me?" Sol's voice almost sounds childlike.

Stillness stretches between us. Above, warm station lights flicker. Everything I thought I knew was wrong. Isolde didn't want me to be Wilder. The world didn't stop spinning because I said no to my father, and now, she's asking for my forgiveness, giving me the choice to refuse her when she's all I ever wanted.

"Please?" she whispers, and my heart fucking breaks.

I pull her close, and the press of my mouth against hers muffles her gasp. She melts into me, grabbing on tightly and kissing me back with all the wild longing I have desired from her for years. I remember the first time I saw her, the first time she kissed me, and that first *I love you.*

Gods, she feels like home.

I want this. I want her for the rest of my life. I want her beside me, every damn night and morning. I want her, *always.*

"I love you, Isolde Faez," I mutter softly against her mouth. "Do you love me, too? Even if I am nothing special?"

She parts her lips, tongue flicking against mine.

"You are special to me," she whispers.

"Yeah?"

"Yes." Her nails bite my shoulders. "I fucking love you."

I groan, drunk on emotion. "We should get out of here before they lock us in."

"Or"—she grins—"we could fool around in one of the empty train cars."

My pulse thunders. "What if we get caught? It would be awkward for two Blades to get arrested."

She laughs, the low, sultry sound sending shivers down my spine. She grabs my hand. "Come on, before I change my mind."

"Too late. All sales are final."

Isolde glances back as she climbs the steps into the first empty train car, eyes gleaming with challenge. She pulls me up with her, then drags me against her for a deep, rough kiss that leaves me dizzier than nicotine.

"Don't worry," she whispers against my lips. I hold her close, unwilling to let her go now that I have her. She's mine, and I won't accept anything less. Finally, my world feels right. "This time, I'm all in."

CHAPTER FORTY-SEVEN
LEIGH

"READY?"

I don't get to answer. Wilder hoists me up, bridal style. I gasp, tightening my grip around his neck. He gently kicks open the bedroom door, carrying me over the threshold into our darkened suite. I'm still in my wedding dress, and I'm itching to get out of it. My cheeks are flushed from dancing. A smile stretches across my face.

I can't fucking believe it. We are married.

"Let's get some lights on in here," Wilder says.

I blink, adjusting to the darkness. Wilder waves his hand, still managing not to drop me. Dozens of candles burn.

Soft-looking rose petals litter the floor and the bed. My eyes water. It is beautiful, like a moment straight out of a scene in a movie, and it's Gianna's doing. When I see her again, I must thank her in a big way. She honestly thought of everything, while I was morbidly focused on the portal. Everything is exactly as I imagined: beautiful suite, soft candlelight, achingly handsome husband. I'm the luckiest girl in the universe.

Using my hand, I wipe a tear from my face. It's hard to believe I traded my soul for Aradia's several hours ago. Without thinking about the big picture, I trapped myself in Mictlan. I'd been so focused on repaying Aradia for everything she did for me and our country that I hadn't thought about how my choices would impact me or my future. I'd been brash, and that brashness almost cost me my life. Not to mention this perfect moment.

We left our reception early, and I have no regrets. Our marriage is about us and no one else.

Wilder sets me on my feet, gripping my hand as if he's afraid I'll disappear. I squeeze him back. I'm not going anywhere—today or any day. We are bound through sickness and in health. Till death do us part.

The gods gave us another chance. I'm not going to squander it.

"It is beautiful."

"Perfect," Wilder replies in a whisper.

I face him, feeling the intensity of his gaze. His green eyes glow with an inner light, and I can sense their penetrating power stripping me bare. My hands tremble as I struggle to remain still under his focused attention. He looks at me with such adoration it's clear that he loves me, and there's no way to express how happy I feel in this moment. He is gorgeous and loves me enough to want to share his life with me. Our souls are bound, just like our hearts.

I want to show him how much I love him and how thankful I am that he didn't leave me behind, even after I begged him to.

"There was a moment where I didn't think this day would ever happen," Wilder admits.

I caress my thumb over his. His skin burns with the warmth of his solar powers. I place his hand flat on my chest. His eyes widen. "You feel that?" He nods. "*I'm* real." His heartbeat is like a caged animal. "*You're* real." I moisten my lips. "I'm not going anywhere without *you*."

"Promise?" he rasps.

"Promise."

I press my lips against his. Wilder kisses me back, breathing life into me. Deep-rooted frost melts from my muscles, and I coil my arms around him. Our kiss turns molten. His touch is nothing short of a brand. My tongue teases his lips, begging for entry. He gives me what I want and more, massaging his tongue with mine with expert strokes.

I'm his, no matter what.

Wilder draws me closer. I chase his kisses, eager for more—another taste, another touch. I swallow his love like nectar, until I am drunk on his touch, drowning in his kisses. I thread my fingers through his soft hair and give a gentle tug.

"I want to eat you up," he murmurs against my lips.

"I'd like that."

We erupt like a supernova. I gasp, and his tongue dives into my mouth. I suck on it, savoring his taste. Wilder grips me around my waist too tightly, suffocating me, and I retaliate by pulling his hair, drawing a delighted groan from deep within his chest.

My pebbled nipples rub uncomfortably against my dress.

"Get me out of these damn clothes," I demand, untying his hastily retied bow tie.

Wilder undoes the silk buttons, but it's not fast enough.

"*Hurry.*"

Wilder pulls the loosened fabric apart, tearing it into ribbons.

I yank the skirt down until it encircles me like a halo on the floor, and stand in my fancy white lace underwear. Wilder stares at me, his pulse jumping in his throat.

"How'd I get so lucky?" he breathes.

"Touch me."

Wilder releases an appreciative sigh. He kneads one of my breasts over the fabric with one hand while unhooking the bra with the other. The strapless garment joins the rest of my belongings on the floor. He stoops, sucking one of my nipples into his mouth. I gasp, burying my hand in his hair, holding him against me.

Heat spreads between my thighs until it is unbearable.

I undo his pants, then grip him. He sucks in a breath, and I slide my hand up and down his throbbing shaft. Wilder kisses my neck, teeth grazing the tender flesh. He reaches behind me, palming my ass with both hands until his thumbs hook into the elastic of my panties. I release him. He slides my underwear down my shaking thighs, and he crouches to the floor, eyes locked on mine.

"Lift." He taps one calf, then the other, until I am completely nude.

With hooded eyes, Wilder slowly rises, unbuttoning his shirt. He takes it off, and I barely blink. My mouth waters as he kicks off his patent leather shoes. They go skidding across the hardwood floor. He removes his pants next until we are both naked and panting. He's godlike, glorious, and I want more from him.

We lunge for each other. Our limbs and tongues entangle.

I cry out. It hurts how much I love him. My heart expands *painfully* with each reverent touch and kiss. I let it. The pain reminds me that I'm alive. That we made it out. *Together.*

Wilder massages my slick entrance with skilled fingers.

I moan into his mouth. *Fuck.*

He kisses my lips, trailing them over my jaw. Every soft touch cuts me open, and I bleed for him all over the rose-petaled carpet.

Wilder draws back to look at me. Tears sting my eyes as if I have perfume in them. I take his hand and guide him to the large bed. He sits, and I climb onto his lap. I straddle him, rubbing my wet center up and down his hardness. His gaze travels south, watching my every movement with starving fixation.

"I've been fantasizing about this moment—about you—all day," I whisper hotly into his ear. I lift. He grins as I sink onto him. My brows draw inward.

"Fuck you feel amazing," I whimper.

"I've fantasized about you, too."

I take a deep breath, then another. "Say my name." I grind against him, taking every inch that I'm able. "*Say it,*" I demand again, searing his skin with messy kisses as I lift and lower my hips. A force builds and builds inside me.

Wilder grabs my ass, rearing up inside me. "Leigh," he gasps.

I shake my head. "My full name."

Wilder kisses me deeply. My insides coil tighter. "Leigh Amaris Raelyn-Dunn."

I moan. Yes. "Again."

"Leigh ... Amaris ... Raelyn ... *Dunn.*" He accentuates the words between deep thrusts that leave a mess in his lap.

"Shit, I'm yours," I whisper, breathless.

Wilder chuckles, then holds me tighter as I lift and drop my hips. I squeal as he lifts me. He flips us around, lowering me onto the bed with him on top. He looms over me, and I widen my legs, cradling his body between my thighs. Sliding into position, Wilder eases his way back inside me. His attention never leaves my face as he feeds me every torturous inch of him.

My eyes roll back as I arch. Gods, will it always feel this goddamn glorious? "Right there, yes, you're so good at this."

Wilder pistons his hips. My moans start soft, then get louder as his movements turn more erratic, both of us chasing the release we so desperately crave. I tighten my thighs around his hips, keeping him deep inside.

"Wilder."

"Yeah, princess?"

"I love you."

Wilder curses. He pulls out, then drives himself back in. I could die like this. But ... I go when Wilder goes.

Together.

"I'm close," I warn.

Wilder presses his forehead to mine; sweat lines both our brows. "A little longer."

I nod weakly, my orgasm cresting.

Wilder sits back on his haunches and positions me back on top of him. Back in control, I am more desperate than I was before. My orgasm is imminent.

Wilder sinks his teeth into my left breast. I scream, chanting his name as I come.

His hips jerk, one final thrust before he pulses inside of my still trembling body. I hold him tighter, nails leaving half-moon marks on his tattooed skin.

Neither of us speaks.

We sit silently as the candles surge around us, breathing heavily in the rose-scented suite.

I don't need to say a word. My reverent touch says it all.

I will love him forever.

EPILOGUE
WILDER

Three Years Later

"I DIDN'T WEAR the proper shoes to traipse around the city at night!"

I chuckle. Leigh is wearing a short red dress and spiky heels. Her straight hair cascades like a golden sheet down her back, faintly scented with violets. Her jewelry is simple, but knowing her, it probably costs a fortune. She looks perfect, but then again, my wife always does. "Relax. It's a surprise, and we're almost there."

I cover Leigh's eyes as we walk down the last stretch of the graffiti-lined street in the Burned-Over District of Borealis. This area is now well-known for its nightlife and festivals, a stark contrast to when I rescued her from Eos's bomb six years ago.

It's just after eleven p.m. Pedestrians crowd the sidewalks, cars honk at every stoplight, and even though the Spring Equinox is still a week away, people are already celebrating. The bars are at capacity, lines spill onto the sidewalks, and thumping music mixes with shouts and laughter. There's bound to be trouble, but that's not my concern tonight—it's Soter's. My Domna knows how to handle things without me.

Tonight is about Leigh and me.

Soter already warned me that Leigh will leave the moment she figures out my plan. He might be right; what I'm considering will cause pain, and she'll do anything to avoid it. She always says she's a baby when it comes to pain. But a bet's a bet. Leigh won't let me down—she hasn't in nearly three years of marriage. Besides, this was originally her idea.

We pass beneath a neon red sign that reads Tartarus. My smile widens.

Fuck, this is going to be fun.

"You ready?" I ask.

Leigh sniffs the air. "What's that smell?"

I pause. The air reeks of paint, ink, and stale cigarette smoke.

"That's the smell of fun, princess." I grip the shop's smooth door handle.

She exhales a shaky breath. "Ugh, fine, but can we hurry up? I'm getting anxious."

I laugh. "Your wish is my command."

We step into a spacious reception area with brick walls adorned in glow-in-the-dark graffiti and hanging LED lights from the low ceiling. Curtained-off rooms branch off from a central space filled with framed licenses lining the walls and red vinyl chairs. Behind the counter, a green-haired girl covered in tattoos smiles at me. I wink back. Diana and I have been planning this for weeks. I even told her not to take no for an answer if Leigh protests. I know my wife; she'll cave. She made me a promise, and she never breaks her word, not since we got married. That's part of what makes her a great queen.

"Okay, surprise," I say, uncovering Leigh's eyes.

She blinks a few times, then gasps. "A tattoo parlor?"

I nod, a wicked smile on my lips. "We had a bet, remember? Soter and Isolde's second kid—"

"You want me to get a tattoo?" She backs toward the door.

"The deal was if they had a girl, you'd get a tattoo of my choice." I waggle my eyebrows for effect.

Leigh crosses her arms over her chest, but she's grinning. "Absolutely not."

Diana slides a consent form toward us. "He prepaid and everything," she singsongs.

Leigh glances at Diana. "I'm sure he did." To me, she says, "You're insane if you think I'm going through with this."

I give her my best reassuring grin. "Come on, Leigh, it's not that scary. It's just a little ink."

But she shakes her head, biting her lip.

My smile falters. "Are you actually scared?"

With a little puff of laughter, she looks me dead in the eye. "No, baby, I'm not scared." Her smile widens. "I was going to tell you at dinner, but the restaurant was swarming with press … but I see no excuse now."

I pause, concern rising. "What is it?"

She slips her hand into mine, squeezing it. "Wilder, I'm pregnant."

The bottom drops out of my world. My future rewrites itself in an instant.

"Pregnant?" I may float away.

"Yes."

We've been trying, and it's something we both want, but I didn't expect it to happen so quickly. It's only been two months since I stopped taking the contraceptive brew. Don't people usually try for months or even years before conceiving? Is it too soon? We've been together for nearly six years. Maybe I'm overreacting. I'll have to tell Soter right away. Get him prepared. I'll need to cut back at work, cancel night shifts, and be home more—we need to figure out a nursery and call our parents … Will Mom be her doctor, or is that weird?

"You're turning green," Leigh says.

"I—"

Leigh rubs her thumb across my knuckles. "Hey, breathe. Nothing has to change unless we want it to. I don't want you giving up the things you love—I love our life. This baby is something we both wanted, Wilder. It's a blessing, not a catastrophe."

I breathe out slowly. "Of course it's not a catastrophe," I murmur, tearing up and grinning all at once. "I just want to be there for you." I place my hand against her flat stomach, which'll soon swell with my child. *Holy shit. We're having a baby.* "Both of you."

"Then, just be the man I fell in love with."

I lean down to kiss her. "I can do that."

I glance at Diana, who is pretending not to eavesdrop with a very obvious smile. "Well. We need to reschedule," I say to Leigh, feeling thirteen different emotions at once. All of them are happy.

She lifts her chin in a lopsided grin. "I'm not against commemorating big moments, so maybe you should be the one getting tattooed tonight? Diana did stay late and all. I'm thinking my name, or something equally as nauseating."

I laugh. "You want to mark me as yours?"

Leigh nudges me playfully. "I thought you already were." She glances pointedly at the ring on my finger.

"Hmm," I muse, teasing her. She narrows her eyes. "I'll do it."

Leigh grins, eyes soft and burning with something that makes me nervous. "Yay! I knew you would."

Diana laughs and waves me over. I sit in the seat intended for my wife, bare my chest, and wait for Leigh to finish signing her name so Diana can use it as a stencil. Once we've prepped everything and wiped my skin clean, Diana gets to work. Leigh watches as her name—her real, sophisticated, queenly signature—gets etched in the space above my heart.

She brushes her lips over my ear and whispers over the sound of the tattoo gun whirring, "Forever."

I smile. "And then some."

ACKNOWLEDGMENTS

Wow, here I am again, writing the acknowledgments for my third book, and the final one in my first series! Where do I even start?

First, I'd like to thank Jim Henson. Thank you for directing *Labyrinth*. You simultaneously haunt my dreams with the ballroom sequence and the David Bowie codpiece, which might actually be a nightmare? Hard to say. But without you and that movie, this book wouldn't exist.

And to the Duffer Brothers. What do you mean *Stranger Things* is over? The Upside Down was a loose inspiration for Mictlan. Leigh and her ghosts are integral to this series, and the idea of her visiting a ghost realm in this book was a concept I've had in mind even before the first book.

Next, Ian, can you believe I finished my first series? Your love and encouragement made it happen. Without you and the boys, my life would be very lonely, full of ghosts in my head, but you remind me to keep one foot in reality and the other in fantasyland. Thanks for keeping me grounded.

Emily, we've known each other for almost six years now, and I can't imagine my life without you. I talk to you more than I talk to most of my own family. What does that say about me? You're the best coach a girl could ask for. Without you, Leigh and Wilder wouldn't exist, or they'd be more bland than off-brand Cheerios.

Many thanks to my Nana, whom we lost earlier this year. You nurtured my love of fantasy and storytelling at a young age, making me believe in elves and mermaids and letting me turn the jacuzzi into a full-blown music video set complete with color-changing lights. I miss you every day and wish we had more time together.

Therese, you continue to amaze me with the beautiful covers you create! I know your artwork is a big reason readers are drawn to this series and give it a chance, so thank you for sticking with me!

Erin, my endless thanks to you! I appreciate all your help keeping me organized, beta reading *Last Breath,* helping me make the romance shine, and always believing in me.

Laura, thank you for your continued support in helping me get the military language and weapons usage right! I appreciate you teaching me how silencers actually work, and just so you know, Wilder's body-temperature regulation moment when he goes through the portal is all for you.

And of course, to my street team, thank you! You continue to champion these books, share them with others, and make this series feel like something truly special. I hope it means as much to you as you do to me.

Finally, thank you to everyone who picked up *The Eleventh Hour* books. Without you, I'd still just be a girl with a dream instead of an author living it.

Here's to the next great adventure!

ABOUT THE AUTHOR

Brit K.S. has always been a voracious reader of many books — but all her favorites have kissing in them. Growing up in Laguna Beach, CA, she wrote stories, plays, and truly awful poetry that didn't improve with age. At college, the boy next door stole her heart, and in 2021, they tied the knot in England with a ceremony that was equal parts Elfhame and Starfall. Brit currently spends her time in Atlanta, GA, with her husband, their two fur babies, and many, many cups of iced coffee.